The Particular Appeal *of* Gillian Pugsley

a love story

Susan Örnbratt

The Particular Appeal of Gillian Pugsley
Susan Örnbratt
www.susanornbratt.com
www.lightmessages.com/susanornbratt
sornbratt@lightmessages.com

Published 2015, by Light Messages
www.lightmessages.com
Durham, NC 27713

Paperback ISBN: 978-1-61153-111-4
Ebook ISBN: 978-1-61153-112-1

For Grandma
I hope your poems have finally found their home.

When I grow old, my prayer will be,
To find content,
In memories of how I tried as days sped by,
To do a little good —
A helping hand,
A kindly word,
A tear for tears,
A burden shared,
A load made less because I cared,
And hope reborn, where lived despair.
And when at last my youth has gone,
My memories dim, my story told.
I pray that peace will bless the days,
Still left to me when I am old.

Chapter 1

I HAVE A MAGNIFICENT OBSESSION. One that hasn't marinated or stewed but has been gobbled up faster than my withering body can digest. Life. If I look down at my crimson coat and scarf covered in Scotty dogs, I'm sure I'll start to laugh. Who in their right mind would wear something so festive to such a dreary place? But my barometer always seemed broken when it came to expected behavior. And I wasn't about to fix it for anybody, including this doctor.

Leaning back on his chair, the hospital wall behind him is stippled with pockmarks like a worn institution. But what I remember most clearly about this place was the joy in holding my granddaughter in my arms for the first time. I swaddled her in apple green pixies, getting a look of horror from the nurses' station. But I glared right back as two sets of white clogs slunk behind the desk. *They* couldn't see my granddaughter's eyes light up with wonder the way I could. Of course, it was over twenty years ago; now I'm afraid I'm the one who needs to be swaddled.

I close my eyes for a moment trying to forget where I am, but the hum of his pager plucks me from my trance. Look at him sitting there. Now, I've seen my fair share of sulky lumps, but this doctor champions the lot. If he only knew what a grand life I'd led, I'm sure he'd be tapping his toes by now. Poor thing, trying to muster up the strength to tell me the worst.

"Mrs. Pugsley," he says, clearing his throat and looking as though I am his one and only patient. I can tell because he's flushed a warmer shade of pink and his eyes look as though they'll well up at any moment. I couldn't have asked for a kinder doctor. "I'm afraid I have some bad news."

Suddenly I'm not so sure about him. Bad news doesn't sit well with a name like Pugsley, as distracting as it's always been. The first time I heard it, it jangled my nerves. *Angus Stanley Spencer Pugsley.* How cruel could a mother be? The poor scamp wouldn't have a hope in a month of Sundays attached to a name like that. But I love it now and wouldn't change it for anything.

"Perhaps you should get your things in order," he says, not knowing what else to say. I'm sure he's right, but I don't know what my *things* are. I have this big nose of mine. That I know. Wherever I glance, left or right, I see its shadow pestering me. I wonder if it's true what they say, that noses never stop growing, because mine is now far too unwieldy for my head. Angus' really got in the way, I thought, toward the end. I sigh, my chest crumbling inside me. *Angus... how I wish you were here.*

A puff of air suddenly reaches my lungs, snapping me back to reality. But of course he isn't around to help; he usually wasn't. Angus preferred to be waited on hand and foot, bless his heart, but he wasn't about to get it from me. The least he could have done was show a little discretion when he tried to get it from the likes of Charmaine Dipple. Good God, the way she flaunted her appendages. Well, good luck, I said to him, but he was back groveling within a week. I find it a wonder sometimes how I miss him so, but soon enough. *Perhaps up there you can dote on me.*

I FEEL MYSELF ON UNFAMILIAR GROUND, walking away with an insidious gob of cancer feasting on my body. But I won't spend another minute in that hospital until I set things straight. I suppose without knowing it, that's what the doctor meant. A nasty chest cold it was when I walked in and a nasty chest cold it shall be. The family doesn't need to know anything different… for the time being anyhow.

I walk along the sodden bricks to the car park with my arm coiled in my granddaughter's in a country where I never thought would take my last breath. Granted, I wish I were walking to my fiery Mini Minor in the old country instead where Angus and I spent a number of years. Mildred was a loyal car and I always felt like a champion driving her. Even Leslie, the watchmaker in Ascot, would step onto the threshold of his shop just to eye my arrival. Oh yes, Mildred in her pearly white overcoat knew how to draw attention. Instead, this little pixie is kindly fetching me yet again. What Gilly wouldn't do for me!

ALTHOUGH GILLY OFFERS TO COME UP, I want to be alone. My flat isn't much, but it's where her grandpa drew his last breath, and I want to feel near him. It's been quite a day after all, and tired has come to have a new meaning altogether.

I plop into my cushy pink lounge chair and gaze over the other seven high rises that surround me. They all look the same—gray. Gray in a London that couldn't think up a name for itself, so it has echoed the original's for nearly two hundred years. I suppose it's flattering really; truth is it made me feel at home instantly. I dare say I even take kindly to Canada's version of the Thames, snaking its way through all the names that are dear to me. Still, it's not the real thing.

And it's certainly not Ireland, my first home, apart from the weather today. But I see the balcony door hasn't been washed for months. Yet if I squint my failing eyes to the rain now trickling down the railing, I can feel something resembling relief. I wondered when it would be my time. Now I have only weeks; months if I'm lucky. Just a cruel blink to sum up a whirlwind of eighty-nine years.

I don't want to say good-bye.

I don't want it to be the end.

I can feel my chest crushing my bony frame as I draw a breath. I never used to notice my age unless I looked in the mirror. But where I used to sashay, I now lumber; I'm afraid I can't bounce back from this wobbler. All in all, I feel perfectly morbid, and I don't think I like it. Angus would knit monkeys in his grave if he saw me like this.

It's extraordinary how time flutters by. Another early autumn with the bluest of blue skies and I can't imagine being anywhere else with my granddaughter. Three days, two and a half hours have passed, but I refuse to count. I'm on a mission here, and the fire sizzling underneath me isn't doused yet!

"Here's a good spot for us to sit, Grandma," Gilly says while brushing some pine needles off a bench. "But watch your step."

Springbank Park is full of benches by the water. And if you're lucky enough, the odd rowing shell will glide by while ducks by the dozens take life at an easy pace. The number of times I'd walked past the old stone pump house only to be caught off guard by the sudden bellowing of a coxswain. It always riled me until I realized how much fun it looked.

"Yes, the Canada geese have been at it again, I see." A smile curls up at the corners of Gilly's mouth. The first smile I've witnessed since the news spread of my illness. My nasty chest cold didn't fool a soul.

"Are you comfortable?" she says, her eyebrows now arched above her new glasses. The black rims suit her being such a pretty thing—her fair hair lying in folds on her shoulders.

"Of all people, you are the last person I want doting over me, do you hear?"

"I know. It's just… well."

"For a young woman who's never been lost for words, I beg you not to start now. You are a writer, Gillian Pugsley, a woman of words and we share the same name for a reason. You are as stubborn as I am and don't for a second let that go to waste. If you're wise, it will serve you well. You must nurture this love of yours and no matter how many rejections those deplorable agents send, you must never stop writing."

"It seems like only you believe I'm a writer, Grandma. Sometimes I wonder myself," she mutters, lowering her chin.

"Look at me. Go on, look at me, Gilly. Do you wake up in the middle of the night thinking of words? Do you leave bits of paper all over your flat with new words or expressions scrawled across them? Do you go for walks then find you are beside yourself when you've thought of precisely the way to word something and you're without a pen and paper on hand? You begin to recite the phrase over and over until you arrive home. And once you do, you sigh a great relief when you've managed to scratch it down as quickly as possible?

Not because you have to. Not because someone is telling you to but because you can't bear the thought of not getting it down on paper?"

Gillian wears a look of amazement in her eyes. "How do you know? It happens to me all the time."

"My dear, *you* are a writer. You don't need to be the next Margaret Atwood to tell a great story. You just need to read and write. The more you do, the stronger you'll become. I didn't have this same luxury. Good reads were hard to come by in my day, and writing was for the foolhardy. It certainly wouldn't have put food on the table. In those days practicality was a necessity—especially during the war."

"Are you telling me, *you* wanted to write, Grandma?"

I feel an ironic chuckle reach my breath. "If you recall, I said you were stubborn, as stubborn as me. It may not have been practical to write in my situation, a young woman caring for those around her, working too many jobs to count while the world was at war, but do you think for one moment that would have stopped me from writing? Not a chance."

"I… I can't believe it."

"Dumbfounded twice in one sitting. Not a good sign my dear. But fear not, the words will come again."

My eyes now travel the shoreline, enjoying the serenity of the river. And the sun makes the water glisten like a thousand green sequins tickling the surface. I was wrong to imply the Canadian version of the Thames was anything but lovely. Imitation or not, it has its own charm, narrow and the color of jade with magnificent oak trees nearly clutching the opposite bank. The odd leaf has changed color—yellow, red. Soon there will be too many to count. A lively selection of mallard ducks scurry toward a little girl who's tossing hunks of bread into the water. Gilly reaches over to clasp my hand.

"Grandma, I don't want you to go."

"I know dear. That's why I asked you to bring me here." A curiosity springs into her eyes. *Yes, my Gilly is back.* "Please," I motion to my handbag sitting next to her on the grass. "Inside you'll find a leather folder. Will you give it to me, dear?"

I glance at the folder now resting on my lap. I still find the grouted pattern affecting, although others would consider it dull. Moreover, I can smell a faint tinge of the hide almost as though it were new. This big nose has its uses after all. Tracing the edge stitched in thin leather strips, I unlatch the hardware on the front.

"I won't bother reading these to you. They've never had an audience. I'm afraid the words would jump off the page and run for the hills if I let them loose. But I know that if anyone can catch them, you can. They are yours now. Perhaps you can do something with them one day." A tear begins to swell in my granddaughter's eye, though I see she tries her best to draw little attention to it. "I could say that I have nothing of value to leave behind, or I could say that I have everything—a sublime tale aching to be told. Lay as they may be, these poems hide a grand story, a story of life and love. A story that will soon belong to you, Gilly."

I thumb through the pages sighing, my fingers stiff from years of arthritis. But for the first time in weeks, I don't feel the crushing in my chest. This breath gives me freedom, if only for a moment. I gaze fondly at my granddaughter who is whirling with emotions. I can see it as plain as day. My eyes travel downward, examining the wrinkles folding over my skin, my plum veins far too confident. My hands are withered, aged from writing and living the words in this folder—a folder that took a lifetime to fill.

I look into Gilly's eyes—that tear now falling to her jawline. Her young, smooth hand replaces mine on the leather as she tucks it in her arms. Through another tear brewing, she suddenly looks quizzical.

"If I'm called Gilly all the time, why doesn't anyone call *you* that?"

"Only one person ever called me Gilly," I say, feeling myself drift into reverie for a moment. "I loved your grandpa. If ever there was a tattered slipper to grow old with, it was Angus Pugsley. But there was another... before your grandpa. *He* called me Gilly. My first love and in some ways a love that cannot be measured by time, a love that has never grown old." There's a long silence between us.

"His name was Christian and he came from a place you once visited as a child, yet far from where I grew up. A small town on the Bruce Peninsula, well... not much more than a harbor for fishing boats at that time."

"Tobermory?" she utters, likely wondering how I'd met a Canadian in those days.

"That's right." I feel a smile working its way into my cheeks, and if I dare say, a playfulness in my tone. "Oh yes, Christian," I sigh throwing my chin back, gazing up at the treetops that shelter the park. "I'd only ever told two people about him. I'm not sure why in retrospect. Perhaps it had something to do with the times or perhaps my father. It wouldn't do to have the daughter of a prominent Irish Catholic architect bring home a Canadian fisherman. *A colonist!* I can hear him say. I don't think I would have lived long enough to go to my next confession. I can hear the meddling church ladies now, tarnishing every last morsel of my delicious love affair, not that I gave a pickled onion what anyone thought—except Daddy. Ironically, I've always thought Father Kelsey would have approved. He was quite like Christian in ways, adventurous above all. Yes, I would have had his blessing, I'm sure, and a little slap telling me to go get him."

"I never knew you were so feisty, Grandma," Gillian says nudging my elbow, trying to look spirited.

"I wasn't always eighty-nine you know."

"Tell me more," she begs.

"Our story—*my* story—is in these poems. I leave the rest to your imagination. After all, you are a writer. You might consider them a gift or a life sentence, knowing they will likely leave you with bags of sleepless nights, words and frustration churning in your head. But aren't the possibilities glorious?"

Curiosity has snatched my granddaughter now. I see it in her eyes. I dare say I can almost see words fluttering down around her like soft snowflakes trying to find their place on the ground, arranging themselves into sentences. She lowers the leather folder to her lap. I know what she will do, what will drive her. She opens the little blue notebook tucked inside. I see my poems drawing her in. I remain quiet, yet somehow I feel my granddaughter's words begin to unfold my story. Somehow I feel those fluttering words bring it back to life. She is a talent, that one! I draw another peaceful breath—no crushing. It feels lovely. I gaze once again at Gilly, the words around her now whirling into a fury, yet not a sound leaves her lips. Oh, how right I was about her. She's getting my story spot on.

I may have left her dangling in ways, but the details will come. She looks up from the page and smiles, an understanding between us that no one else shares. And though our embrace is warm, it's the first warmth my shivering body has felt in weeks. It seems to me that I'm unable to control my emotions after all. I feel a swelling in my own eyes now—something I've tried to avoid. What's more, I feel incredibly close to this creature in my arms.

When I squeeze out the tears, I notice the river begins to spread, the grassy bank opposite us folding backward. Gilly's words are happening already! She's caught me off guard. I'm not sure I'm ready for it… but it's thrilling. The grand oaks crank themselves to attention, opening up the sun to the water, while their leaves tremble with striking energy. Fallen acorns by the hundreds begin dancing upward, making way for a slew of delivery boys scooting past on vintage bicycles, three hauling carts filled with newspapers, one milkman with bottles making a terrible racket, and a fifth lagging behind with a basket of live chickens. Odd.

I squeeze my eyes again—sure I'm seeing things—then follow the current to the trestle bridge that now grows into something more substantial, lined with stone guard rails on either side. The pavement just over Gilly's shoulder rolls away, and in its place sprouts a cobblestone path leading to a street filled with merchants and huge front-grilled cars put-putting along, all resembling each other in one shade of black. What's more though, a clock tower, perhaps Big Ben, it's hard to know, clangs its third quarter as hurried passers-by ignore its patrol over London. High Street is something to be relished with its myriad of shops as the widespread grass of Springbank Park in Canada's pint-sized London stipples into something extraordinary, a time where men tipped their hats to bid "good day." The London I knew as a young woman.

I feel a renewed energy pulsing through me, and when

I glance around, my granddaughter is nowhere to be seen, vanished from my arms. I clutch my hands now rich with moisture, veins barely visible. The sagging I once felt in my eyelids has disappeared, and my sharp eyesight is restored. Even my nose seems to have shrunk a size or two. I'm wearing a coral knit dress, cinched at the waist, draping softly to just below the knee with a fine twirl to it if I turn quickly. I remember this dress. I always felt lovely in it. But this hat tilted to the side. I never liked the damned thing. I much prefer letting my hair ripple effortlessly like Greta Garbo's. Yes, I dare say I'm quite like Greta Garbo in ways… sultry when I want to be—or better yet, a *vibrant intensity*. Although no one knows me that way *yet*, something tells me someone is about to.

I am seventeen years old, far from my home in Ireland. I must be visiting my sister Beaty. She always insisted that I wear a hat and wash my hands upon arrival. When I look up, the knocker beckons me. It is 1931, and I am in London, England at last.

The trees are in full leaf,
The gardens full of flowers,
We swing into the hammock
To dream through sunny hours.

But soon the birds no longer sing
The only sound is pattering rain,
The English summer once again,
Runs true to form, and we the same
In soaking garb, look on dismayed
Through a misty veil this summer's day
To the sheltering porch so far away!
And so it goes from year to year
Hope unfulfilled!

And then one day, from morn to night
The sun shines on without a break,
Our greetings fly along the way —
"Oh isn't this a lovely day!"
And being rare, none can deny
The joy we get on this wet Isle,
When skies are blue, instead of gray,
And rain-filled clouds have rolled away!

Chapter 2

"Ahh, look what the mouse dragged in!" Beatrice said sprightly while kissing Gillian's cheek. "Do come in dear." Gillian felt an instant tingling inside to meet with her sister again. "Don't you look scrumptious in that hat! It's from *Harrods* if you recall."

"How could I forget? You remind me every time I wear it."

"Yes, well..." Beatrice said, brows darting straight up. Gillian could swear she'd flattened her hair somehow. Made her ears stick out. "Oh, stop fidgeting with your dress. It's lovely just the way it is. No doubt you must be terribly exhausted after your long journey. A nap will do you good. First, go have a wash up." Gillian rolled her eyes hoping she had noticed—the tingling inside falling away quickly. "You remember where the loo is?"

"Yes, Beaty. Why would I forget?"

"That's a girl."

Honestly, unless Gillian's mind was playing tricks on her, she'd swear her sister had just scooted her along. When would she realize she was a grown-up now? Seventeen years old! Beaty had already left Ireland by the time she was sixteen. No. Beatrice hadn't changed a bit—still ruly and in charge. *It's no wonder Daddy let her venture abroad; clearly he wanted to get rid of her!* Gillian had to wait an extra year— too impulsive he'd always say. But secretly she knew he only wanted to keep her around.

Anyhow, Gillian felt frustration pinching at her brow, knowing full well it would soon layer itself like a sickly sweet baklava and she'd barely stepped in the door! Even worse, Beaty never seemed to notice these things. The way she treated her like a meek, inexperienced fledgling—ten years the younger! How she managed to get this far in life must have been a mystery to her sister. But she was the only Beaty that Gillian had, and she'd have to do. It was kind to take her in after all. Still, she wasn't her mother, and she'd do well to remember it!

GILLIAN OPENED HER EYES. A stream of sunlight gushed through the partially opened shutters while shadows painted curious images on Beaty's guest room walls. Their evening catching up was lovely, like old times, at least for as long as Gillian could hold her eyes open. She felt as though she'd slept for a week. Too long really. She was aching from head to foot. Her toes scurried from the bedding for a peek and some fresh air. Yes, they were still attached to her, and that window was begging for a little attention.

She couldn't see much with the guest room being at the back of the townhouse. Why couldn't she have had the front room? From there she could spy Westminster's cricket boys in Vincent Square, or better yet, watch the groundsman's comings and goings for signs of a frothy mystery in the making. Then again, you could see the *real* goings-on from the back room. Her gaze travelled the white cladding adjacent, pausing briefly at the reflection of some trees in a neighboring window before finally landing on one smallish window beneath a fire escape. If she cocked an eye and then the other, she was quite sure something steamy was at play through that curtain and that her wishes alone could summon it right off the rod. Whatever they were up to made her feel like a Peeping Tom, embarrassed but curious, as she slid discreetly to the side.

Gillian could hardly peel her eyes away until a cat rummaging through some bins in the garden stole her attention—just for a moment. She wondered what it would be like to have someone touch her that way. Squinting for details while the silhouettes were melting into one, the moment felt daring. Indeed, the cat down there should run for cover, otherwise her curiosity might just do him in—for good. She glanced back at the curtain, certain her first interlude would be a mix of fear and great discovery. Sometimes when she was alone, she would close her eyes and imagine what it was like. Her body felt sensations now that could be toxic for all she knew. No one talked about such things. But it didn't stop her from feeling them.

A light knock at the door snatched her attention. "Gillian, are you awake?" her sister whispered while opening the door.

"Yes, I'm over here."

"I'm glad you're awake. I trust you slept well. You were out for nearly twelve hours."

"Really? Was I?"

"Traveling will do that, you know. I bet Hollyhead was a nightmare, then all those travelers packed on the boat like sardines no doubt."

"I'm sorry, what did you say, Beaty?" she mumbled, once again dazed by the rapture behind those curtains.

"Never mind," she said while throwing open the shutters on both windows. "What a spectacular day, isn't it?"

"Yes. I can't wait to see London again."

"In time my dear," she said while busily fluffing up Gillian's pillows then tucking the bedspread under the mattress. "I think you should get dressed then join me for breakfast. We have plenty to discuss."

That's exactly what worried her. If Gillian knew her sister, she had something up her sleeve along with that hanky of hers. And what kind of twenty-six year old stuffed something like that up her sleeve? She wasn't going to snag many boys that way. Anyhow, Gillian knew her father wanted her to find work, but surely a few days to soak in the people and sparkle of this place wouldn't give him indigestion, would it? Might cripple Beaty, though, straying from her plans like that!

Beaty's townhouse was lovely with its high ceilings and plenty of room for a growing family. Too bad she didn't have one. Might have had something to do with acting like a prude well beyond her years. That would scare off even the Colin Tuckers of this world. He might have been shy all right through that spotty face of his but underneath Gillian just knew there was a suave blue blood aching to come out. But even *he* was no match for Beaty. Gillian supposed with her sister taking on the role of their mother—or at least trying to—to all their siblings would spoil anyone's heyday. Pity really. Gillian was too young at the time to understand why her sister had up and left—London was a world away after all. Now, Gillian had a sneaking suspicion that it was all in pursuit of boys. She wasn't sure if she'd entirely forgiven Beaty for leaving her. It was a bit selfish really when she was needed at home in Longford. Even if she had found a husband, she could never admit to their father that she'd fallen for an Englishman. Bet she was hiding one under the staircase though. Gillian would have a peek later to be sure.

Poor Daddy, Gillian thought. *Two of his daughters abandoning Ireland as though it would become a faint memory. Oh, how wrong he could be at times.* He needn't worry; she had no intention of finding a man here—of course, if one should happen to find *her*, perhaps he'd be worth a tiddle. Oh, she could hear her sister now, *that's not a word!* Well it was to her! On second thought, she wouldn't want to face Daddy either. He'd either disown her or throttle her at once. Gillian was certain it was one of his greatest fears that any of his seven daughters should marry an Englishman or worse yet a *foreigner*. Trouble was, she found them absolutely charming.

WASN'T THAT JUST LIKE BEATY, laying the table to match the weather? She'd even brought out Mommy's Belleek teacups and matching pot.

"The daisies are lovely, Beaty," she said grinning while eyeing one for her hair.

"They do make you feel springy, don't they?"

"Mmm... yes they do," Gillian said tucking a daisy behind her ear, despite Beaty's nose twitching in disapproval.

"It's getting more and more difficult to stretch funds these days. Fortunately, I have a dear friend who has a tiny greenhouse at the back of his garden," she said patting the napkin on her lap as though it were creased.

"His?" Gillian's eyebrows sprang right up.

"Yes. Horatio happens to be a man, but don't go getting yourself into a tizzy; we're merely friends."

"You mean the way you and Father Clare's alter boy were *just friends*? Don't forget I'm the one who saw the two of you kissing behind the rectory."

"You were six years old!"

"And you should have known better."

"That's neither here nor there, I can assure you." Quiet filled the air for just a moment.

Caught red-handed, Gillian thought, *that was why her lips were suddenly pursed. Didn't like it then. Didn't like it now.* Truth was, Gillian felt horrible when they'd been caught and could feel a tear running down her cheek at the time. Beaty couldn't sit down for a whole week after that. It was no wonder their father let her go to England—as far away from that boy as possible. Fortunately, Beaty couldn't hold a grudge for long and Gillian liked when she traded in her apron for a scandalous cardigan, surprising her with a frisky kind of truth. "But if there are any developments, I'll keep you posted." Yes, a glint in those eyes proved she wasn't as innocent as she wanted everyone to believe. Perhaps Daddy would need to overcome his prejudices after all.

It was times like these that Gillian wished they had their mother. It wasn't Charlie's fault. She thought sometimes their father blamed him. But loads of women didn't make it through childbirth and even though he was irritating, she thought she'd keep him. Anyhow, he had the life of Riley with seven older sisters mothering him as though he were helpless. And he knew how to milk it. Was a miracle he learned to tie his own shoelaces!

Though Gillian missed her mother, she hardly

remembered their times together. She missed most of all the *feeling* of having a mother, of having someone to look up to, someone who would champion her cause when no one else cared to listen. She glanced up at Beaty. She was busy putting two sausages and a grilled tomato on Gillian's plate alongside a rather soppy-looking egg. She looked so happy to have a bit of company. Gillian supposed in a way, she'd filled Mommy's shoes after all.

"How's that?" Beaty said setting the plate in front of her. Gillian smiled back, grateful to have such a sister, even though her ears *had* grown since yesterday. "Now listen, Gillian, I understand you'd like to have a looksee around town. We have all weekend for that, but come Monday morning, no sooner than the magpies start rummaging through the bins in the back, you have an appointment."

Gillian nearly choked on her sausage. "An appointment?"

"Yes, with a Mr. Nigel Hardy. He oversees an estate owned by a maharaja of India. Can you believe it? A real maharaja!"

"Why on earth would I have an appointment with such a man?"

"It's well-known that the maharaja has come to England on business for years. He's like a prevailing wind through these parts. Admittedly, now that England—and much of the world for that matter—is seeing the likes of the Great Slump, he has made the wise decision to move his family here in order to clean up the awful mess that has come of his fortune."

"How do you know that?"

"Well, it's only a guess, but I would bet my last shilling on it. He'd need to protect his money, and I dare say it would be difficult from the other side of the world."

"What does that have to do with me?"

"Simply put, he needs a nanny."

"A *nanny*? Isn't he a bit old for that?"

"Gillian, I can promise you it wasn't easy finding work. Employment is scarce. Everyone's scraping by these days. It took a little trickery on my part but happy to do it, my dear."

Good God, she just winked at me, Gillian thought. But Gillian knew her sister meant well, whatever was up her sleeve with that hanky.

"It was a Wednesday morning and the bank was slow," Beaty continued. "I knew something was stirring during elevenses. I thought I would do some investigating on your behalf. The *only* place to start was Winifred Beastly. You know the one. She brings tea to Barclays' patrons whilst waiting for their appointments. Always with her ears pointed straight up. You know," Beaty said with a devilish grin, "working in a bank has its advantages. The things I learn about perfectly respectable people would horrify you. Do you know that gossipmonger knew well ahead of Mr. Tyler himself that his wife was playing Parcheesi, that God awful American version, with Harry Thicket every Tuesday evening? The little snippet! Well, apparently the bank's postman had a slip of the tongue when he let on within earshot of Winnie that one of his colleagues had delivered directly to the maharaja's residence in Kensington of all places."

"So, how did he find out about the position?"

"Well, it turns out that he'd had a little fling with one of the maharaja's landscapers."

"Janey! A woman landscaper?" Gillian gasped. "How thoroughly modern!"

"That's the juicy bit—every landscaper employed by the maharaja is of the male persuasion. In the end, of course, the bit about hiring for a nanny position was an absolute bore. Not a soul was interested in that—except me. So they agreed to see you straight away. You would be well taken care of—room and board and a little pocket money on the side. Daddy has already wired me saying that he approves, provided you have Sundays free and are treated like the respectable Irish girl you are."

"But I don't want to be a nanny." Gillian felt a nervous uncertainty crinkle into her expression, knowing she had said or done something wrong—quite like the time she'd peered at her classmate's test paper with that foul beast sitting at the head of the class, glaring from her desk. Suddenly Beaty quite resembled that teacher!

"I was afraid you'd say that," Beaty said with a frown. "Listen, it's just something to tide you over until the times settle down and something more profitable can come along. You've always fancied writing. Maybe once you get a little experience under your belt, you can look for work at a newspaper or something equally as exciting. For now, beggars can't be choosers. You'd do well to take my advice on that."

Gillian couldn't quite decide whether she should be grateful to her sister or hit her! Before she realized it, the words were slipping off her tongue, "Have you done something with your hair, Beaty?"

"Yes. I have it ironed. Do you like it?"

THE WEEKS ROLLED BY SO QUICKLY Gillian hardly noticed. She loved her new job. Beaty was right to nose around. It had been a wonderful way to introduce her yet again to

London. She was always out and about with the children. They were well behaved and not as whiny as she'd expected. Shashi, the little one, was as sweet as your favorite wish. It was like looking in a mirror, really. On second thought, she was always looking up her skirt—not her own but Gillian's. The child fancied her stockings. Gillian had a faint memory of doing the same to Auntie Rosalind. Her dresses always looked good enough to eat, like big meringue cakes with all those layers and layers of petticoats! Samir, on the other hand, was always pulling his sister's hair when his parents' heads were turned. Of course, if that was the worst they got up to, then she could count herself lucky.

Her favorite time of day was telling them stories when they were tucked in bed. They had an agreement—if they told her a story about India then she told them two stories about Ireland. They never complained and very cleverly managed to seduce her with never-ending questions about Ireland's countryside and people. They were so curious. Gillian adored that about them. Even more, she adored their gorgeous droopy eyes begging for her attention. She never did figure out how to tell them no.

Shashi and Samir were particularly creative when they were at their weekend home in Wentworth Estate. There, the deal was two stories of India and one of Ireland.

Gillian had Sundays free, but she preferred to stay and stroll the gardens, reading big, fat books by the pond. Oh, the whole of Virginia Water was such a pretty place. She couldn't imagine what her father was going on about— economic slump. What slump? She'd never seen so many large homes. If she squeezed her eyes shut then opened them quickly, she could almost see a far-off version of herself actually living in a place like this, pram, husband and all.

Not in an estate though. No, she'd prefer one of the small carriage houses on one of the old properties. Of course, the county of Surrey would just have to wait. Her to-do list was being checked off rather nicely, thank you very much. Case in point, not a single item had anything to do with marriage.

In the meantime, she enjoyed her weekends in Wentworth Estate. The gardens were full of flowers—they even had a hammock. When the sun wasn't being lazy, sometimes Gillian and the children would fall fast asleep, swinging gently under the trees. This was when they'd dream through sunny hours until the pattering of rain tickled their noses. It nearly always came—the rain. Sometimes she liked it. Sometimes she loathed it.

"Gillian?" Shashi peeped. Looking down at the child cradled in her arms, she was as sweet as lemon drizzle cake. *How does anyone grow such thick eyelashes at that age?*

"Yes, darling?"

"Do you want to be married one day?"

"Well, I suppose that would be nice. But only if Mr. Right comes along."

"How will you know him when you see him?"

"Hmm, good question." Gillian paused for effect. "Well, I guess he'll need to have a good pair of hands."

"Why?"

"So he can build me a house."

"What kind of house would you like? One like ours?" Gillian glanced over her shoulder at the monstrous residence behind her, scowling just a little.

"No, I don't think so."

"Why?"

"It's far too big."

"Our house in India is much bigger. This big!" Shashi

said stretching her arms out wide.

"Yes, I'd imagined as much. But I'm afraid both are too big for me. I'd like one the size of a mushroom."

Shashi giggled, "Mushrooms are too small to live in."

"Not for me. Wherever I turn, I want to see my family, and when they're little rascals like you and your brother, I'll sweep them into my arms, scoot out the door and run as fast as I can through the flowery meadow to the edge of the knoll—stopping short of course! We'll all drop to the ground then roll down in tumbles, and when we reach the bottom, we'll gaze at fluffy clouds, finding animals until our breath returns."

Shashi smiled then tucked in a little closer. Hammocks were wonderful things.

SCHOOL HAD BEGUN for the children now. Of course, the rich sent their children to all the best schools. But it did free up a portion of Gillian's day, so she was grateful. Gillian liked to visit with Beaty as often as possible, for she knew she must have been lonely in that big townhouse of hers, and with her reduced hours at Barclays' to boot. Sometimes she thought it might do her good if she insisted on bunking up with her, but Gillian knew she'd never hear the end of it if she resigned from her job. That was something one didn't do in these slumpy times.

The children were in different schools of course, with Samir enrolled in a particularly strict one for boys. Gillian thought they were too hard on such young children, always disciplining the way they did. Samir learned very quickly that fidgeting in his seat wouldn't do, not one little iota. Trouble was, the poor thing needed to go to the loo constantly. It was bad enough at home where he had the freedom to go to the toilet whenever he wished, always biting his lip the way he did until the very last second. She could imagine him in lessons burrowing a hole in his bottom lip, quivering and gyrating while he sat on his hands, too afraid to raise one of them in order to ask for permission to leave.

Father Denney, the school's headmaster, saw it firsthand without a doubt when he had visited the Reception class for an impromptu read. Samir described every detail of his horrific experience to her through floods of tears. It broke her heart. Gillian had a right mind to flatten that wretched man. Beaty would have said two Hail Mary's after that thought... but not her, no way! Honestly, how could he be so blind? Wasn't it obvious when a child needed to go to the loo? The beastly creature probably became a priest because no woman would have him!

All the headmaster apparently saw from the corner of those woggly eyes of his—yes *woggly*, there was no adequate word for them so she might as well make up her own—was this little Indian prince, a real honest to goodness *rajkumar*, trying to balance himself on his heel, which had been tucked underneath his bottom in the hope of holding it in. Of course *rajkumar* was a word she never would have known before she met the little muffet. How sweet of him to teach her a little Hindi. You know, she could now count to ten and say "How do you do?" and "Thank you very much." Beaty was quite impressed and had told her that she should become a translator and start her own organization fostering a positive social arena around the world instead of becoming a writer. Gillian had no idea what her sister was blabbering on about. On the other hand, Gillian had noticed her ears twitching whenever she'd learn how to say something new.

Well, when the headmaster had asked Samir what he

was doing, of course the boy was instantly flustered and started to make up all sorts of stories. Father Denney took no nonsense whatsoever and very coolly asked the class to "carry on." Everyone knew what that meant. According to Samir, the headmaster curled his index finger precisely three times right in front of his "big fat nose." Samir followed him at once with twenty-six horrified little eyes staring at him. He told Gillian he could see them from the back of his head, every last one of them ogling from the rows and rows of desks. There would have been twenty-eight, but Sebastian Waters was absent that day on the suspicion of head lice.

The long corridor had stretched from the time Samir arrived at school that morning, the Reception class at one end and the headmaster's office at the other. Nearly half of the year had come and gone now, and still, he remembered that walk being the worst part of all, with Father Denney's key chain clanging from his fists as he marched in front of him, his long shadow magically appearing. Behind the priest followed a little prince with a stream running down his leg. Samir hardly remembered the sting of the ruler—just that walk. Gillian had noticed Samir never drank now before bedtime, and she'd seen his morning juice discreetly fed to the English ivy sprawling over the center of the breakfast table. She didn't blame him a bit!

Although Shashi's school wasn't run by Jesuit priests like her brother's, it *was* run by a slew of nuns who could stare down the Pope himself. Even so, Shashi's spangled eyes melted their hearts straight away. Fortunately, both children were in day school, though there were plenty more who boarded. Gillian felt sorry for them really, hardly seeing their families. Although that would have been heavenly from time to time when she was in school. Her only escape had been the meadow at the back of the garden. And even then she'd still manage to get stalked by little parasites claiming to be her siblings—and always at the climax of a good book!

Both Shashi and Samir were able to come home for lunch except for Fridays when Benediction took precedence. There were many pupils of other faiths who were exempt from Catholic practices, but the maharaja liked them to attend mass and felt it built character to know first hand about the world around them, despite everything being in Latin. Gillian liked their father. She didn't think of him at all like royalty. Besides, she was sure he thought of her as more than just as a nanny—not in the way a filthy mind might think. Even Beaty had warned her about "ill-considered notions," always appearing cross-eyed whenever she'd meet the maharaja, sniffing him out like a bloodhound. True, Gillian didn't know him, not really. It was only that he and his wife, the maharani, treated her quite like part of the family. They made her feel a part of something, patching up the tiny gap that was always saved for homesickness.

Just last weekend at their Wentworth home, Gillian was included in a lovely celebration to honor their tenth wedding anniversary. She was the only one in attendance who was not Indian, so she was instantly chuffed. It wasn't at all like one might imagine—not the least bit stuffy.

There were two men sitting on the floor, one that resembled a pouty, overstuffed doll, his skin like porcelain. Gillian had an urge to tap it and see if it felt like one of her dolls. This man was in charge of the two very tall candelabras. The other was as hairy as they come—not the candelabra but the man. They must have used some kind of paraffin for the fire since there were no candles. Gillian didn't dare ask questions. The maharaja and his wife were standing above one of the candelabras, waving a small flaming chalice. The maharaja's dress was a very plain white, but his wife wore her usual breathtaking colors and fabrics, both wearing a boa of tightly knit flowers.

All of the guests, sixteen if you counted the tiny woman who just stared, not moving a single muscle, proceeded to whoosh their hands over the flames then touch their foreheads. Gillian hadn't a clue what she should do. She sat there, gobsmacked by it all. They were playing with flames for ages it seemed, even swirling a plate of flames above the maharaja's head. Good God, she thought he'd catch fire! Wouldn't it have been marvelous if Beaty could have been there? She'd have been bewildered with their fixation of foreheads. The guests kept touching and wiping the maharaja's and his poor wife's brows as though they hadn't cleaned properly. *If anyone tried to do that to an Englishman, he'd swat them like a fly,* Gillian thought.

There was more food than Gillian had ever seen in one room—each plate wafting with a dizzy aroma that could knock out even the air around it. The whole evening was playing with her senses: the music, the dancing, the colors, the flavors that made her eyes water. She couldn't help but forget about the world outside. For those few hours, she felt like a newborn pixie discovering her magical world for the first time.

The smell of incense from that evening lingered even now in her mind. Sometimes she liked to hold a piece of the children's clothing to her nose when they had returned from an event. It took her to a far away place. Beaty thought it was ghastly and liked Gillian to wash up twice when she dropped by. Beaty was harmless of course—just didn't understand their ways.

The children had taught Gillian so much about their culture, and here they were far from their homeland. She couldn't have been more impressed with them really, settling in so well to a strange country with mostly their nanny for comfort. They'd given the sun yet another reason to smile each day, and when it was cloudy, Gillian took its place. As pokey as her room might be, the door was always open for them.

Tonight the children were tucked away in their dreams rather early. It took them no time at all after sneaking down for something sweet before bedtime. Since she was in cahoots with them, they'd made a promise to settle down quickly and kept to it.

In the corner of Gillian's room stood a long oval mirror tilted on its feet. As she appraised her clothing, a simple blue day dress with cap sleeves and a cardigan over top, she thought the garb of today was sadly becoming more and more drab. She saw it around London every day. The slightly more daring shades of violet and orange from the twenties were becoming rather queer in this decade, she thought, muted somehow as though they'd been soaked in tar then scrubbed on a rusty washboard a hundred times too many. She loved a bit of color and wouldn't let the difficult times take it from her life. The way some people looked at her—honestly, it was as though they thought she was insulting the era. They couldn't fool her. She knew what went on after dusk. That was when backless gowns and adornment on sleeves and ruffles stepped from their cars. No one wanted to be dreary, not really!

Gillian slipped her cardigan off her shoulders then unbuttoned her dress, letting it drop to the floor. Her new pink knickers to the waist felt gorgeous against her skin, and her bra made her bust look like something from the cinema. She smiled, lightly gazing at her figure, but her hair was a right mess. When she whisked across the room searching for her brush, her grandma came to mind. "A girl's hair is her crowning glory, so brush it well." Another smile. Gillian missed her. A deep sigh took her to the towering window where the night sky was calling.

Gillian unlatched the hardware then opened the windows wide, letting in as much of the cool, damp air as possible. It was freezing against her bare skin. It felt glorious. Little shivers danced on her skin as she looked upward through the smoky clouds. There was hardly a sound; though the house was so large it wrapped around its own courtyard, not a soul could be found at this late hour.

The stars somewhere behind those clouds begged her for more attention. Gillian wondered what her future held and if she'd be standing here at this window a year from now. Two? No. She couldn't imagine so. Either way, the chill took her breath. Perhaps there was a man out there, somewhere near or far, looking up at the same stars at this very moment and wondering about her, a girl... no a woman... he had yet to meet. A man she had yet to meet. She threw her head back running her fingers from her chin to the hollow of her long neck. She stopped there, daring herself to caress her breasts and feel them against the cold night air. Gillian slipped the strap of her bra off her shoulder, almost feeling him touch her instead. She knew he was there, perhaps an ocean or two between them, yet she felt him just a breath away.

The window was left slightly ajar as a faint glow from the sky peeked at her bed. She slipped between her sheets feeling beautiful and smiled at the thought of him.

NEARLY A YEAR INTO GILLIAN'S EMPLOYMENT NOW, and Mr. Hardy had called for a meeting. It was hard to get past the lines across his forehead. They made him look like a walnut. Mr. Hardy informed her that the maharaja and his family would be returning to India indefinitely, but they wanted Gillian's services to continue. Thrilled wouldn't begin to describe her excitement at being offered such an opportunity. She had always wanted to see the world, and she and the children had grown so close.

A telegram the following day read:

ORIG LONGFORD IRELAND

GILLIAN MCALLISTER C/O BEATRICE MCALLISTER 33B
AUBREY CLOSE LONDON =

NO DAUGHTER OF MINE SHALL MOVE TO INDIA
= OVER MY DEAD BODY = MR. SAMUEL SEAMUS
MCALLISTER +

A second wire arrived:

ORIG LONGFORD IRELAND

GILLIAN MCALLISTER C/O BEATRICE MCALLISTER 33B
AUBREY CLOSE LONDON =

ENGLANDS ECONOMY IS SUFFERING BADLY = IT IS
BEST YOU COME HOME AT ONCE = YOUR FATHER +

Wire number three:

I WONT GO TO INDIA BUT I REFUSE TO COME HOME
= PLEASE UNDERSTAND DADDY = YOUR DAUGHTER
GILLIAN +

She could see him scowling through the airways now, his lips vibrating under that shaggy moustache of his, curled at the sides as though a ferret had fallen asleep under his nostrils, "Disobedient little imp!"

Wire number four:

FINE I HAVE ARRANGED FOR YOU TO TRAVEL TO
CANADA FOR THE SUMMER SINCE YOU ARE YOUR
MOTHERS DAUGHTER OBSTINATE = YOUR AUNTIE
JOYCE AND UNCLE HERBERT THERE HAVE AGREED TO
TAKE YOU IN FOR THE TIME BEING = THE QUESTION
REMAINS WHAT TO DO WITH YOU THEN = PERHAPS A
CONVENT IN TIBET - DONT BE ALARMED I AM NOT
DISOWNING YOU YET - YOUR GREATEST ADMIRER
DADDY +

Gillian spent the next several days trying to imagine why on earth Daddy would want her to go to Canada of all places. She needed to let the idea soak in. Honestly, she was furious with the man. India sounded so exotic—all those spices! Canada sounded, well… wild. She felt a tingling in her nose, hard to tell if it was pollen or excitement.

At long last, an answer… she hoped.

What a lot of waggle this telegram business was. Everyone she'd ever known had been put off by them—nothing more than unwelcome news stitched into the paper most times. Here she'd been sitting restlessly, waiting for the darned thing while her father was enjoying every moment of her turmoil. He knew she had tiny champagne corks for toes. She wanted to know—why Canada!

Wire number five:

DEAREST GILLIAN = HAVE I LET YOU STEW LONG
ENOUGH = WHY CANADA YOU ASK = BECAUSE YOU

CANNOT TAME A WILD BOAR +

Wire number six:

DEAREST FATHER = ARE YOU CALLING ME A PIG +

Wire number seven:

IF THE HOOF FITS MY DEAR +

Wire number eight:

I DEMAND A BETTER REASON FOR LEAVING CHEERY
LONDON +

At double long last she received a proper letter in the post from Ireland, just days before she should leave for a country that both excited her and terrified her. Gillian held it in her hand with a potpourri of emotions, wondering what Daddy might say. She slipped her nail in the envelope, tearing gingerly along the edge. She slid out the paper—just one piece—then unfolded it. To her surprise, Daddy had written only a few lines after his salutation.

1st of May 1932

My one and only (that's not to dismiss my seven others of course),

Cheery is it now? I hardly think so in these times. You want a good reason? Perhaps this will soak in better.

Obstinate = adventurous = fascinating = you

Why Canada? Because it needs to be stirred up by the likes of Gillian Rachel McAllister!

Your very proud father

Post Script – May I remind you that you are in no position to demand anything from me. However, if you are in need of even a peanut, don't hesitate to ask.

Do be safe and mind your manners.

Post Script Yet Again – Perhaps your cheekiness has cushioned me after all, otherwise the grief of losing you to adulthood would surely kill me if I didn't dislike you just a little bit. Now, a word of advice— you are the loveliest girl Canada will ever have seen and you will attract plenty of young men. Because you will draw such attention, you need to remind yourself of the blood that runs through your veins—the meat and potatoes blood of the Irish. Be wise my dear, but above all never think of yourself as anything other than absolutely fantastic.

The note fell to Gillian's side. All that pacing, and for what? A silly note that told her nothing. She drew a breath, deep and soothing. His words began to settle in nicely until mini gasps of air reached her lips, causing an instant rush of longing for Daddy's arms—his words far from nothing. At the same time, Gillian felt like a goddess. How did he manage that? She supposed that she'd been wrong. She had all the details for the journey that Daddy had sent two weeks ago, and now he championed her cause, a cause that had been blazing inside her since she learned to walk. Maybe she *was* a wild boar after all, but clearly Daddy didn't think she was the least bit piggish. A smile crept into her face. She would save this note for all time.

Why must I remember
The things that are gone
The sunshine, the shadows,
The lilt of a song;
Of flying feet dancing
O'er green velvet sward
Of winds softly whispering
My love to the world!

Why must I remember
And suffer again
The anguish I knew
When my tears fell like rain
And all my joy died
And now all is pain
Since my beloved
Has passed down the Vale!

Chapter 3

1946

CHRISTIAN HUNTER PULLED in the oars to his rowboat that rocked gently on Georgian Bay. Nothing could stop him from watching the sun sink into the bed of watercolors sleeping on the horizon. The Bruce Peninsula had just about the blackest skies in all of Ontario. Perhaps this is because it was tucked away, far from the lights of the big city, but Christian thought there was more to it, as though this narrow strip of land wanted to shut itself out from the rest of the world. It took a special breed to live out here where dirt roads trembled through the forest, crawling their way toward the shoreline. Christian was used to the isolation, having lived here most of his life. But the sunsets leading up to the black... those a man could write stories about.

Christian swallowed the air like it was his first taste of something sweet. Today was chilly even for midsummer. He could hear the masts clanging in Little Tub Harbour and relished their familiar sound mixed with the lapping of water. Still, nothing beat his rickety dock nudged into a hidden cove lined with milkweed and sycamore trees.

Dozens of Monarch butteries just within reach flirted with him occasionally while laying their eggs on pods that looked like prickly cucumbers. In moments like those his troubles would vanish as though they'd floated away on a fluff of silky milkweed floss.

The house Christian had built was nothing to speak of, but it was comfortable and had a good-sized porch with roll up netting to keep the mosquitos out in the evenings. His parents' empty place still sat on the property, but it was too far from shore and he wanted the water at his feet. Christian rented his parents' old house out every so often to earn a little extra money. And the crop-dusting wasn't half bad either. He'd nearly dusted three hundred acres of farmland on the Peninsula last year alone and fished with the best of them. More than a little loose change, that was.

There was that clanging again in Little Tub. It really did stir him up like an old melody. He often imagined that ghosts from all the shipwrecks sitting at the bottom of Georgian Bay somehow played a hand in that song. Those were the same ghosts that haunted his nights when he was a child after his father would tell tales of their ship's demise—tales that had been passed around so much they'd gone ahead and knotted themselves good. His dad wasn't trying to scare him, just turn him into a real man. Because out here on the Peninsula, that's what *real men* talked about. As a boy Christian would dive down, hoping to catch a glimpse of a wreck. It wasn't hard either, not with water that clear. Christian believed the Great Lakes were like a tonic, soothing to the eye and a boost for the soul. He felt it every time the winds drew him in.

Most of the fishing boats had worked themselves back to the docks. Christian kneaded his callused fingers still sore from the day's work. He'd had to finish up his neighbor Griffin's woodshed before heading across the Atlantic. One blister on Christian's palm just wouldn't seem to heal, and it bloodied up every time he'd swung a hammer in the past week. Rowing this boat didn't help much. Christian picked at the skin wishing he had something to lean back on.

CHRISTIAN'S EYES TRAVELED the waters edge. *Griffin. What a character!* he thought, shaking his head as bits and pieces of their past skipped like stones across the water with a final plop, settling into his mind. Griffin was one of those seasoned fishermen who'd outgrown his waders—too old and a belly so big it was nearly tearing at the seams. He mumbled badly, but for some reason Christian never had trouble understanding him, probably because he didn't say much.

Griffin wasn't one to give advice either, but he had a way about him, something Christian noticed years earlier when he was only nine or ten. With all those ghost stories chilling up the tide, Christian had imagined washed up pirate bones and skulls and would search endlessly along the rocky shoreline. Every time a treasure would masquerade as part of a seagull's carcass, he'd clean it, sort it, and add it to his collection. He liked giving them pirate names like Captain Ripper St. John and his first mate Snarky Cutter. They were his favorites. He stashed them in a box he'd carved from some driftwood.

Christian didn't have the bones any longer. When his parents had run out of food one nasty winter, Griffin said he knew of a pirate who could use those bones and would pay a hefty penny for them. So Christian sold them to Griffin who sold them to the pirate. That night, Christian's family sat down to a real roast beef dinner with not a cabbage in sight!

Nearly a year later, he'd gone into Griffin's run-down woodshed to get some kindling when he saw his old driftwood box poorly hidden behind a scrappy beaver trap. Christian opened the box and smiled; not a bone was missing. But there was a note inside, something *he* hadn't added to his collection. It read, "This treasure belongs to Christian Hunter. And I'll knock the block off anyone who says otherwise!" He never looked at Griffin the same way again.

CHRISTIAN ROLLED BACK his shoulders, trying to loosen them, and let his eyes fall back on the sky. They couldn't stay away for long. Truth was, the bay could be hotheaded when it wanted to be. That's why so many ships had gone down in these parts. But not tonight, and not his creaky boat.

Christian could see a string of lights along the harbor beginning to rouse, reminding him that nightfall was quickly approaching. Tobermory was peaceful at night. In fact, it was pretty much peaceful day in and day out. Most outsiders would think it was dull as sin, but they couldn't be more wrong. This was a place filled with life untarnished by shops and city bustle. The best place to see that was down by the water. And the best age to enjoy it was when one was still small enough that buttercups and ladybugs didn't go unnoticed.

Lazy days were welcome here, but in the same breath hard work never seemed to be far away. Truth was, Christian was the laziest, most ambitious person he knew. If he had nothing to do, he'd go out and dig a hole in the ground. It was impossible to know what a feeling of satisfaction that was until one had done it.

City dwellers were like scraps popping by their abandoned cottages, left behind to collect winter dust until the dandelions came out again in droves. Commercial fishermen would come in on the tides and drift out with the next wind. All in all, if a man didn't mind his own company and was neighborly when it wasn't the slightest bit convenient to be so, then he'd get on just fine here. But nothing was like digging that hole to set things straight.

Trouble was, Christian couldn't bury his memories in there for good. Somehow, they kept digging their own way out. That one summer never went away. The summer of 1932 had marked him forever.

SHE WAS EIGHTEEN YEARS OLD and he had just turned twenty. Christian's rowboat now idled on the water as though it was helping time stand still. Christian drew a deep breath; his thoughts would clear on the exhale and then grow cloudy again. At thirty-four, he'd found her image was beginning to fade. The exception being her broad smile and the luster in her green eyes—they were as clear today as they were fourteen years ago. Of course, nothing compared to that cheeky mouth of hers.

Christian glanced down, his breath deserting him. He'd never met anyone so high and mighty before while perfectly at home with the down trodden. A chameleon. That's what she was. Every color was tailor-made for her—usually worn to make others feel at ease. And they did. He'd never seen anything like it.

Then of course there was that accent of hers. What could he say about that? She'd get furious when he'd call her "leprechaun." It was true, she really was his lucky charm, his own walking four-leaf clover. He knew it the first time his eyes fell on hers. Christian swallowed, trying to focus on the bay, trying to focus on the present. He'd tried to drown her out with other women, and for a moment he thought it might be working. Then they'd get too close and he'd push them away so fast it made him dizzy.

Christian reached into his pocket and pulled out the newspaper clipping he'd cut out a month ago. Carefully unfolding it, he pinched the edges so the breeze wouldn't take it away. The fading light made it difficult to see, but it didn't matter. Christian had burned the image into his head long before. He couldn't be sure it was her, but the resemblance made him tremble. It was a short article about healing a town after the war. No mention of her name, just a throng of people standing posed in front of what looked like a hospital in an English seaside town. The setting looked just how he remembered from his brief stint in the RCAF in '42. He'd flown over a myriad of towns just like it, each one blurring into the next. Yet there was a landmark here, in the corner, one that Christian thought would guide the way.

He drew a breath then leaned over the oars. Maybe Griffin was right. Maybe she hadn't left because of him or because of her father. When Christian showed him the clipping, Griffin's hand shook so badly, he could hardly hold it. Everything shook on him these days, and he couldn't read a thing without a magnifying glass. But it was the look of fear in Griffin's eyes and the trembling on his lips, a trembling that had nothing to do with age that was driving Christian to move ahead. He'd never seen his friend that way in all these years. One look at Gilly and the lines in Griffin's face told a horror Christian wasn't sure he wanted confirmed. He didn't want to believe what Griffin had suggested. Most days now, Griffin didn't even know himself. He was an old man, confused for such a long time. One minute he'd see his late wife frying up bacon in the kitchen, the next he wouldn't even remember he'd been married. No. He was a mixed up old man, and as close as they still were Christian couldn't trust Griffin's memory. But the possibility alone was enough to make him book a ticket across the Atlantic.

Christian tried during the war to find her, but things were different now. Only he wasn't sure if he was traveling to prove Griffin wrong or to prove him right. Either way, Christian had to go, and this time there wasn't a village he'd leave unturned. There was no war to get in his way, no air force to cut his leave short. He'd find that landmark. He'd find Gilly McAllister... his beautiful, stubborn, lucky charm.

THE LAZY WATER suddenly grew restless beneath the small boat. Christian brushed the bristle on his chin with his fingertips. His hair fluttered in the breeze. It was cool, so he rolled down his shirtsleeves from the elbow then his twilled cotton trousers that had been folded once up.

This place was toying with him now as an evocative sound punctuated the fall of night. The long, mournful wail of a loon called out to his partner, crying, "I'm here, where are you?" Christian felt pity for the bird; he, too, knew the loneliness of the night.

Christian rowed to his dock then took up the oars, tucking them securely under a tarp next to his boathouse. After pulling the boat along the dock, he dragged it to shore through tall reeds and lily pads, finally rolling it on its belly to rest on tufts of grass until the bay came calling again.

Sleep came easily. Christian's last waking thoughts

were of the *S.S. Empire Brent* leaving Halifax in just three days—a ship he'd be on. He imagined Gilly greeting him at the docks in Southampton but knew it wouldn't be that way at all. He'd have to ransack England first.

Give me your love for this is true,
I am as rich in love as you,
And any love that I may owe
I can pay back to you and more.

Give me your love knowing this is true
That I can repay all that's due,
So give me your love
Oh, give me your love.

And with this love we stand secure
Against the "ups and downs" we all endure,
Together we face the darkest night
Together we smile when skies are bright.

When at last the days of youth are gone
Love will bless our Evensong.
So give me your love
Oh, give me your love.

Chapter 4

GILLIAN WAS STILL UPSET over what had happened at the farm last night. She was sure Mrs. Hemsworth would lose the baby and found herself walking on eggshells all morning for fear the telephone would ring with panic again. The phone didn't ring, and the surgery was quiet this morning. Dr. Pilkington had arranged his instruments for the third time and was interrupted only by Gilbert Brody who had pinworms. As long as he walked around with that pig next to his side, those parasites were bound to keep reappearing. Like roaches, they've been around since the dawn of flesh and could easily wrangle their way into Gilbert's backside again. *Quirky critter!* she thought. Not the pinworms— Gilbert. Albeit he was scruffy and always looked as though he'd just crawled out of bed, Gilbert was an easy soul—not a rumpled temper in him except when his bottom was on fire. He should be well thankful for a little castor oil instead of moaning about how it slid down like a land slug.

By now, Gilbert had long gone and Dr. Pilkington looked exhausted. It wasn't easy dealing with Mrs. Hemsworth.

She never stopped buzzing about the sordid affairs around town, affairs of which she had no proof. All the while she was wailing with pain. "The worst of all," she cried, "is those two *fisherwomen*," she called them, "who spend as much time rolling in the hay as they do rolling in on the tides." She grew a belligerent glare in those crooked eyes of hers, "Lesbians! I'm sure of it!" When Gillian had wound a bed sheet into a muzzle and offered it behind her back, Dr. Pilkington smiled and nodded. They were very close to following through with it until Mrs. Hemsworth whipped her head 'round and caught them in the act, throwing a beady glare Gillian's way. She was sure the doctor would have preferred her to faint for a few minutes just so he could concentrate. In the end, Mrs. Hemsworth fell asleep and the baby would be all right, provided she stayed on her back for the next week.

Dr. Pilkington had dropped Gillian at home just before 3:30 in the morning. She would have driven herself, of course, except that her motorcycle had its own ailment—a flat tire. Neither of them could have had more than four hours sleep before they were expected at the surgery again. Gillian was grateful for the slow pace today and was hoping she and the doctor could make it an early evening.

"Gillian," the doctor said. "How would you feel about lunch down by the pier today?" He shrugged. "I think we could both use some fresh air."

"Well, I'm not going to turn that down," she said with no need to consider. "Shall we go straight away?"

"Why not? That is, unless Gilbert comes back itching again."

Gillian smiled as she finished labeling some blood tubes.

It may not have been rugby union season on the Isle of Man, but Gillian noticed a group of men scrimmaging on some grass opposite the pier. The sound of men banging up against each other had a rather satisfying ring to it, she thought. Yet her gaze travelled to a curly string of nautical flags flapping from the one and only sailing boat moored in the bay. There were plenty of distractions down by the harbor and an unshakable belief that Port St. Mary would crawl out of any postwar dribble taller than when it had been sucked in.

Gillian refused to see what cleanup needed to be done. It was just to do it and get on with it. Never for a moment would she deny herself the pure pleasure of taking that tiny space in time to see the beauty shining through a field of ugly. She wondered if Dr. Pilkington felt the same and if any of the ruckus surrounding them stirred him. When she saw he was more interested in the potted dahlias along the roadway, she smiled knowing that *his* tiny space in time was filled with the scent of sweet clematis, dog violets scrambling into trees, honeysuckle sneaking through the hedgerows between cottages, and shrubs of yellow gorse that he'd pass on his drive out to her. All of it brought echoes of life to a village that was otherwise raw with wartime residue.

"Shall we sit here?" he asked motioning to a narrow wooden bench, more like a non-upholstered kneeler in front of the pews at church than anything else. Though it sat at the edge of the pier, Gillian still looked down considering the spot. Apart from seagull droppings and perhaps one or two puffins marking their territory and an infinite number of possible slivers to be had, it was perfect. And it was always lovely to see the doctor without his white coat. Some drapey gabardine slacks held up by braces and his white shirt unbuttoned just enough to see a hint of chest hair. Not that she noticed! But before she could answer and test her resilience, the grocer's wife blundered down the concrete, squealing like that pig of Gilbert's the day he was born.

Iris was a round woman and was in great competition with Marjorie, the seamstress down the narrow street with the thatched cottages. They both fancied Iris' now husband. In fact, their rivalry for him was held sway until he got a taste of Marjorie's Manx bunloaf at the Mad Batter Bake-off in the late thirties. Hers tasted like sawdust, apparently, not the rich fruitcake it was meant to. Gillian wasn't living on the island at the time, but rumor spread like an unpleasant virus. Before she had even settled on the island, the information was dumped in her lap, so to speak, from who else but Mrs. Hemsworth.

That grocer, he had a terrible sweet tooth and suffered horribly during the war. Even today with all the rationing still in effect, he showed signs of twitching. But in *his* eyes, you couldn't mess with a bunloaf. He'd always say the haunt of smugglers didn't bring in spices only for recipes to be ruined two hundred years later. In the end, he knew that he couldn't live the rest of his days digging out seeds from his teeth. So Iris had duly won his affections. The only thing left to tolerate was Iris' tightly-wound bun bobbing on the top of her head like a dinner roll. And it was headed this way now.

"Dr. Pilkington! Yoo-hoo, Dr. Pilkington!"

"Yes, Iris, what is it?" he asked, waving his hand for her to slow down. She was so out of breath, she nearly toppled into the water.

"You won't believe it, but Mrs. Hemsworth just rang me. Said she was looking for you but you were nowhere to be found."

"Well, that's because I'm here," he said exasperated.

"Yes, I can see that," she said licking her fingers then patting down those few strands that escaped her bun. "I told her I would find you at once. She's in great pain, you know. Sounds like the baby is on its way to me."

"I don't think so, Iris. We were just there last night. I've told her she needs bed rest."

"Doctor Pilkington!" she said with an icy tone and pinched eyebrows pointing straight at Gillian. "Are you going to take that chance? If that baby comes out sideways and lives a crippled life all because you wanted to eat a bit of lunch with your chum here, you will never be able to look in the mirror again," she said shaking her stubby finger in front of his nose.

"Iris, apologize to Gillian. There's no need to bring out the boxing gloves," the doctor said coolly.

Iris stretched her brow, tilting her chin like a told-off teenager. "My apologies," she said to Gillian. "I'll accidentally drop an extra packet of Typhoo tea in your bag the next time you're in."

"That will be lovely, Iris, thank you," Gillian said, holding back a smile.

"Right," the doctor sighed. "Are you up for it again?" he said to his *chum*. "We'll eat in transit."

WHILE ON THE WAY, Gillian felt as though she was in danger of smacking some sense into that woman. Yes, last night was a worry, but Dr. Pilkington was a good doctor and managed to rotate the baby without a problem. Nothing that a bag of frozen peas wouldn't cure! The problem was, Mrs. Hemsworth was a real crying wolf and loved attention.

Most times, they'd arrive to a woman picking currents in her garden, looking as fit as the last time they'd been rushed out to the farm. But the main problem was that the doctor could never be sure if she was telling the truth. And that was precisely why they were headed there now.

The ground underneath them was still spongy from rain during the night. It couldn't have let up at all, the way Gillian's low heel sunk beneath her today. Even the lane to Mrs. Hemsworth's farm proved uncertain. Dr. Pilkington left the car on the main road just to be safe. After examining his patient, he declared that Mrs. Hemsworth was not only fit to deliver this baby, she could likely run Port St. Mary, hail down the *RMS Queen Mary* and triumph at the Highland Games in the same breath. Though no one could deny the baby was en route, was it necessary to ring the doctor with every kick, twitch, and pop?

Gillian didn't think the doctor quite understood the woman's motives. After all, when she thought about it, Dr. Pilkington wasn't exactly hard to look at. He could be a little stuffy, but underneath his stiff hair was quite an attractive man, she supposed. Gillian deliberately avoided taking the idea any further. They had a professional relationship only, although she *had* found his company pleasant. She hadn't had much time in recent years to even consider a man and those available had been off at one of the air-to-air firing ranges or schools for air gunners up at Jurby.

In the early years of the war, there was one soldier who'd taken leave at Port St. Mary. He was lovely and had spied her in a meadow picking poppies the color of red nail varnish. They'd seen each other several times, but it was no good pretending it would lead to anything. Every time he had tried to make advances, she made some excuse to pull away. One time too many, and he was gone. She'd never heard from him again.

Dr. Pilkington was different. She'd seen him almost every day for the past three years and considered him a friend of sorts, though she didn't dare call him Reggie. Her sister Beaty would be horrified knowing she called a professional man like Dr. Pilkington by his given name. Not that she gave a worm's whiskers what Beaty thought, Gillian reminded herself.

"Oh damn," the doctor said, snapping Gillian from her thoughts as the farm grew distant behind them.

"What is it?"

"I forgot my bag. Can you believe it?"

"It's only because you were anxious to get out of there," Gillian said consolingly.

"Hmm, that woman!" he said twisting his lips. "Listen, you go on ahead. I'll meet you at the car."

"Right! See you shortly," she replied.

THE DAY WAS CHURNING into a breezy afternoon, but rainclouds were distant and Gillian was sure they'd keep at bay, at least for the time being. Beneath the sky, the barley moved like velvety chartreuse. The wind always had that affect. Although it would take a drought to dry the earth, Gillian was grateful to have a bit of blue sky. As she approached the car, her good fortune fell away when she noticed the tires on the left side had sunk into the spongy earth. The ditch was luring in the car whether it knew it or not, and she wondered if this day could get any longer.

Taking a deep breath, Gillian decided not to be a moaner. She never liked moaners. Instead, she got behind the huge rump of the doctor's Rover, her fingers spread like twin peacocks, then pushed, almost believing she could make it budge. In a matter of only a few minutes, she'd sunk into the mire herself. It may as well have been molasses trying to set her feet free. When she finally managed, the last straw was in turning the engine over. Since the doctor always left his ignition key in the glove box, all it meant, really, was pulling the starter key. Though she'd never driven a Rover before, it couldn't possibly have been too different from her motorcycle. She smiled as the engine spluttered, begging to take her home. It was only to move onto the road and the doctor could fly right in. But when the molasses nearly cemented her foot to the accelerator, the wheels spun wildly, causing a terrible howl from the back of the car. When she looked into the rearview mirror, she could see the doctor standing there. What could she do but run around to see if he was still living? He was. The trouble was with the pool of sludge around the tires. Gillian felt like someone had pulled the rug from under her as she slid like a fool to the bottom of the ditch.

"Good God, Gillian, are you all right?" the doctor shouted.

She glanced at her skirt now waist high with legs that looked as though they'd been dragged through a mud bath. She turned and looked up at him then began to laugh.

"What's so funny?" he asked.

"You! You're filthy." She'd made a mess of him, splattering dirt in every direction.

"You should see yourself." He stood tall at the top of the embankment, hands on hips and shaking his head but wearing a wide smile. "Here, let me help you," he said as he shuffled down the hill.

He sat down beside her, his sleeves rolled to the elbow.

As the wind flew over the barley, they laughed at the last twenty-four hours.

"Did you ever think you'd lead such an exciting career, Gillian McAllister?" he asked with a smile, making the dirt crinkle under his eyes. "And I suppose you didn't think tumbling would be a requirement."

"Not quite," she admitted. The doctor reached over and softly moved a strand of hair from her eyes. When she met his gaze, the moment felt new to her. The feeling was new.

"There, that's better." He smiled tenderly as the moment stretched out... until an uncomfortable feeling pulled their gaze apart—as though they both knew they were about to cross a line.

The doctor sighed as they now sat quietly listening to the sound of wind sweeping over the land. As Gillian watched his eyes travel the horizon, that feeling came over her again. It was the first time she'd really noticed how fit the doctor was, or perhaps the first time she'd admitted it to herself. His shirt had torn somehow, revealing a small snapshot of his shoulder. She studied his face, trying hard to be discreet. It was smudged with dirt and small pebbles; his hair had broken free from the tonic he used, falling gratefully over his forehead. Just for a moment it seemed not quite as black.

This was the first time he didn't look polished, and the first time she allowed herself to see how attractive he was. While she was being honest with herself, she could admit that on Sunday mornings, she'd find herself wandering past his townhouse in the hope he might join her at mass. It was always lovely to have a coffee afterwards and chat about the week, then stroll along the curly lanes through town. When she thought about it, she'd always arrive home later feeling quite agreeable. That wasn't such a bad thing, was it?

"You know Gillian, I think we make a good team," he said in all seriousness. "Apart from *that* of course." They both glanced up at the car then smiled. But the doctor's expression quickly weaved into something more... well, *more*, she thought. Gillian bit her lip, wondering if there was something happening between them. She hadn't really felt a spark in the past, though he was a bit dishy like this. She had an urge to ruffle his hair but didn't. And she had never come close to considering a life with him outside of the office. She was thirty-two now. Maybe it was time to look at things differently? He had a lot to offer and he *was* good-humored. Everybody in Port St. Mary admired him, and goodness knows Beaty would lap it up. Gillian sighed, *her* eyes now traveling the horizon.

"Gillian," the doctor said nervously. And it was in his slight tremble that she knew it was coming. "Have you ever considered... well, I mean, considered *us*?"

She felt her chest plummet in that single syllable, that simple word, those two letters. "Us?" she said as though she'd been struck over the head. "Of course. As you say we make a good team and..." And for a reason she couldn't understand, she now drew stiff. "And I wouldn't change a thing."

As she turned to the field, the silence was deafening. She could sense Dr. Pilkington's eyes lower, and it broke her heart. What had she just done? It probably took all his nerve to ask such a thing. It was sweet, really, but the silence was thick and she couldn't bear it. She took a deep breath. No it wasn't sweet at all, it was revealing and lovely and what did she do? She had dismissed it like it meant nothing. Like she didn't know where the conversation was headed. This time, she wanted to smack some sense into *her*self. Why did she push everyone away?

"Right then," he said making way to his feet and reaching out to help Gillian up. *Always the gentleman*, she thought. Suddenly there was a part of her that wanted to kiss him, just to see if she could feel that *feeling* one more time in her life. In any sane mind, there was no reason she couldn't. Maybe he had hidden talents, and it could be thrilling to peel away those layers. Though that did sound lewd, she always enjoyed a good challenge. Maybe he had saved the rascal in him just for her?

She was afraid no test romp would compare to that feeling she remembered. Maybe it wasn't meant to. That feeling, after all, had been tucked away in a past she'd tried with everything in her to forget. Yet she hadn't forgotten. Gillian sighed. Though it was only a summer, she knew a part of *him* poured out of her in every verse she wrote, in every breath she took, and in this case, she sighed again, with every rejection she gave.

Once they sorted the car out, Dr. Pilkington drove Gillian home and wished her a pleasant evening. She felt small.

THE SUN WAS LOWERING in the sky with dusk sneaking its way into yet another day on the Isle of Man. With Ireland at her back, Gillian stood facing her cottage in the countryside, the rumbling of Dr. Pilkington's car fading away in the distance. The few neighboring homes made it feel quiet, even lonely perhaps. Gillian cherished this place nestled by the sea, a place of her own that she was finally able to call home.

After having a bath, making a cup of tea, and thinking of all that had happened in the past twenty-four hours, Gillian took her little blue notebook to the patio out back. Writing in verse was all that she could manage to soothe her ache. She felt proud of her spicy ways and preferred to let her tears fall into words on paper instead of feeling sorry for herself.

Gillian glanced at the sea, waves swelling and falling on themselves. It was like a thick-woven fabric in blues and blacks, always at play in one way or another. Gillian never tired of the scene; whenever she needed to be filled up again, she'd sit by the edge of the crag and soak it all in. She sighed deeply then set down her notebook with a stone on top so it wouldn't fly away.

The sea was whispering to her again as she wandered closer to hear its wisdom. As she curled up, wrapping her cardigan around her knees, thoughts of the near kiss today sat uneasily on her mind. Gillian had never quite understood moderation before and settling for mediocre didn't seem right. Not that Dr. Pilkington was mediocre. He'd make a marvelous catch for anybody, but she couldn't imagine living without passion.

Gillian's gaze followed the horizon as thoughts of *him* came floating back. She could feel her chest rise and fall with a mix of sadness and excitement. Kissing Christian Hunter that summer, a mind-boggling fourteen years ago, was like tasting holy wine for the first time—each and every time— daring, intoxicating, as the last remnants of childhood slipped through her fingers.

THEY HAD AGREED TO MEET at Big Tub Lighthouse in the early evening, just before the sun would paint a masterpiece across the Georgian Bay sky. It was still light enough that she could see every detail of his face, the way his eyes drooped and how his shaggy hair tickled his ears and neck. He was wearing a T-shirt as white as the lighthouse and trousers the color of the flat rock surrounding them, rock that looked like walrus skin.

With all the confidence and cheekiness he'd shown since they met, Gillian watched as it washed away into the bay replaced by a sweet vulnerability. It was *this* boy, the lonely little boy she sensed inside, that was making her fall in love. But it was all happening so fast, like a carousel spun out of control as she stood just inches from him with her back against the lighthouse. She marveled at how he touched her in one place yet she'd feel it in an entirely new spot altogether. Gillian had never experienced this before, though it was lovelier than anything she'd ever known. He was feeling the same, she was sure of it. This would be her first real kiss—it should be a kiss to remember.

Christian slowly drew Gillian's arms above her head, cupping his hand over hers. He pressed against her body, just enough to make her shudder. And as he slid one hand down her arm, along the side of her clothed breast then to her waist, she could hear little gasps coming from her mouth. She begged inside for his lips to touch hers and felt tormented by his restraint. At the same time, she loved the feeling of his confidence working its way back. She was eighteen and all she wanted to do was ravage him. But he basked in teasing her as he skimmed his lips down her naked arm then across her clavicle, her blouse gathered at her chest. As his lips caressed her neck, her hands still pinned above with one hand, she could feel her chest rising and falling with anticipation. It seemed to Gillian that the warmth of his breath, as sensual as their kiss promised, might cause a frenzy in her. She'd already felt fairy tickles streaming down her back, making her jolt. Christian stopped just a breath away. She opened her eyes almost dazed with now both of his hands clasped in hers above as he gazed through those droopy, baiting eyes.

The wind from the bay shuffled past as the sky swirled into a mix of tangerine and crimson while Christian leaned in and put his lips on hers, slow and sultry. And as she lowered her arms to her side, she felt the little boy escape him entirely. More than one to remember, this was a kiss to be revered.

GILLIAN COULD TASTE the salty air on her lips now, smiling at the memory. But that's all it was—a memory. And although the wind wanted to set her straight, a seagull floating on that same breeze reminded her that something so sweet had a right to drift softly in her heart.

Gillian watched the seagull set down on the stony beach below. From this perspective the pebbles looked like a nubby blanket warming the shoreline, until the tide crashed through. She liked this time of day when the sea darkened under rolls of thick cloud and her old cardigan proved its worth just enough until it got too cool. In minutes there would be no beach at all.

Gillian sighed, having questioned her actions more than there were breaths to breathe. How could he ever forgive her? She'd left a letter for him on her auntie's porch, knowing he would come looking for her. It was brief and to the point. She had to return to the UK. *After all it was only meant to be a summer holiday,* she had written, *and her father had expected her.*

It wasn't fair running off like that. But there was no other choice and she couldn't regret her decision when it was made to save him. Though she'd considered going back to find him too many times to count, especially in those moments of weakness when she sat crumpled after enemy planes thundered above, Gillian always pulled herself together. But it was in their last kiss, a kiss that felt remarkably different from their first, that she sensed he could feel a good-bye in it. It was the love behind it that she hoped he would remember. All she asked of her auntie, if anyone had come looking for her, was to let things remain in the past. Somehow she knew her auntie had understood. There were no more words spoken about it.

But there were words written in a scrawly sort of writing, the letter Gillian dusted off and brought out to the edge of the crag with her, a letter she'd read only once before, a letter that her auntie had forwarded to her fourteen years ago.

November 30, 1932

Dear Gilly,

Every evening, I walk over to Big Tub Lighthouse hoping you might show up. But you never do. I listen to the loons calling out to each other hoping you'll answer. But you never do. I sit in my rowboat watching the beavers like we used to, thinking I'll hear your laugh again. But I never do.

If somehow this letter finds its way to you, I want you to know that I would have asked you to stay. And I would have only asked once. You have a mind of your own; trying to change it is too big a job for a crop duster on the Bruce Peninsula, I think. So maybe I'll never know if I did something wrong, something to drive you away. I figure it was just easier for you to leave the way you did. I'm okay with that now. I was pissed as hell before, but I'm okay now.

Gilly, I'm not even sure what to write except that you changed my life forever. Truth is, few ever get to know a love like we had, and it doesn't take an old soul to figure that out. If I could wish it twice for just one person, it would be you. Ours may have only been meant for a summer, but I want you to know it was the best summer of my life.

I'll always love you,

Christian

As the letter flapped in the breeze, mixed emotions toyed with Gillian. She could still see ghostly words slumbering between the lines all these years later—a man calling out to her but hearing no reply. She was sure this acute nostalgia would only last a moment, and then she could return to the life she had now. Maybe she really should consider a relationship with Dr. Pilkington after all. He was a good man, and it was a good life despite the war. Hers was now a life cloaked in honesty and hard work with hidden hopes that one day Gillian could live with the choice she'd made—a callous choice that no matter what would have hardened Christian over time. She had to live with it because one thing was for certain, Christian Hunter could never learn the truth about what really happened that summer.

In winter sitting by the fire,
We dwell on things to be.
The earth no longer robed in white,
But dressed in tender green.

Bringing us as days pass by,
Nearer our summer dreams!
The fury of the winter storms,
Gives place to calm blue seas,

The gulls no longer claim the shore
Where they have reigned supreme!
But summer days are very few,
The sun a buttery cream.

So while hoping for the best,
We'll ready for the worst.
By heeding common sense,
That to prepare oft time prevents.

Chapter 5

1946

THE PARTYGOERS HAD WORN themselves out. They'd already teetered back to their cabins before the clouds opened up showing off the real night sky, the one known only to the open sea. A smattering of men on the lido deck were engaged in deep, meaningful debates while their ritual of preparing a cigar, gazing at it tenderly before slicing its head off with a polished guillotine cutter, secretly summoned its own string quartet. Puffs of smoke swirled from their dialogue topped with a nightcap of cognac now that the women were long gone. Christian leaned against the railing wondering about their lives, wondering if these men were as settled as they wanted everyone to believe.

They were all so formal even during the day, dressed in their suits that Christian thought looked strangling. Some pranced around in their argyle vests hoping to woo a pretty stranger, not always sure if gender mattered. He felt disconnected to them as though he'd been watching some moving picture for the past seven days. Frolic whirled along the decks—something that surprised him. He'd expected at least a dash of misery considering the liner was headed to a land crippled from six years of warding off the Nazis. But the spirit on board was infectious, naïve perhaps. High society at sea with a somber mood waiting for them on the other end, he was sure.

Each day, Christian would watch passengers poaching deckchairs then saving them for others. It made him laugh the way they snapped straight up, on the lookout like meerkats poking their heads from their burrows. He was glad he wasn't that way at all. On the other hand, he thought it was wonderful that people were seizing the day, making their own joy in what could easily be considered a cauldron of mixed emotions with the end of the war leaving a tragic mess to clean up. They certainly wouldn't be able to breathe spirit into the ruins without an air of cheer in their stride.

He turned from the gruff voices that now broached the subject of England's state. They seemed to be guessing just as he was doing. It bored him quickly, each wanting to sound more *up* on the current status of England's people. Christian hoped that Gilly had come to her senses and returned to Ireland, safer from the turmoil and constant threat of bombers—although even Ireland's neutrality couldn't stop all attacks. As much as he hoped she was safe, he knew she'd never have left somewhere she felt needed. In the same breath, he found himself admiring her stubborn trait even as it drove him mad. Her affect on him hadn't changed.

Christian's eyes widened when he noticed a young couple tucked away under a staircase that led to the bridge, the aroma of the captain's pipe no doubt wafting through the grated treads. Either they were considerably daring, or the passion outweighed the risk. He was envious of their reckless joy and knew that would have been Gilly and him all those years ago. He sighed feeling a certain peace in that, then turned away knowing the moment was meant only for this couple.

The ship was nearing the English Channel. Although he couldn't make out any sign of the coast, being so dark, Christian knew the morning sun would bring it to light. His eyes sailed freely up the ship's black smokestack, its white stripe sharp against the sky, then over to the crow's nest that climbed into the stars. A great ocean liner with a history, he thought. He'd overheard an officer mention how it served as a hospital ship until just recently and how it had brought his brother back home where he belonged. There was something admirable in that. He could feel his lips curl at the edge—a silent understanding among wounded soldiers. Christian glanced down remembering.

The night air was cool now—a little too cool. He pulled his tweed flat cap down slightly at the front trying to stay warm then turned up the lapels on the jacket he'd worn a hundred times, drawing them together with his hands.

"Excuse me, sir?" a lanky steward said approaching him. "I'm afraid this deck is for first class passengers." Christian felt himself grimace, wondering how the steward had known he wasn't one of them. Then he smiled widely. He could see in the steward's eyes that both men were cut from the same stone. Just when Christian was about to say good night, the steward had slapped him on the shoulder and offered him a cigarette. Christian took it in gratitude even though he would never put one of those things to his lips.

"Thanks."

"Have a good night." The steward nodded then moseyed off, his hands crossed at the back. Christian turned to the railing again for one last look. He studied the rolled-up paper of the cigarette pinched at the ends, appreciating the gesture, then flicked it into the crests of waves all trying to snatch it at once.

WHEN CHRISTIAN OPENED HIS EYES, he could feel it instantly, a force pulling him to the deck, drawing him toward something special. He threw on his trousers, his undershirt barely pulled over his sinewy abdomen while making his way toward the gangway. The sky was clear and the railing free from what he'd suspected would have an onslaught of passengers wanting to get a glimpse of the Isle of Wight. The deck was surprisingly calm with just a smattering of people. When he looked up and felt a rush of cool air brush his shoulders, the Isle seemed an arm's length away. It was enormous. Christian felt like a child seeing something magical for the first time even though the Isle wasn't new to him at all.

The chalk cliffs were as stunning as he remembered, slicing straight into the water. He recalled how they wrapped around much of its coastline and was pleased to see it again, especially from this angle. From the air it affected him differently. At first sight, Christian thought the island resembled a colossal iceberg strangely topped with the greenest of green grass. There was a mist in the air today that made it feel like something from his imagination—a beauty that couldn't possibly be real. But it was real. He glanced at an elderly couple next to him who were equally as taken by the sight then smiled, a kindly nod in return. He wondered if moments like these needed to be shared with at least one other human being to be truly appreciated—otherwise what was the point?

The Port of Southampton was waiting for him at the

end of that stretch of water now staring down the bow. Christian curled his hands around the railing of the deck, feeling its moisture. The mile-wide inlet that sheltered the port was hardly the spectacle that the Isle of Wight was. No, that island could well be accused of impersonating a Venus flytrap. Its beauty snared you, slowly feeding you to the bowels of England.

Christian had once visited Southampton, and even though it wasn't a pleasing town with inspiring buildings, it was surrounded by some of the most beautiful countryside he'd ever seen—not a rare beauty in these bowels either. There was plenty of English landscape to be admired—that was if you could overlook the devastation in the height of the war. Christian could see it all best from his *Tiffy* when his squadron would fly low over the countryside on its way back from the mainland. That Hawker Typhoon was the only thing between him and meeting the rain gods in person, so he got rather chummy with that fighter plane and did something in it he never thought possible—pray. Pray to whoever up there would listen. He didn't care who or what, just that they'd listen. So he'd met Southampton from the air and from the ground and appreciated this place, filled with hardworking folk and some of the humblest tramp steamers on the water.

The ship was now approaching the docks, so Christian returned to his berth to arrange his one and only bag, a backpack that he'd saved from his time in the military. He didn't need much, just a change of clothes—something warm and something to keep him dry—for the rain was sure to come. He was able to strap his outerwear to the backpack and knew he'd manage to wash his clothes one way or the other. His toiletry bag, coupled as a first aid kit, fit in the front pocket of his canvas backpack nicely. It was roomy—huge compared to civilian packs he'd seen on the road. It had a rugged construction and served him well, but the best part was that it freed up his hands. It was just what he needed on this trip.

Christian made his way to a communal washroom—toddled would be more accurate—with the floor feeling like a conveyor belt. He took a moment at the mirror above a small sink. He turned the tap cold then felt the running water rush over his hands, scooping it up to throw into his face. His bristle was short enough not to bother shaving today. He never liked that chore and would sometimes go weeks without bothering. He could get away with it being so fair in color. It didn't really matter what anyone thought anyway—except maybe Gilly. He sighed heavily, feeling the ship rolling underneath him and finding it tricky to steady himself at times. Staring almost through the mirror, his mind drifted back to another time, to a moment when life was perfect.

THE HUMIDITY REMAINED high all week in Tobermory, but there was a light westerly breeze coming in from the bay that caught folks off guard every so often. Granted, that day the only two people by the shoreline, well on Earth for that matter, were Gilly and Christian.

"Like this?" she said in a velvety voice as she scraped the straight razor along Christian's jawline. He could feel the sharp edge taking the hair and cream along with it and gazed into her eyes knowing she had him right where she wanted—under her spell. A sudden glint in her eye and he knew she was up to no good. She couldn't have had more power, a straight razor in hand, her hair falling perfectly without even trying, and a sundress conveniently falling off one shoulder. His eyes sprinted from her plump lips down her skin to the clavicle and just beneath, her breast swelling with each breath she took. Her scent in the thick air drove him mad.

"So you think I'm a leprechaun do you?" she said reaching over to the tree stump on which sat a well-used washbasin and just under its rim, a frothy shaving brush. She swirled the brush in more cream then drew it down his naked chest, daring to shave what little hair his twenty-year old body had. Flicking the blade in and out of its handle, she stood in front like a panther waiting to pounce, her loose dress provocatively pulled above her knees.

Christian felt an eyebrow rise while he calmly smirked from one side of his mouth, lather left on the other side of his jaw. "I'd be careful if I were you. That thing's pretty sharp."

"You know," she said glancing over her shoulder at the bay just steps away, "leprechauns can make things disappear."

Both eyebrows rose this time, "You wouldn't."

"I think you look rather charming with half a beard. If you're not careful yourself, you might just walk around like that for the rest of your life. Leprechauns can be quite mischievous you know," she said with a cheeky leer.

Gilly slowly backed away, clearly knowing she didn't stand a chance, and swiftly turned running like a feline as fast as she could through the reeds, tossing his razor to some rocks on shore. Straight after her Christian ran, both of them waist high in lily pads and soaked from head to foot with all the splashing. When she lost her balance from his playful push, she struggled to plant her feet firmly in the softened stones underneath, so instead she managed to make her way to a large rock sitting just under the surface. She sat there catching her breath, a moment of quiet.

"Don't move!" Christian hushed.

"What is it?" she asked, returning his whisper.

"Can't you feel it?" Gilly shook her head while the sun danced on her skin, her wet nutty-brown hair running down her back. "There's a dragonfly sitting on your shoulder."

When the words left his lips, the world stopped. He could see in Gilly's eyes how intoxicating it was for her. She smiled at Christian in a way he'd never seen before. The iridescent wings of blues and greens rested their quiver against her skin. She looked sensual and completely relaxed.

CHRISTIAN DREW IN A LONG, deep breath then threw back his head. He'd carried that image of her framed in his mind for fourteen years.

A bellowing of the ship's horn drew Christian from his trance, bringing his image back to the mirror. It sounded again, only this time long and guttural, a pending doom in its call. He rubbed his jawline, noticing that his blister wasn't sore anymore. He studied his palm. It was finally healing.

A basket of facecloths sat on a ledge just above the sink. As he dried his skin, he looked into his eyes and for the first time had doubts, wondering if what he was doing was crazy. She would surely have a completely new life, maybe even her own family. A small part of him hoped she had, for he wanted to find her happy with a full, rich life. He wondered what he'd do if he found that to be the case—smile perhaps and wish her well. He couldn't really know.

CHRISTIAN HAD NO SOONER stepped off the gangplank when he noticed a series of what looked like Morris Tens, five of them in a row, sitting along the dock. He knew this model first hand since he'd driven one when he was here during the war. In his search for Gilly, he had met a couple that lived in the New Forest District. Percy and Pickles Spooner. He'd never forget names like those, and he'd certainly never forget two of the most eccentric people he'd ever stumbled upon. That same couple was at the top of his list now to visit. They may not have been able to help him four years ago, but he was certain they knew the coastline and would recognize the landmark in the article. Christian reached into the chest pocket of his jacket then sighed knowing the article was secure. He'd need it this time.

He spent the morning in town revisiting sights that remained standing and getting his bearings straight. It wasn't easy. Poor old Southampton from the bottom of the Avenue to the docks had been more or less flattened just about as badly as four years earlier… except Bargate. There it was still standing, stubborn and proud a building that didn't just mark the main gateway to the city but to Christian represented the strength of the people in it. The center of town reminded him of a great phoenix that could rise from the ashes. And it had already, on more than one occasion. He remembered how vulnerable it was, a port like that. It was a target that even the English Channel couldn't ward off. Christian could see in the eyes of the residents—morale here couldn't be broken, only bent. His eyes traveled over the rubble that hadn't yet been taken away and stopped every so often to admire the buildings that withstood the attacks. The air grew thicker with tiny droplets as the day wore on. And as the salty, industrial trail followed him, the clouds couldn't decide whether to gush down or not.

Christian preferred being by the docks, inhaling the

heady odor of fish and oil and found himself heading back in that direction. He passed a long line of workers dangling their legs over the dock and eating lunch from brown paper bags. He expected that he'd feel like a foreigner, whatever that meant, but he didn't. He felt connected to these people and liked that they nodded to him and tipped their caps.

"Alright?" one said through a nearly toothless mouth.

Christian assumed the man thought he was looking for someone or something? Or maybe it was obvious he was a foreigner. "Actually I'm looking for someone… well a place, really. Maybe you can help me?"

"You American?"

"No. Canadian. I was a fighter pilot here during the war."

The man's eyes traveled over him with an air of understanding in them, "Good ol' Canadians. What can I do for ya?"

Christian reached into his chest pocket to take out the article. "Do you recognize this place?" he said unfolding the paper and placing it in the man's blackened, stained fingers. The dockhand studied the photograph then slid his fingers along his jaw.

"Could be anywhere."

"But this lighthouse in the background—I've never seen one like it," Christian said. "Even in my time here with the air force."

"Don't matter none. Lighthouses in the UK come in all shapes and sizes. Too many to count anyhow." He shook his head, "Sorry mate. 'fraid I don't know it." All seven of the workers sitting there tried to help, but none of them recognized the lighthouse. It was just the beginning, so Christian wasn't bothered. No. He had to focus his attention on getting to the Spooners. Why they would know this place over a bunch of shipyard workers he couldn't be sure. It was just a hunch. And if they didn't know, they'd know someone who would.

A COACH TO BROCKENHURST STATION and rides hitched from two kind country folk brought Christian to the Spooners' garden gate. He noticed a new sign bearing the words,

HONEYSUCKLE COTTAGE

HOPE YOU BROUGHT A PINT—

OTHERWISE OFF WITH YOUR HEAD!

Christian smiled knowing he had the right place. The cottage hadn't changed a bit, apart from the added wine bottle feature in the front yard. On closer examination, it had to have been Pickles' handiwork—a wooden post with branches, each carrying its own bottle. Must've had over fifty of them. When Christian walked through the gateway he could see each one had a date written on it. He scanned the yard just a little more. The grass was overgrown and the clay roof tiles needed repair, not to mention the cladding chipping off the side of the cottage. A few trees had been cut down to bring in light, he figured. Otherwise the place was still nestled in the woods, hidden from the world. He could hear some crackling coming from the bushes near the house, then sighed when two nightingales broke into flight from their own ruckus.

Christian worked his way up the path to the front door with a strange sense of familiarity. Of course he had been here before, but it wasn't that. There was something in the air. Something that made him feel as though he was coming home. He tapped the knocker then waited. No answer. Maybe they were out, but he thought a wander around the back wouldn't do any harm.

As he turned the corner, he stood for only a moment when a screech nearly toppled him flat. Before he knew it, Pickles was climbing down from a tree house wearing oven mittens, shouting for *Mr. Spooner* to get down from there "this instant… it's Christian!" She wailed. "He's come home!" She nearly barreled him over, dungarees, feather boa and all, squeezing so hard he could only wheeze. From the slit of his eye, he could see Percy watching his step carefully.

"Well, blow my elderflowers right off their stems! Let me have a look at you!" Pickles' eyes twitched as they swept over him. "Good gracious, what have you done to yourself?" she said, her eyes full of tenderness and curiosity. She sowed kisses into his cheek and the other. "Look at you all scruffy. Still as gorgeous as ever I see despite your laziness. We'll fix that!"

"Christian!" Percy offered his hand and threw the other around him. "What a surprise! We were just having afternoon tea."

"Dinner already?"

"No, just a cup."

"Do you always drink tea in a tree house?"

"Well, not every day," Pickles answered for her husband. "Why? Is that strange?"

Christian grinned, shaking his head. "Not at all," he said, wanting to be polite.

"Mr. Spooner will take you inside, won't you dear, while I snip some parsley for supper. You *will* stay for supper, won't you?"

"I'd like that. Thank you."

Percy still towered over him. He looked thinner than Christian remembered. His nose resembled a potato and a man could get lost in those eyebrows. Christian smiled just as he had done when he first met this odd couple. "What are the oven mitts for?" Christian asked Percy as they headed toward the door.

"God only knows! I think all the bombs loosened her brain a bit."

CHRISTIAN WAS PLEASED TO SEE his friends hadn't really changed. Their spirit was still alive and thriving. And he couldn't have felt more welcomed.

"I'm afraid food rations have become even stricter since the last rumble of war, Christian, so we make do the best we can. Poor old Mr. Spooner here has had a terrible craving for humbugs lately, but they're about as scarce as a carnivorous billy goat. I'll never forget almost two years ago to the day, we were visiting Mr. Spooner's elder sister in London. Weren't we, dear?" she nodded to Percy. "She wouldn't listen to us, the buffoon. We had told her umpteen times to come and stay with us where it was, dare I say *safer*. Well, to make a long story short, her local sweet shop was called Nellie's. It was in an old carriage house on Buxley Road. Just a day after our arrival, a doodlebug landed too close for comfort and Nellie's was hit. Scared the life out of us! Although sweets were rationed severely at that time, on that harrowing day there were Liquorice Root Sticks and Catherine Wheels, Nipits, toffees, and Jelly Babies scattered everywhere, but not a humbug in sight! Poor Mr. Spooner," she said patting his lap. "Children were coming out of the woodwork to nab what they could from the remains," Pickles sighed, "and there's Mr. Spooner digging through the rubble to find his precious humbug. I can tell you, humbug or not, we weren't short of sweets that day! Thought I'd have a hole in my teeth by the time supper rolled around." She sighed again, "So I hope you can forgive the measly portion of bread on your dinner plate, Christian. Flour, I'm afraid, has found itself in the same predicament as our beloved sweets. Of course, I've been very naughty. If you sniff hard, you might just smell the makings of this week's flour ration in the oven—the remnants of that loaf of bread," she said glancing at the now empty basket.

"The meal is perfect just the way it is," Christian said rolling back his shoulders and feeling more comfortable than he had since he started his journey. If he ever came across a bag of humbugs, if he had to beg, borrow, or steal, nothing would stop him from getting them for Percy. He glanced around. The table was laid in a hodgepodge of items. Not a single dish matched and the chairs were three over-stuffed lounge chairs they had pulled from their tiny living room. Pickles had a taste for the gaudy, but Christian found her style charming. It suited her. Kitsch at its finest.

"You know, we're only rationed two ounces of margarine per week, times two of course—a gross substitute for butter. The first time I saw it, I thought I would gag—a glob of yellow swimming in the center of a white slab. Very puzzling indeed. I thank heavens every day for Elspeth."

"Who's that?"

"Elspeth? Why, she's our cow. We were fortunate to inherit her after the demise of Mr. Warrington, our neighbour. You'll have to say hello later. I think she's wandering the woodland at the moment. Mr. Spooner will see to it that she's safely in her stall before sundown." She gazed at Percy who was paying little attention. "Won't you, dear?"

"I can't imagine how tough it's been on people here for so long. I'm sorry."

"Don't be sorry, Christian," Percy slid in. "We've managed just fine. We took the war in stride and we're doing the same in the aftermath."

"Yes," Pickles smiled tenderly at her husband. "This war has made us resourceful and there are those who have far less. We had no children of our own to send off to God knows where in the hope they might survive, never knowing how they were getting on. Can you imagine the nightmare for those children and the unbearable grief all those mothers have gone through? And now, they're scrambling to find their babies again. It breaks my heart. Such a senseless thing war is—doesn't solve a bloody thing, does it Mr. Spooner?"

"You're right about that," Christian said while spooning up the last of his mashed potato. Dinner was simple but tasty, and in some ways he didn't feel as though any time had passed since their last meeting. He thought they would talk about it, how they'd taken him in for a short time while he was on leave, just for a weekend. How Percy had nearly run him over in his Morris Ten when he'd hopped over an old stone wall, escaping a paddock with an angry ram. That's how they'd met. The wheel had nicked his leg. It was barely a scratch, but Percy and Pickles seemed to feel obliged to help. Pickles nursed him back to health, and truth was, Christian liked the doting. It was something he hadn't had in eons and it reminded him of his mom. He certainly didn't get any coddling back at base.

They wanted to help him find Gilly. They really did. They showed her photo to everyone they knew, but it was hopeless. She'd left London and so had her sister Beaty. A shop clerk down the road told him that they weren't going back to Ireland, at least Gilly wasn't. That's all she knew and that's all Christian knew. He had thought about contacting her family in Ireland but knew how her father felt about *the Canadian*. A Canadian he'd never met. If Gilly's story were true, Christian figured he didn't want his daughter staying in a country so far from the family—so far from him. He couldn't blame her father. She was a treasure that no father in his right mind would want to lose. Yet after talking to Griffin, he now knew that in the end Gilly's father had nothing to do with it.

"Love," Pickles said taking Christian's hand, "why have you come? You haven't said."

"I guess I haven't." He glanced at Percy across the small, round table then into Pickles' endearing eyes. "There's something I want to show you." He asked Pickles if she wouldn't mind bringing over his jacket from the hook beside the front door. "Thank you." He reached into the chest pocket and took out the article.

"What's this?"

"Will you have a look, see if you recognize this place?"

Pickles studied the photograph but Christian saw nothing in her eyes that revealed she knew of this place. "Oh Good Lord, Christian, I know what this is about." Her eyes pinpointed his longing for a girl he once knew. "This is her, isn't it? This is the young woman you were searching for four years ago... Gilly."

"You remember her name," he said surprised.

"How could I forget? I see it now. You're still in love with her." Pickles stroked his cheek with the back of her hand. "Oh, my dear, you're in for heartache. A whole war has passed between you two."

"Let me see that," Percy insisted. The room was silent and now filled with the unmistakable odor of bread pudding that Pickles had in the oven. An egg timer broke the silence, and she was in the kitchen a moment later. Still not a word from Percy.

"Do you know that lighthouse?" Christian asked. "It looks like a bullet."

"Mmm. It does, but I'm afraid I don't recognize it. It could be anywhere." Percy grew silent again, cupping his jaw with his hand. Christian studied him as much as Percy studied the photograph. When he suddenly pinched his brow together, Christian became curious. Percy reached to the windowsill where a large, round magnifying glass was sitting. He brought it to his eye then the silence grew again.

Pickles returned, scooping a pile of bread pudding into Christian's bowl.

"Smells delish, don't you think?"

"Yes, thank you," he said pointing his chin up but leaving his eyes on her husband.

"Well," Percy finally said moving to Pickles' chair, "if you look here above this doorway, there's a symbol. Can you see it?" He turned to Christian. "It's hard to tell, but if you look closely, I think it has three legs on it." Christian had a look through the lens then nodded. "Do you know what this three-legged symbol means?" he said, his bushy brow arched.

"No."

"It's the Isle of Man. No doubt about it. They're proud of their red flag and fly their three-armored legs wherever they see fit, even above doorways. Port St. Mary is the only village I know that has this." He pointed to a jetty that crawled into the sea, barely visible in the corner of the photograph. "It's the longest, straightest one on the island next to Douglas, and from what I can see, this is a small place, far from the bustle of the capital."

CHRISTIAN LAY IN A FOLDAWAY BED that had been set up for him in the sunroom at the back of the house. Pickles wouldn't hear of him lodging anywhere else. Bunking up with them was perfect, and he was grateful. He liked the sunroom. It was where he stayed four years earlier and like then, the sounds of the night were soothing. The woodland wrapped around him echoing each one; the goldfinch that wouldn't sleep, twigs snapping under foot from a red squirrel or hedgehog, and the whirling of wind around the trees and past his nose through the screened-in walls.

As his eyes traveled the room in the darkness, signs of hard times remained. The silhouette of a mesh bag filled with onions and shallots hung from the ceiling against the dark backdrop. On a table in the corner, a jug of milk covered with muslin soaked in a basin of cold water trying to catch the draught. He would never look at his refrigerator the same way again.

Christian yawned, stretching his arms wide over the edge of the bed with quiet thoughts of the past resting on his mind. He thought about Pickles' bottle tree in the front yard and the meaning behind it. She had explained during coffee that each bottle represented an air raid that she and "Mr. Spooner" had survived. They hadn't enough bottles in all reality with over fifteen hundred alarms in their neighboring Southampton, fraying their nerves each time. They had kept wine or bottles of water in their shelter hidden under the forest canopy. The next morning, suffering from a bit of *Divine Punishment* (Pickles' term for a well-deserved hangover), they'd date the bottle then add it to the tree. But those sirens, Christian could see her hand quiver just at the thought. He remembered them from his time here and felt a genuine empathy for the people in the south. The Luftwaffe terrified them.

Something Pickles said still lingered on his mind when she had talked about Gilly and how he wanted to find her. "You can't go back. Nothing good ever comes from it." A part of him knew she was right. They may have loved each other once, but... No! He couldn't think one way or the other about it. He wasn't going there to charm her or expect anything apart from peace and closure knowing she had survived it all. Maybe, just maybe, he'd find out what really happened, if Griffin's suspicions were right. If he found her with a husband and children, he knew that she'd have made that life incredible and he'd be happy for her.

Christian pulled the blanket over his shoulders then gazed through the darkness. He never knew what Gilly saw in him, why she was attracted to him. She often said he was different from all the boys she'd ever met. He imagined she was right. But he knew it wasn't about conquering a Canadian in the wild. They were drawn together plain and simple.

Gilly understood him. He knew that but struggled to understand why she'd left. He would've moved anywhere for her, but she didn't give him the chance. She didn't want to take him away from his home, the place he was most comfortable. At least that's what she said in her good-bye letter. Christian sighed, unsure of his decision to go to Port St. Mary in the morning. But he knew not even his own nerves could stop him.

Even though he couldn't heed the Spooners' warning about long-lost love, somehow he knew they were rooting for him. Christian's eyes fell shut with a sobering feeling that tomorrow he could be standing in front of the woman he had never stopped loving.

For I was born with wandering feet
They wouldn't stay in place,
The urgent need to travel on
Was my only saving grace.

And so I sailed thro' winter storms,
Where icebergs loomed above gray seas,
And when at last I reached the shore,
Found earth frost-bound as if in sleep.

And so I sailed towards the sun,
Where skies are blue and soft winds blow,
And thought at last I've found the place
Where I will stay—but no
The urge to travel on remained
And so I said farewell again.

So I, my wandering days now done,
Tread English soil from whence I sprung,
My youth is spent, my questing feet
Content to rest, and no more seek!

Chapter 6

Canada—1932

Mr. and Mrs. Herbert McAllister
Undisclosed Address, Pretty Place Only
Toronto, zone (numbers aren't important) Ontario
Canada

10th of June 1932

Dearest Beaty,

Don't you just love Auntie Joyce's stationary? I
knew I liked her for some reason. Who would think
to put a beaver and Celtic cross on a letterhead? Only
someone daring—that's who. It makes me smile.

In any case, I hope this letter finds you well and
in love... perhaps? Horatio isn't nearly as stuffy as his
name implies. I'm glad I had the chance to meet him.
He grows the loveliest flowers; you were right about
that.

I have been anxious to sit down and write to you
every detail of my adventure up to now. Oh, I dare
say, you'd be proud of me lapping up every morsel—

odd as some things may be. But not the boys! They're gorgeous, hardy looking, like a new recipe, really. Everything's new, not old and grim like your first edition print of Anna Karenina. Even the kind, old gardener next door confessed he was nearly fifty years old! You should hear him talk. His dialect sings in your ears. When was the last time you could make out what an old person said? Oh Beaty, Canada isn't at all what you'd think. Not a soul runs about wearing a Mohican headdress, you know. Whatever gave you such an idea?

Uncle Herbert and Auntie Joyce met me at the port in Halifax as planned. I didn't have to wait a moment for them as I always had to with Daddy. On the long drive to Ontario, they told me that they had been well warned not to arrive late or he'd see to having their heads put on platters for show at family reunions. Uncle Herbert found that to be rather amusing coming from "an old fart like him," he said, "a man who's never been on time in his life."

They live in Toronto, as you well know, but tucked away in a place called Rosedale—not quite as "in town" as I would have liked. I'd sooner be roosting above one of those Witt streetcars here where gossip could slither up the cables and be served with a good hunk of morning bacon. Shame really. I'd love to be in the thick of it. There's a wonderful ravine, though, at the back of their garden and a gorge nearby for secret strolls and fantasy. That keeps me busy for hours. Uncle Herbert is often sent out on the hunt for me before the night keeps me trapped until dawn. Wouldn't that be exciting? Their house is large and rather stately, but the people in it are far from snooty. They are just as I remember from our times together before Mommy died—happy to dig out a stubborn potato from the dirt with the rest of us. Too bad I can't say the same for the neighbors, especially one brazen minx who spoke ill of Uncle Herbert at the grocers.

But my goodness, has Uncle Herbert put on weight! When he laughs, his belly jiggles, and he's balding now. Tries to hide it by sweeping strings of hair across his head as if it wasn't obvious to everyone that their days were numbered. By the time summer is over, I plan to have him polishing that head of his, proud that it shimmers in the moonlight. His moustache is a copy of Daddy's while he seems to have a dislike for fedoras. I think he blames them for his balding. He's also taken up saying "eh" like the locals after all his statements. It's only been three weeks and I'm finding I do the same.

Auntie Joyce calls him Pop. Don't know where she got that from, which by the way is what they call fizzy drinks here. Have you ever heard such a word? Isn't it delightful? I want to use it in every sentence but have chosen not to for fear of tiring of it like Uncle Herbert's steak and kidney pie. He's becoming quite Canadian, you know, wanting to drown everything in maple syrup. Have you ever had steak and kidney pie with syrup? I think, in this case blending the two cultures is a mistake. By the time he's sixty, he'll be completely bald with no teeth!

He got the pie and syrup idea from Mr. Thorthborough around the corner, I was told. Must have been having a bit of fun with him, don't you think? But doesn't it feel as though you're lisping when you say his name? Go on, say it, Beaty. I know you want to. Timothy Thorthborough. I can't help laughing myself. What a delightful name to make you so aware of your tongue like that, eh? You see, Beaty, I can't help myself. I want to say "eh" all the time.

Auntie Joyce is a character in her own right. You know, she wears an ill-fitting angora jumper every Saturday evening when they go to play bridge at the Davenport's down the street. Makes her bosom look enormous. Trouble is she's a bit podgy everywhere so you can't tell one lump from the other—except in that jumper! Ordered it from one of these catalogues, you know. I quickly understood her reasoning when I caught a glimpse of the Davenport's domestic help bending over in their strawberry patch by the hedgerow. He looked like something sent down from the heavens—a cousin to Thor, perhaps. I'm sure even you would have been watering at the mouth, Beaty. The lovely thing about it is, Auntie Joyce doesn't seem to notice her dimensions at all and will wear the most spirited clothes.

And if you're wondering or worse yet, concerned, I'm not bored for a second. Both keep me wildly entertained with that Mexican piñata they have hanging from their big oak in the garden. They replace it every week. Not the oak, the piñata. Must have a stash somewhere. God knows where they get such a thing! I keep meaning to ask, but I get sidetracked by the fever of this place. You should see Auntie Joyce with a stick. Last weekend, she chased Uncle Herbert all over the garden, threatening to swat him if he ogled

Livingstone's Grocers' cashier one more time!

My goodness, Bea, you've never seen so many trees! Canada's full of them. If I only had a penny for every single one. Uncle Herbert tells me that I will have plenty of time to count all the trees this summer as they intend to take me to the Great Lakes. I wonder what's so great about them. Can't possibly be true that you can't see the other side, but I'm just aching to find out. Of course, Lake Ontario is only steps away from here, but it's the smallest of the lakes, Uncle Herbert says, and we're going somewhere much grander. They have a small summerhouse, apparently in a place called Tobermory, so I'll be sure to let you know if the rumors are true. Do you remember our stay in Tobermory, Scotland all those years ago? Such a happy memory when Mommy was alive. Although I was very young, it's one I remember. As you can see, Canadians seem to have an appetite for borrowing British names. There's even a London here with a Thames River, if you can believe it.

I realize I've been writing far too much. "Willywigs!" I can hear you say like our head mistress at school. Do you remember her, the one with the moustache? "When will she be done with it?" she'd say. For some reason you, too, seem to think I am garrulous by nature, but if I were you, I'd have a good stare in the mirror, especially when it comes to Winifred Beastly tales, although I admit, they do have their appeal. At least I got to the important bits. If you're interested in learning all about my journey, I'm afraid that will have to wait. Auntie Joyce is calling me for supper, I think. There's an irritating buzz from the first floor and she does this funny thing with her eyes when you're late.

I'll be sure to write again soon. A squeezy hug as always,

Love,

Gillian

Post Script – I think it's time you put some freesia on the table before they're finished for the season. I'm quite sure the scent would lure in Horatio.

As GILLIAN LAID THE TABLE for supper, a waft of shepherd's pie floated from the kitchen—worlds apart from the ever-present curry in the maharaja's home. She hoped the children were happy to be back in India, but the truth was there was nothing like a plate of shepherd's pie to make you feel at home.

"Do add one more place setting, won't you, dear?" Auntie Joyce said.

"Yes, of course. Who's coming to dinner?"

"Well, it's a surprise really. If I told you, it would spoil the whole thing." The wheels in Gillian's head started turning instantly. It couldn't possibly be a neighbor or even one of Uncle Herbert's colleagues with shepherd's pie on the menu and nothing formal on the dining table. At least she wouldn't have thought so. It must be family, but it couldn't be Roderick; he was at Queen's University at Kingston, all the way on the opposite end of the lake—too far to drive for supper. But he was their only child and Gillian hadn't seen him in donkey's years. They used to play together all the time when they were little. Daddy wasn't too pleased that Uncle Herbert had gone ahead and accepted a position in Canada, breaking up the family like that. But it must be Roderick. She felt giddy at the thought. How would he look as a grown-up? Bet he was so Canadian now; maybe he even picked up their accent.

GILLIAN WAS RIGHT ALL ALONG—it *was* Roderick. He'd come down from the university to visit, all because of her. And what a feast for the eyes he turned into. His hair had gone dark and his eyes even darker, but in a mysterious way. She was sure he'd have the pick of the lot when he earned his degree. It was fun to see him again, only now he seemed a little embarrassed by Auntie Joyce's doting. He remained his quiet self, but the two cousins had never needed to say much to one another. He always said she did enough talking for the both of them.

"Would you like to take a stroll?" Roderick asked Gillian. "The evening air is fresh and you look as though you could use a stir."

"Do I?" she questioned, wondering how she must look.

"Yes, you two go off now. Your father and I will clean up," Auntie Joyce darted in.

"Will we now?" Uncle Herbert said turning down the corner of the newspaper stuffed in his face.

"Are you sure? I'd be happy to help," Gillian offered.

"I know you would, dear, but you and Roderick haven't met since you were children and now look, you're both all grown up. Take some time, just the two of you. I'm sure you have piles of catching up to do."

Roderick kissed his mom on the cheek then snatched Gillian's cardigan from the back of the chair. Thinking he'd changed and would drape it over her shoulders, he instead tossed it into her arms with a smirk to go with it.

HE WAS RIGHT, the evening air was lovely—not quite as

humid as it was earlier. They strolled the gardens nearby for ages it seemed, nodding to passers-by as they, too, chatted endlessly. No doubt they looked like an item to strangers, Roderick tall and devilishly handsome with her arm coiled in his. But it was that swagger of his that drew eyes from all directions. There were so many questions. She wanted to know all about his Canadian adventure and she suspected he wanted to know the same about her. The moments of quiet between them felt like whispers of curiosity.

As easy as their reunion felt, Gillian couldn't help this feeling that Roderick was holding back. Surely such an adventure as moving across the Atlantic at the ripe age of eleven would stir up all sorts of stories. But no, there was something... something behind those mysterious eyes. She decided to press him just a little. Gardens filled with roses and manicured paths and perfectly polished stars couldn't possibly unearth deep dark secrets. No, Roderick needed to be taken to the wild. The gorge perhaps with the moon spying through the treetops would do nicely.

"This is more like you, taking me to a place like this. Roses are pleasing but they aren't really you, Gillian. This gorge suits you much more," Roderick said when they arrived.

"Do you like it? I come here all the time."

"Not at night, I hope."

"Why? Because you think I'd lose my way?"

"No. I'm quite sure you're like a cat."

"A cat?" She felt her brow arch at the insinuation.

"Yes, with night vision and on the prowl. It's only others I wouldn't trust if you really want to know," he said while taking her hand as they climbed down to the path below.

She took her hand back, thank you very much. "You can't

live your whole life not trusting others, Roderick."

"You're still as stubborn as you ever were, aren't you?"

"That has nothing to do with this conversation and for God's sake," she shouted back, "I am *not* stubborn!" She started to laugh then ran as fast as she could to her favorite spot, an enormous tree fallen across a dry riverbed carpeted in rocks and small rounded stones.

After teetering across the trunk as though they were on a tightrope, they found a comfortable spot to sit and dangle their feet—hers peeking out of her new wide-legged trousers. Oh, she loved how easy they felt, high on her waist and long on her leg. It was very dark now, but the moon did its job nicely, casting just enough light so she could see Roderick's expression and a hazy shimmer on the low ferns lining the path.

"I'm glad you brought me here. It's been ages, but when we first came to Canada I frequented this place nearly every day after lessons. I'm glad you like it, too." He turned to her, "And I'm glad you're here," he said with a sudden serious expression, his brow pinched together. She was right. She knew there was something.

"What is it, Roderick? What is it you're not telling me?"

He sighed deeply, his chest swelling up. He held his breath for just a moment long enough to worry her.

"Well, since you ask." He looked away, but his eyes worked themselves back to hers. "I think I'm one of those."

"One of what?" she asked curiously.

"You know, *those*... a homosexual."

"Good Lord! Really? Oh how thrilling! I've never met one before." Gillian could feel herself gasp.

"Thrilling?" he laughed. "My, you are a character Gillian McAllister. I've been mulling it over for years."

"Well, what are you doing about it? No good being all talk you know."

He suddenly looked a bit pale. "The truth is I haven't quite decided about it."

Gillian felt a *snittering* coming on and no one could tell her that wasn't a word. It perfectly described how she was feeling! "Well, you either are or you're not. Which is it?"

Roderick took a moment to ponder. There was that chest swell again. "I did get rather cushy with that gem father brought home from the office last Christmas. I saw the way he gazed at me from behind the platter of sweet potatoes. Then before I knew it, my forearm was nearly grazing his as I passed the turnip. Mom was livid I passed across the table like that, but I could see his appreciation."

"Well, there you go. It's settled."

"I'm afraid it's not as simple as that."

Now Gillian was really getting agitated. "Hogwash! If you're concerned about what others might think, you'll never know the joy of a buttercup again. Everything will slowly begin to look gray and your mood will match—every waking hour. You will become a sourpuss and no one, not even me, will want to spend another moment with you."

"Is everything always so black and white with you?" Roderick dribbled.

"My dear cousin, far from it. I see every shade, every hue known to mankind. I see sparkle where you see matt. I see possibilities where you see obstacles. What a bore it would be if you were anything but what you are, Roderick. But I still will not want to spend another moment with you until you get your story straight. Everyone else can go roll in stinging nettle!" She leaned over to kiss his dishy but witless cheek then darted straight up, trying to keep her balance on the log. "When you've come to your senses and admitted it to yourself, our code shall be a wink across the room… two winks if you're adamant." How dare he glare up at her with those eyes turning all puppy on her! "Only then will I be able to say that I know one personally."

GILLIAN'S ROOM WAS COZIER than the one at the maharaja's. There was a pretty bedstead with a canopy that reminded her of her parents' and a small sitting area with a fireplace. Although the room was a good size, Auntie Joyce had managed to fill it with so many family knickknacks, which proved to be less strangling than they were haunting. Gillian was sure her great Auntie Essie's dog, Miss Marple the Boston terrier stuffed with a sly expression pressed into her face, had yelped mysteriously during the last full moon. The knickknacks reminded her of Daddy's prize fowl he had perched under the crown molding of his study. Those glassy eyes gave her nightmares, the way they followed her.

She plopped into the small, velvet settee at the foot of the bed, Miss Marple tucked behind the drapes and out of view. As Gillian ran her fingers along the curves of the paisley pattern, she wondered if she was too hard on Roderick. She didn't think so. No one should be concerned about what others think. If he was a homosexual, so be it. She'd love him just the same. She didn't particularly care what went on in anyone's bedroom except her own anyhow, and if he wanted to prance around showing off a new flame, she'd jolly-well hope so! She'd do the same. On second thought, being a peeping Tom at Beaty's was a bit thrilling. The act reminded her of sneaking a sip of Daddy's sherry when his back was turned. She knew it was risky, but she couldn't help herself. Twice, Beaty had to peel Gillians eyes from the window. Perhaps she did care about other people's love lives after all. Regardless, she hoped to get a wink from Roderick one day soon. He was only staying for the weekend, so she daren't say it would happen now, but she'd hold out for Dominion Day. At least he was coming for that. She knew Beaty would disapprove of his "recent confusion," but she'd come around. Beaty loved him just as much as Gillian did.

Gillian was glad that she found some time to write to her sister. It must have been hard for Beaty. She didn't really want Gillian to go. Beaty's wit had turned to porridge in the days before she left. Her constant advice was suffocating.

"Now be careful not to pick up their dialect! You know how the colonies have butchered the English language over the years. Separation has its downfalls!"

"As far as I know, Canada's no longer a colony," Gillian said, her tongue like a sharp blade of grass.

"Perhaps not, but it remains part of the British Empire and that is likely the only reason Daddy considered sending you there. Of course, India is, too, but *that's* a whole other matter. Foolish I think. He always was soft when it came to your whims. And yes, yes, I know Canada was *his* fanciful idea; that's neither here nor there. I *do* worry about you, Gillian, even though I am well aware that you would happily wrestle a grizzly if you got half a chance! Oh, you can be too impulsive, and one of these days… Good Lord, I shudder to think!"

GILLIAN TUCKED INTO THE SETTEE, oddly missing her sister. There was something comforting knowing that Beaty was watching over her. And now she was a world away. Gillian didn't like when they quarreled, although they left on good terms. They always did. It was only that Beaty worried about her travelling to a new country, which Gillian quite understood. She didn't know what to expect either. As embarrassing as it was to admit, somehow Gillian had expected fashion from the turn of the century; she expected to stick out like early morning mist—always pleasing to the eye. Sadly, Gillian fit in like a pearly glove in the city.

The one thing that appeared to distinguish her from Torontonians was her expression. The clerk at Eaton's in town gazed queerly at her when she said she needed her fishing hooks within a fortnight. She wasn't sure whether he was more befuddled by the timeframe or her wanting to go fishing. Later, Auntie Joyce unveiled her Eaton's catalog, which unleashed a beast in the aging woman—an honest to goodness beast. Gillian was sure she might be spoiled with a little something, but her Auntie was bedazzled and there wasn't a thing Gillian could do to get her attention. Apparently she used their mail order service regularly but never got it right with the sizing. Bless her! She confided in Gillian that when the postman rang, her eyes would shift in all directions, worried that one of the neighbors would spy her purchase. "Rosedale is like that you know," she said with one arched eyebrow, like a sleuth.

Fortunately, Uncle Herbert had quite a sense of humor and had no desire to keep up with the Jones' despite where they lived. It was a fact. Just yesterday, Gillian had overheard two of their neighbors saying the most degrading things about her uncle behind the root vegetables at the corner market. Telling Beaty was best, although she hoped her sister wouldn't press for more details if she replied. Imagine criticizing him for wanting to celebrate Canada's birthday with his niece in an apparently beautiful part of the country, whether it was a suitable place to visit or not. *Hussy!* Gillian thought at the time. The one with the ugly hands. Gillian saw her fingering the parsnips then putting them back. Every time she'd think of her, Gillian would have nightmares about those hideous paws.

Gillian rustled her bottom in the settee trying to shake away the thought—feet up, cushion snug in her lap. Frankly, the people of Toronto weren't the least bit stuffy, but in Rosedale, sometimes the nostrils here were flaring wider than in Wentworth Estate. Pretty place—Rosedale— though life grew juicier the further you got away from it. That was why Gillian was anxious for Dominion Day. What a splendid name for a country's birthday. Though Uncle Herbert called it low-key, she hoped he didn't mean dull. The last thing she wanted was to become a hermit tucked away in the woods. How would that look? She'd end up growing warts in all the wrong places, and over time her hair would matt and bunions would confine her to a rocking chair— back and forth, forth and back on a pine-planked porch while playing a ukulele and spitting tobacco into a bucket! Still, it did sound exciting. Gillian couldn't wait to see what was lurking in this Tobermory place. A whole summer by the Great Lakes, not just one day. The mere thought of it wrung out every sour notion Gillian ever had, even that of becoming a hermit. A lake so big you couldn't see the other side and so fresh you could drink from it. Georgian Bay and Lake Huron, named after the Indians Uncle Herbert said, side by side. She wondered if she'd meet one—an Indian that is. Gillian bit her lower lip in anticipation.

EIGHTEEN DAYS HAD PASSED since Roderick left and again returned—still no wink. He hardly said a word to her upon his arrival yesterday and was conveniently absent from the morning breakfast table. Well, two could act like that if he wanted. She'd help Auntie Joyce prepare a picnic lunch and see to putting a jar of gumption inside labeled, *Roderick— three tablespoons a day unless you want the gray haze stuck to your eyes permanently. Four tablespoons and you'll actually see a buttercup again.*

When Gillian looked at the top of the staircase, Roderick stood on the landing as though he was royalty—two-toned brogues and all! Perhaps he had expected rose petals to be peppered in front of him as he entered the kitchen? Cheeky thing considering he hardly noticed the feast she and her auntie had prepared.

Auntie Joyce had lined the picnic basket with a blue gingham cloth. The basket alone looked good enough to eat, but when she darted up her finely plucked eyebrows at her sourpuss son, Gillian knew for the second time that she liked her aunt for good reason.

"Well, get a move on Roderick," Auntie Joyce spat. "I'm not growing any younger, you know."

THE SUN WAS A STUNNER TODAY. The car was finally packed and a newly arrived letter from Beaty was clamped in Gillian's fingers. Roderick had spent the morning pouting like the little boy who waved to her from the boat in Dublin. She knew he was still moaning over the other weekend, but once he simmered down, he'd see that she was right. Shame he'd have to return for summer studies at the university. A few short days in Tobermory probably wouldn't do much to loosen the stick from his backside. He'd make a fine solicitor, solving everyone else's problems but his own!

Gillian glanced his way feeling no mercy whatsoever as he climbed into the backseat. Not even a flutter her way.

Served him right, spineless jellyfish. Instead Uncle Herbert deserved her attention. He loved his DeSoto. And Gillian loved the way her uncle admired his own reflection in the black finish, giving a little polish with his elbow. She didn't know a soul in London who had his own private car, apart from the maharaja, of course. Her uncle winked at her as he slid behind the huge steering wheel.

"All set?" he called out.

"Yes, of course we are Herbert," Auntie Joyce snapped, wearing a huge brimmed straw hat. She had changed it twice since breakfast. "Now stop stalling. We don't want to be late for the festivities. We have a long drive ahead."

As the tires rolled over the stone drive, Gillian glanced over her shoulder at the house vanishing through the trees. That feeling had returned, suddenly and piercing. The same feeling washed over her that night at the maharaja's. *Someone* was out there—for her. His breath was closer now. She knew it. She could feel it drawing her toward him and feared she wore the same glazed expression as the woman behind the neighbor's curtain at Beaty's. But as Uncle Herbert turned the corner, a brush of wind made her gasp, washing away all evidence of sheen. She took a peek in his rearview mirror just to be sure.

Looking down at Beaty's letter whispering her name, she paid no mind whatsoever to the wheezing coming from that *creature* sitting next to her. He was eyeing her but she refused to give in and stuck her nose up just a little. The envelope. She tore along the edge, wondering if Beaty could have possibly received her letter already.

21st of June 1932

Dearest Gillian,

This is your sister, Beatrice writing—the one with the very impatient glare searing my finest stationary. Can you see it? It's staring right up at you this very moment. In my wildest dreams, I wouldn't have expected for it to take you three whole weeks to write to your sister. Let me top that with a glop of double cream. Three whole weeks. I can only say that the blow has been cushioned by our dear father, who has informed me—twice now—of your inherent safety, and dare I say imminent vagary, knowing you! Yes darling, that means whim. You can add that to your list of words and please don't go deforming that one, too. Being a writer doesn't give you a license to invent your own words, does it? I wouldn't be surprised in the least if you had already secured a summer job at one of those papers they call magazines.

I'd be wary of these catalogs you were telling me about if I were you. You can't imagine what the world is coming to. Just the other day, Winifred Beastly nearly had a coronary on the spot. We all thought it was the Spotted Dick she'd had for elevenses. When she came to, her nose was buried in Harvey Nichols' spring catalog. There was no further explanation needed. We saw it with our own eyes—women's undergarments advertised on the page next to men's leatherback diaries! Can you just imagine the things they'd write? Someone should have these magazine editors arrested on the charge of indecency. To add insult to injury, the woman stood up, breaking wind right in front of Mr. Tyler. Vulgar creature.

Now, to answer your question. No, I do not like Auntie Joyce's stationary. I find it preposterous to put a rodent on the same page as a Celtic cross, insulting in fact. You can see straight away the ill-effects such a wild place as Canada has on the brain. Now we have evidence. I beg of you Gillian, please do not go nutty yourself. I'd be quite embarrassed to admit I had a mad sister. But I promise that if it happens, I shall come to visit you at the sanitarium every Sunday after mass. You may find me sporting a headscarf and a fine pair of sunglasses. I've seen them at Marks & Spencer you know—cost a fortune, the silly things!

Speaking of Marks & Spencer, I was feeling adventurous and wandered over to the "unmentionables". They've come a long way in hosiery, you know. I gave a lacey corset a try. I don't like the new term "girdle." Makes me feel like a cow. When I envisioned it with stockings, I immediately saw a trollop staring back at me in the mirror. In the bright light of day, I might say it was not for me, but since Horatio wasn't expecting me until half six, I bought it. Not the one at Marks & Spencer, far too dear, but nearly a copy at Prudence's Pinafores on the corner, just down the way. She carries a nice variety for these times and for a pittance in comparison.

Now, you implied in your very delayed letter to me that Auntie Joyce has seen better days in her style. I think you should take that angora jumper and bury it deep in that gorge you told me about. Don't go wearing it yourself, otherwise you'll wind up in the throes of passion with Thor down the street. Oh that would be something, wouldn't it?

By the way, wherever did you get the notion that I didn't like your nonsense, Gillian? I get quite a kick out of it, for your information. You can never write too much for me. I shall be the first in the queue to buy your debut novel. Of course, I'd expect a small dedication, for I know that I've been quite an influence in your life. Now that I've got that off my chest, I shall wish you the most marvelous time this summer by the Great Lakes. I envy your spirit, going so far from home. I'm afraid England is as adventurous as I can manage. You really are a marvel, my dear! Mommy would be so proud.

Do write again soon. I don't want you to become a stranger. And please tell me all about Roderick when you meet him.

My love to you all,

Beatrice

Post Script – Mr. Thorthborough kept me in stitches for ages. I spent the whole next morning at Barclays asking everyone to say his name.

Post Script for the anything but fainthearted – Never mind that hussy in the grocers. She can go ahead and spread her peacock's tail somewhere else!

As I sit alone in the old armchair,
My thoughts wander back through the years.
And see again in the heart of the fire,
The pictures I made of the things I desired.
Of my youth and my hopes and the promise of love,
To be mine in the future with life at the flood.

The fire's shadows recall things long past,
How we walked hand in hand down a flowering path.
When each sunrise brought beauty that went through the day,
And each sunset brought peace as light slipped away.

And while the fire dies, it still leaves a glow,
Of comfort and warmth though the flame has burned low.

Chapter 7

My GRANDDAUGHTER'S CAR is already pulling up the long drive leading to my son's horse farm. Such a curly road he built as though trying to dodge any number of oak trees that swindle sunlight from the farm's entrance. He always was a tree-hugger, my son, but in a good way of course. True, there's nothing quite like the feeling of breaking free from that checkerboard of trees to sprawling paddocks with white board fences that roll with the hills. From a distance, the farm looks like waves of white sheet music pasted on unbound green parchment. Only the score would depend on the season, and today it's playing the coo of a mourning dove on the eaves trough next to me. I notice the gutter is fat with autumn leaves. I would have loved growing up in such a place. My son has more land than he can manage, but it keeps him as happy as Larry and that's all that matters.

London, Ontario may well be known as corn country, but there are plenty of horse farms surrounding it, and Arva is just a stone's throw away from the north end. Before my license was snatched from my purse, it took me only three minutes from the Eloise Teas tea room to Masonville. I positively loathed all the traffic. I much preferred taking the country road past Sunningdale Golf and Country Club and over to the west end to get to my square of concrete jungle.

Though it wasn't an attractive pile of flats, we'd made it our home when maintaining a garden became too much for even an enthusiast like me. I can't count the number of times my son barked about Angus and me moving into the "guesthouse," as he likes to call it. But I wouldn't hear of it. No matter how I considered it—twitchy left eye, index finger hanging from the edge of my lip, or in a drunken stupor after eating a slice of Angus' Christmas pudding—all I could see was my daughter-in-law's fictional smile through gritted teeth. One should never live that close to their in-laws. Case in point and thank God for that, Kate replaced her.

I'm here now staying in the main floor office-turned-guest room for "easy walkabouts" my son says. What he really means to say is "easy access" for paramedics. They know it's only a matter of time, and it's true that I can't manage on my own now. Soon enough I'll be led to the hospital. So I want to enjoy every moment here, including watching my granddaughter as she now closes the door to her car and scampers over to her Shetland pony, Ballerina. Always looks as though she'll get her big head stuck—not my granddaughter but the pony, of course—the way she pokes it through the white boards of the fence with a wagging tail in excitement to see Gilly—like a dog greeting her master.

Gilly adores that old pony, and nothing gave me more pleasure than to give it to her on her fifth birthday. Angus and I saved every penny for two years just to see how high she could leap with joy. She didn't disappoint. Springs on her feet, I'd say.

Every so often I wonder what's happening over there in the guesthouse where Gilly's been living since she started at the university. Now she's finished, her name followed by a slew of well-earned letters, and slaving away at my story. Somehow though, I suspect there's more going on in that head of hers. But I can't put my finger on it. From my bedroom window, I can see *her* fingers, dancing on her keyboard every evening and then again before the worms get pulled from the earth for breakfast. I would have thought she'd move the desk far away from my prying eyes. I have this feeling she wants an invisible connection between us, like telepathy.

When she thinks I'm not looking, I know she is studying me—like now. She probably thinks I've fallen asleep, wrapped like a cocoon in this lounge chair between the guesthouse and the main house. On autumn days like this, whether my son agrees or not, I march in my crumbling way straight to the patio. And if in my skeletal state they don't take me outdoors when I've been admitted, I will thump the chief of staff until he begs me to leave.

My eyeglasses are thick like hardened fat and leave my nose sore and red—one of the inherent disadvantages of old age that teeters on abuse, in my opinion. So I take the ruddy things off every chance I get. Trouble is, I can't see the details of life so easily without them. Yet, I don't want to hear from a soul that it's too late anyhow. I won't go when the doctors say. I know that. How do I know? Because I just do.

As the cooing of the dove segues into a greedy ruffling of two blue jays, both in a tug-of-war over that single peanut I deliberately placed in the center of the picnic table, I realize they are in agreement with me. No old lady would be that conniving if she didn't have a little spunk left in her. But as I lie here swaddled in this blanket, I remind myself that too much self-reflection can make even a toadstool fall into a deep slumber.

Gilly is giving Ballerina a kiss and a rub behind the ears and that never gets old. Two other horses grazing in the paddock, and I'm afraid without my glasses perched on my nose, I can't see any further. Yet I know my granddaughter will come to check on me in a moment. Perhaps I should wriggle in my chair, otherwise she might think I've joined the heavens without saying good-bye.

"Grandma, what are you doing out here again?" Gilly says, approaching. "You know you could freeze."

"I have my trusty bell, so you needn't worry," I coo like that dove over there.

"An owl wouldn't hear that, and you know it. What if Kate's got the door closed?"

"Well, she has. But she's been spying out that window every time she walks past the sink, and since she's preparing lunch, I feel as though I'm on an egg timer. Every time I don't budge, I hear a tap at the window that widens to a rap. When I turn to look, I swear I can see a puff of air cloud her mouth as she sighs in relief."

Gilly smirks. "You really are stubborn, aren't you, Grandma?"

"And proud of it!" I say, flashing my dentures like a horse. I'm in the mood for using similes today. Since I have those oversized beasts on my mind, I can't imagine a better comparison. Whenever they roll that lip up, I'm quite sure they're mocking me.

"Would you like to come in with me?" she says. "To my place? It's not far, I promise," she giggles winking. Oh yes, I could bundle her up with me and never let go.

"What about lunch?" I mumble.

"I'll go get a tray. We'll have some lunch in front of a fire. Would you like that? I'm sure Kate wouldn't mind."

"Oh, I'd love that, dear."

"You come with me," she says supporting my arm and back while I fight my way to rise. "Are you in pain, Grandma?"

"Nothing that a hardy bowl of soup won't cure," I say wishing that were true.

I glance at the wooden sign Gilly has dangling above the door, like a pub in the old country might have. She's named the guesthouse something cottagey, a name that if I close my eyes for one soothing breath, it takes me back to Ireland when I was a small child. Daddy had carved one for our playhouse, and in magnificent curly writing, it read, DAISY something. I don't remember what the something was but I know it wasn't just Daisy. Gilly's sign is just as pretty: WILLOW DEN, dedicated to the ancient tree that shades Ballerina on those horribly humid southwestern Ontario summer days.

As my eyes soak in the heavy trusses of the lounge, I think Willow Den is a perfect name for it. It feels cozy as though you're standing underneath the umbrella of the old weeping tree outside. There's a cramped kitchenette, and the bedroom isn't really a bedroom at all, just a corner stolen from the room with a pretty curtain of white magnolias for privacy. The bathroom you couldn't squeeze a buttery sponge cake into it's so small, but I'm pleased to see how tidy Gilly keeps it all. It was the old house that came with the property when my son bought it an infinite number of years ago. My daughter-in-law wanted to tear it down, but like his father, my son appreciates the humble things in life and insisted it stay put. I'm very proud of him.

"Why don't you sit here, Grandma," Gilly says while removing a copy of *A Man in Uniform, Let me Count the Ways* from her sofa then fluffing up the back cushion.

"When did you start reading such trash, Gilly?" I ask with high hopes.

"A friend loaned it to me, so I thought I should at least give it a chance."

"Darling, I was hoping you'd say *today* and *because you wanted to*." I glance at her with my nearly hairless eyebrows arched high. "Don't ever try to impress anyone, especially me, or be something you're not. If you want to read a bit of rubbish occasionally, then do so. I've been known to bathe in my fair share of Petunia Petal books," I say winking. "Some of the greatest lessons can be learned from the seediest of tales, I can promise you. If they leave you with nothing more than a good itch, then no harm done!" Gilly looks at me sideways. "What?"

"Just when I thought I had figured you out," she says, "you throw me for a loop again."

"Has anyone ever told you, you speak like one of my white-haired Euchre partners?" I say grinning.

"Where do you think I got all these old-fashioned expressions?"

"Well, I always did want to be a wrangler."

Gilly laughs while fetching one of those... throws... I believe she calls them. They're everywhere, and far too many pillows. But everyone is entitled to at least one obsession.

"Honestly, Grandma, I don't think you're quite right in the head," she says smiling. "What other grandma says things like that?"

"I suspect the ones who know better."

A moment later an overhang with cut timber and some kindling out back snatch my granddaughter from me. I've always had a pinch of the past whenever a fire needs to be started—a day that smuggles a twinge of fear into my thoughts from time to time whether I want it to or not. Even now the word "kindling" from Gilly's lips makes me worry for her. Of course it's irrational. If only I could watch over her for the rest of her days. The crumbling in my chest strikes me yet again, but I have time to hide it before she returns.

As I spy the room, Gilly has set up two TV tray tables in front of the sofa. I haven't seen these in years and could never understand their appeal. It bothers me to think she might not take time to appreciate a good meal, savoring the surprises that come with trying a new spice or relishing an accompanying conversation. Though I suppose if she wants that, she probably scoots along next door to Kate's silver spoon. Ever since she joined our family, Kate's enjoyed spoiling Gilly almost as much as I do. Of course, I only spoil at select times. It's much better to earn your way through life. The best thing I can do for my only grandchild is see to it that she can do for herself. And it's working! Mind you, Kate's such a lovely person and though the going was rough in his first marriage, my son seems to have found the right woman for him. I know because dramatics and my son were never a match. He's so like his father—easy-going, takes a digging machine to get him stirred up. My son always felt hemmed in by the city, too. The farm suits him just as it suits Gilly, always has.

The lovely part of it all is that my granddaughter is as down to earth as her father and proud to board horses, only one of which is theirs, apart from Ballerina, of course. She makes no pretense about money. Yes they have it, but she needs to work hard for her bit, too. Even Kate enjoys a good dig in the dirt. Granted, without the land, part of which they hire out, and the horses they board, they'd be scrounging, I'm sure.

"How's the soup, Grandma?" she says, breaking me from my trance.

"Delicious. Kate worked hard on it all morning." I notice my granddaughter looking at my hand shaking. Drawing the spoon to my mouth, it clangs lightly on my dentures.

"Can I get you anything else? Some bread, maybe?"

"Now, Gilly, stop doting. You know how I feel about that."

"I'm sorry," she says turning to the fire.

I admire her handiwork. "You light a good fire," I say nodding.

"I like them. I'm happy this house has a fireplace." Gilly rises quickly to check that the screen in front is right then sits back down. "Do you remember when we all used to go camping up at Benmiller when I was little?"

"How could I forget? Those were some of my favorite times… with you," I say lowering my eyes.

"Whenever Dad would ask me to help with the fire, you'd always collect sticks with me and make a game of it. I never knew at the time you were trying to teach me math."

"No, dear, I think it was you who was trying to teach me *maths*. Something I'm completely hopeless at, always have been." Just as the words leave my mouth, I begin to feel a little warmth radiating from the hearth. It takes forever to heat these old bones.

"What I remember most," Gilly says, "is curling up in

the tent while you told me a story."

"Yes, a tent I could barely crawl into. Why do you think your grandpa and I would stay in that caravan? You know, the old tent-trailer that folded up and down like an accordion, the one your father had lying around for centuries? I'll never forget the musty smell as though it had been folded down and put in the barn when it was still wet. On the other hand, getting down on my hands and knees in your little tent wasn't exactly duck soup. Sadly, a poppet at seventy-something I wasn't."

"Maybe not, but you were great at making up stories. The way you'd hush me whenever a sound left my lips. You'd make me listen to whispers coming from the fire just outside and ask me if it was the crackling of birch bark or if the others were trying to be quiet. Then you'd make up some grand story of how they were plotting to capture the wind queen who swept through the forest only once every four hundred years and that's why they needed to whisper. And every time a breeze flew past our noses the next day, it was in preparation for her next visit, and no one would ever know what that meant." Gilly smiles. "While other little girls were being told stories about ladybugs and pansies, I was always being told adventures that should have sent me running the other way."

"But they didn't, did they?" I say auspiciously. "They always kept you begging for more. I knew you would be like that, the day you were born."

"Like what exactly?"

"Curious."

The fire swells suddenly like the climax of a symphony, causing a loud burst between the logs. There's nothing as full of life as a fire, the way it mesmerizes people, surfacing the tiniest of memories until it decides to snap them out of their daze. I love that jolt of electricity to my heart every time. Perhaps when the time comes, I should request a blaze next to my hospital bed.

I know the day Gilly is talking about, and why it has stuck with her since childhood. Gilly was only six or seven at the time, but summer after summer she begged her grandpa and me to come. "It's a family place," she'd say. "And we're all family, right?" A woman doesn't forget such words or days like that. It's strange, the way I can't remember less than a minute later if I plugged in the toaster then blame myself for leaving it in all night when I actually did nothing of the kind. Yet I can remember every detail of a day that happened too many years ago to count. There's something puzzling that happens to the brain after giving birth. I'm sure it didn't come with old age. Still, I remember that evening differently. Only a child would pull out the bits that are worth summoning forward again and banish the rest.

After a terrible row between Gilly's parents, I thought the wind queen could blow through the forest picking up the path's ground chips and specks of dirt and churn them into a whirlwind so they could once again fall softly into place. Perhaps it would rid the forest of nasty tongues in the process.

The wind queen was brilliant and should have appeared earlier in the day when we were all by the falls at Benmiller. Well, all of us except Angus. He was napping in the caravan. Gilly had ballooned her beach towel in the air, letting it settle on the flat rock while I unfolded my chair. It wasn't until I sat down that I noticed how the clouds looked like terraced rice fields in the sky. I remember because I couldn't take my eyes off them.

Truth is, the conservation area is lovely there, filled with what I've always imagined are the tallest pine trees on earth. And the camping sites were always well kept, so we were happy to join on weekends. It makes me smile to this day how Benmiller's signpost declares it "Ontario's West Coast." And rightly so! The shores of the Great Lakes are nothing if not coastal. The only missing ingredient is the smell of salty sea air. I do miss that… even today.

The area has always reminded me of Ireland, with its wide chuckling stream, masquerading as the Maitland River before emptying into Lake Huron. I'm quite right, the way it laughs like a cheeky leprechaun past old men dressed to their necks in fishing waders, scooping them up as though they were buoys. If I close my eyes, I can see them now, a dozen men fly-fishing on a Sunday morning as we drive past with our caravan—their heads nearly bobbing in the water.

All the same, the best spots on the river are where it's carved through rock as old as me. I wish bath water would rush over me, smoothing *my* skin the way it leaves the rugged river valley polished underneath. It's a playground for anyone who knows how to breathe. How could it not be with scads of waist-high waterfalls that leave one flapping around like a salmon during migration? That feat alone is worth the drive.

Unquestionably, it was the gripping sky that day, the antithesis of the roar below, that drove me to lie on the rock beside my granddaughter. As we held hands, gazing up at the sky, I told her that if she drew her index finger to her lips and softly *shoooshed* herself, the roar of the waterfalls would fall away, and everything would become silent. With a deep breath, so deep she could feel it in the pit of her stomach, life would become a vision.

"What am I looking at, Grandma?" she said.

"Can't you see that little man up there with the white lampshade on his head working very hard in the field?"

She studied the clouds earnestly, a little squeeze between her eyes. "No, I can't see him. Where is he?"

"Look harder. He's there between puffs sixteen and eighteen." From the corner of my eye, I could see her lips moving, counting every terrace, one... two... three... and so on.

"There he is, Grandma!" she shouted. "I found him."

"Shhhh," I cooed winking. "He needs peace to work."

"Oh..." my granddaughter sighed.

From the same corner of my eye, I could now feel her gaze on me.

"I love you, Grandma," she whispered.

"I love you too, dear."

And when the sky finally drew her in, I turned my head her way then smiled, squeezing her hand just that little bit tighter.

I don't know how long we stared at those puffy fields of rice in the sky, but it was long enough to drown out the squabbling of her parents down the way. And for that, I was grateful.

That evening Gilly's mother pushed it too far. I hadn't raised my only son to fall prey to a negative beast like that. Not for a minute longer would I sit and listen to that garble, and I most definitely wouldn't allow my granddaughter to suffer under a forked tongue. I scooted Gilly to bed at once, and nearly pulling it out of its socket, I left behind my evil eye glaring at my son, for he was the fool putting up with it. He knew I meant business, and thank God, there's such a thing as a last straw. She was gone within a week.

"Grandma," Gilly asked while tucked in her sleeping bag that night, her head lying on my chest. "Why does the wind queen want to sweep through the forest past us?"

"To get rid of the dirt, dear."

"You slept with me that night," Gilly says crinkling her brow, having just recalled. "I remember I fell asleep in your arms. You never left me, did you?"

"No... I didn't."

A tender expression fills my granddaughter's eyes. "You never do," she says, her lip turning up at the side.

I pat her hand. "Life is better now, isn't it? And sometimes stories and books are all that we need to take us away. Isn't that right?"

"But your stories," she says curiously, "I remember thinking you should write them down. You could have put together a fantastic anthology."

"What do you think I am doing now with my poems, having given them to you?" A silence grows thick between us. Somehow I know Gilly is deep in my story by now. "Do you think I don't know what you're doing by that window there till all hours? You don't think I'm awake, do you, dear? But I am, and I know you want from me what I can't give you."

"What are you talking about, Grandma?"

"The answers," I sigh. "You have a packet full of questions I'm sure, but I'm proud of you for not pressing. The poems are yours now, just as I had made clear before. *You* are creating an anthology of sorts, only you are weaving my poems into something much more meaningful, aren't you?"

Gilly doesn't say a word, but I can see in her eyes that it's true. "There's plenty you already know, and it's enough. The rest needs to come from you."

My bowl finds itself empty—a good place to end this conversation. Mind you, I could almost lick it clean, Kate's such a good cook. My appetite will dwindle soon and even her thoughtful gesture of cooking all of my favorites will stop working. I suppose an IV will soon syphon nourishment into me instead of Kate's hearty soups.

I sigh again, my chest squeezing into a knot. This time it has nothing to do with my cancer. I have a feeling Gilly suspects I'm holding back. But she can't know. Even to this day, seventy plus years later, I remember that day as though it was written into my skin like a tattoo. No matter how hard I scrub, it won't go away. I can't let her learn the truth from me. She needs to find out through her own creativity, through her own writing. As grim as that day was, as savage as it felt, it's the greatest gift I can leave her.

It started the moment we met,
Long hours through summer we shared.
In dreamy content, we grew as one,
Our love then quickly declared.

Being together was all we desired,
Then one day our drifting was past.
We had only been skimming the shallows of love,
We are now fathoms deep in its clasp.

But the end of the story is yet to be told,
May years create memories to graze.
Gently as we grow old together,
Till we come to the end of our days.

Chapter 8

1946

THREE-LEGGED FLAG? Christian gazed out the window of the aircraft wondering what the emblem meant. It had been a shaky flight since he left Southampton, but he was grateful there was a flight at all. He'd expected to roam the moors of the North, closer to the Scottish border, before coming anywhere near Gilly. And here he was just two days into his journey, plus his week across the Atlantic, of course, headed to the place where she'd stood for a photograph. Though there was no guarantee she'd still be on the island, it was a start and there was bound to be someone who knew her.

The captain had announced their descent, although Christian couldn't see anything yet through all the cloud-cover. He rubbed his neck while glancing at a passenger across the aisle, noticing the woman's tight grip on the armrest, her head pressed against the back of her seat. He could understand her nerves; he had them, too, but for very different reasons, he figured. He could feel a knot inside braiding itself into something even tighter and tiny shocks nipping at the tips of his fingers. Doubts crept into his common sense again—he squashed them flat when he pictured Gilly's smile.

Christian turned his head toward the rumble of the engines as the plane dipped into the clouds. He hadn't been at such an altitude since his time in the Air Force, and it felt freeing. All those doubts soared behind him in the plane's contrails as he now committed to only favorable thoughts. Just below the propellers, an island dressed in a patchwork of green on green came into view, each square lined with hedges or stone walls. The coastline was rich in the blackest of blues with spots of emerald. While rocky shores and a sliver or two or three or four of sand hinted to tread wisely. He would heed its warning, for he hadn't a clue what he was walking into. From what Christian could tell, the Isle of Man hadn't been trampled on the way Hampshire had. And that sent a rush of comfort through him, knowing Gilly had been there.

THE PLANE HAD ARRIVED at Ronaldsway near Castletown, and Christian was able to take a coach directly to Port St. Mary. He was already finding people to be different here, less guarded perhaps, than in the Hants. No wonder! He'd have been guarded, too, if someone had butchered his home. No. He couldn't blame them in the least. What's more was their ability to get back on their feet and still find a way to laugh. Look at the Spooners and that wine bottle tree. Christian shook his head. There was without doubt spirit lurking in these parts.

Christian arrived around four o'clock and checked into a small inn facing the inner harbor. Christian could see straight away the pride the owner took in this place and smiled when he noticed the three-legged symbol on a plaque hanging on the front desk. It wasn't the first he'd seen either. This town was crawling with them. In some ways it reminded him of the spirit of Tobermory.

The inn was sandwiched between a pub and a barbershop, but the owner explained that because of rationing, the pub's hours were greatly reduced, so if he "fancied a pint," he'd have to wait until dusk. A beer sounded perfect, actually, and it gave Christian time to look around town a little. He first went to his room, thankful that it was on the ground floor. He was tuckered from the journey and wanted to lie down for a few minutes. The room was simple with a washbasin on the dresser next to the bed and a sizable wardrobe on the opposite wall. He'd have to share a washroom with the other guests on the floor, but he didn't mind. He wasn't even sure there were any other guests. The place was quiet and the friendly owner seemed grateful for his business.

Christian unpacked his things, filling only one drawer and using three hangers, but it felt good to organize a little. The owner said if he needed anything washed, his wife would be happy to do it. Christian might just take him up on that offer since he didn't want to look a complete mess when he saw Gilly. He lay on the bed for about an hour resting his eyes and surprisingly not thinking about much at all. He figured things would unfold the way they were meant to; over-thinking wouldn't help. At first glance, Port St. Mary seemed like just his kind of town, and the moment he had arrived, a sense of calm washed over him. How could anyone be stressed in a place like this? He closed his eyes and enjoyed the silence.

A BELL TINKLED as Christian opened the door to the pub. A stocky man behind the bar nodded at him then disappeared through a door. Christian looked around the dark room, wood paneling everywhere, but didn't see a soul. He wandered over to the bar to peruse the list of ales on tap. He could almost taste it now. He liked English beer but wasn't sure if he could call it English on the Isle of Man—Manx maybe? A far cry from American anyhow. He'd gone over the border once to have a beer and swore he'd never do it again. But the Brits got it right. Left a taste in your mouth for more. The man returned wearing an apron.

"Hi ya. What can I do ya for?" he said in a mild, friendly accent.

"What would you suggest?"

"Ya can't go wrong with O'Kell's. Brewed right here on the island."

"Sounds great. Thanks."

The bartender topped his pint with a frothy layer, letting it run down the sides of the glass just a touch. He'd expected it to be warm, which was often the case during the war, but not this time. It tasted even better than Christian had hoped.

"So where are ya coming from?"

"Southampton," Christian answered.

"Not with an accent like that."

"No, sorry, I'm Canadian. I just came from Southampton today. I've only been here in the UK over the weekend."

The man leaned over as if to confide a deep, dark secret. "The Isle of Man isn't part of the UK, mate. Just a head's up on that."

"Yeah, I know. I just don't know how to word it. I guess it's a bit like Canada, eh?"

He grinned, "I'll give ya a history lesson after you've had a few. Or better yet, after I've had a few!" He began to wipe the counter with a cloth he'd just rinsed out. "So how's it taste?"

"Really good."

"Where'ya from in Canada?"

"A small place by the Great Lakes, near Toronto."

"Oh ya? Heard Toronto's nice. Don't know much about it though." He rubbed his chin. "People around here talk about Halifax. I guess they go from there to the big city, anyhow. Lot of families headin' to Canada the last few years. Don't blame them wanting to move their kids to safety."

"Yeah."

"So what brings ya here?"

"I'm looking for someone."

"Oh yeah. What's the name?"

"Gilly McAllister or Gillian I suppose most people would say."

He shook his head. "Don't know it."

"I was thinking I'd ask around a bit, but it's pretty quiet here."

"Ah, not for long. This place'll fill up before ya know it. Blokes like their pint around here. Just have to sneak away from the missus." The bartender put the cloth down then began scribbling something on the chalkboard behind the counter when the bell sounded again. Christian glanced at the door. "Speak of the devil."

A small group of five came in bantering back and forth. "Hi ya, Roland," a couple shouted in unison to the bartender.

"Hi ya chops!" he said, throwing his hand in the air. "How's Mr. Ballard doin' Gil?"

The guy shook his head. "Not good. He got his manhood sliced off this morning."

Christian's eyes widened as he turned to the bartender. "Did I hear that right?"

Roland chuckled. "He's talking about his pot-bellied pig. Doesn't want piglets to force him into that line of work." He glanced at their table, "Walks that thing like a dog." Christian took a sip then set his glass on the counter. "Hey," Roland cut through their gritty voices, "any of you know someone called," he turned to Christian, his brow arched.

"Ah... Gillian McAllister," Christian darted in.

"Gillian McAllister?"

Not expecting any kind of response, he was surprised when one asked if he had a photo. Christian joined them for a beer. He told his story and they told theirs. By that point Christian was on a first name basis with Roland, and this group was a fun mix of old and young.

The guy with the pig twitched a little when he saw Gilly's photo, scratching his backside. He claimed his eyesight was about as good as that pig of his so he couldn't help. Blamed it on pinworms. None of the others recognized Gilly until the bell tinkled again... about two hours later. In walked a middle-aged woman as round as a melon with a small boy scuttling alongside her. She meant business. All chatter stopped as her croaky voice silenced the room, "Barnaby Crowe! I'll have your head if you don't get your lazy arse home and help me with these gran kiddies of yours."

"But nan, you're pulling my arm," the boy cried out.

"Sorry, darling. You take granddad's hand now, and show him the way home. I will just sit down with these leeches and give them a piece of my mind." She glared at her husband, her eyes now twitching in disapproval. "Now off you go!"

As soon as the door closed, the noise in the room rose to

a respectable level, a pub now filled to the brim.

"Where's my pint boys?" she asked gleaming. "Thank God I'm away from that racket. Six grandkids, all under six. They'd drive anyone batty." Christian smiled when he realized they treated her like one of the boys. Jony, they called her. He figured Jony's display must have been a regular thing here in Port St. Mary.

CHRISTIAN SETTLED HIS TAB then returned to his room next door. He tried sleeping, but it was no use. Some fresh air would do him good. When he closed the front door to the inn, he noticed the last pub-goer teetering off down a cobblestone way crooning his own lullaby. Roland was clearing up and wiping the only two tables sitting just outside the front of the pub. Neither table appeared steady enough on the sloped cobblestone, though no one seemed to care. Christian liked that. He nodded to Roland.

"Cheers," he answered back.

Christian wandered across the street to a low stone wall that felt medieval against the night sky cloaking the Irish Sea. He sat down, lifting his leg to straddle the wall. This one leg always gave him problems since the war, but he paid no mind and did it anyway. From this position, Christian could see the town and watch the sea. A few streetlights shone just bright enough to make the place feel both mysterious and strangely approachable. The curve of attached houses lining the road, some three floors high, some two, each unique in its own way gartered by a chimney between them, stood proud against the elements washing in from the tide. He wondered if Gilly had ever sat where he was now, gazing at the same mystery of such a quaint town.

Christian turned his head to the sea, which he guessed

was calmed by the jetty. A handful of fishing boats bobbed gently, and the clanging of a mast on one sailboat reminded him of home. Christian closed his eyes, soaking in every sound. He felt at peace knowing that whatever this venture brought, he'd be okay with it. More than okay. He was grateful for the Barnaby fellow sneaking out this evening for a pint. If he hadn't, he never would have found out about Gilly. Who'd have known his wife, albeit rough around the edges, would turn out to be Christian's savior?

Christian reached into his pocket and pulled out Gilly's photo, not the one in the article but the other one, the one he'd taken with him on his search four years earlier. It was yellowed now but he could still trace her smile with his fingertip, even in the dark. This was the photo Barnaby's wife was more interested in seeing. Of course, she recognized immediately the spot where the article's photograph was taken, but it was this photo, the one he was gazing at now, that triggered something. She couldn't quite place her at first. Her hair was different and she was younger. Not the clearest snapshot. But after two beers, she plopped it facedown on the table and bellowed, "Gawd, blimey! Of course! That's Gillian McAllister. Skinny little thing she is." The last time she saw her, she was sitting at a table with Dr. Pilkington, the town's general practitioner. She happened to be at the doctor's office getting a nostril cleared after an unfortunate pea incident—not Gilly, but Barnaby's wife. Christian thought it was interesting how that tidbit of information just rolled past the others as though it were an every day occurrence in this town.

"They looked rather cozy," she said, "despite the man being her employer. Two odd bods together, I'd say."

Christian could have done without the commentary,

but he wanted to know every detail in case Jony was wrong about the whole thing.

"I know it's her. I'm certain of it," she said. "I had my eyes checked just the other day, in fact. Ruddy things have been giving me problems ever since Gilbert dropped by with that fat pig of his. I could swear there's something seeping from that animal, some God-awful fume."

Christian pressed for more details then finally managed to get an address from her. Well, not exactly an address but a map she'd drawn out on the back of a coaster. It was where he'd find Gilly—at "Dr. Pilkington's surgery."

It was all a bit surreal, like a hazy dream. Christian tucked Gilly's photo back in his pocket and closed his eyes again, listening for the sounds that he knew so well. No loons perhaps, but the washing of the tide on shore was soothing. He couldn't quite believe that only hours from now, he'd be walking into a doctor's office where Gilly McAllister was working. On the other hand, he wasn't the least bit surprised that she'd be employed helping others. He had no clue what he'd say or how he'd behave, even though he'd rehearsed it a thousand times since she walked out of his life.

Christian couldn't help but think how easy it was to find her this time, all because of one photograph in an article. The fact that Percy had a fascination with the Channel Islands and those in the Irish and North Sea couldn't have been coincidental. Christian had never really understood what fate was or how it worked. He just figured everything that happened in life happened because it was meant to, otherwise it wouldn't happen. Simple enough. But maybe, just maybe, he wasn't meant to find her four years ago. Could it be that this was the right time? He was sure she'd have no bad feelings toward him. He'd never done anything to hurt her, but if she had a family, if she was seeing this Dr. Pilkington, then she might be angry with him for showing up out of the blue after all these years. Even so, it was a risk he had to take.

Brooding wouldn't do any good. Christian rinsed it from his mind with the next gust of wind. The air here was much cooler at night than in Tobermory, and he was chilly now. His bed was waiting for him just over there, in this small fishing town smack in the middle of the Irish Sea, a town he never would have imagined he'd visit, yet a town he could fully imagine staying in for the rest of his life.

THE MORNING SUN CREPT quietly into the room while Christian lay staring at the ceiling. He expected his mind to be a whirling mess, but he woke with a confidence he'd always had until meeting this incredible Irish girl. She had a power over him then that made him dizzy at the best of times. She was prettier than he had words to describe, and what he liked best was that sometimes she knew it— you could see it in her walk—and other times she was completely oblivious to it. He liked her unpredictability. Gilly was spontaneous and daring and fun and willful. She made him feel alive. He'd never felt that kind of love before or since.

Christian propped himself up, curious and excited to see what the day would bring. He drew a bath down the hall and soaked for ages. He didn't want to hurry. Something compelled him to take it all in stride. He squeezed the facecloth and let the warm water drip down his torso. He glanced at his chest hair and wondered if she'd notice there was more now. Of course, who's to say she'd even see it. He rubbed a bar of soap that smelled like a strange mixture of talc, hair tonic, disinfectant, and cheap coffee over his chest then lay back, letting the rippling water take it off slowly. Not a bubble to its name. He had a feeling the barber shop next door would smell exactly the same. The tub was small, practically squeezed into a storage cupboard next to the water closet. Every time he'd shift his body, water gushed over the sides, drenching the claw feet and floor. But it still felt good.

As he lay there, his arms draped over the sides, Christian was in no hurry at all. Oddly, he thought Gilly could wait, that she'd waited this long for him to show up, what were a few more minutes? It was almost as if their squabbling had already begun. They had done their fair share of that, but it always ended in lusty moments with no holes in their apologies. On the other hand, maybe she hadn't been waiting at all.

A TWISTY ROAD AND A HANDFUL of paddocks away, Gillian was in her garden cutting roses for her breakfast table. She chose one of every color, each one for each little mood she was sure to squeeze out today. She loved her garden, filling it with as many flowering trees and shrubbery as possible but never once let them grow to shade the cottage in any way. Sunlight drenched the garden this morning, and the only place to be was out in it. She daren't say it would last knowing this island, so Gillian grew to appreciate every moment the sun would gaze down at her.

Today her breakfast table sat just right, in a spot that even as the sun moved across the sky, she'd be warmed. She had a tendency to move the table around to suit her whims. She scraped the thorns on the lower half of the roses then arranged them in a small vase, lastly setting it on the table. It was a table for two, which had never bothered her until now. As she glanced at the empty seat, she had an odd feeling that it should be filled and that her roses would be even prettier had it been.

Gillian reached across the table and took her small, blue notebook. On occasions like this when the white walls and two latticed windows of her cottage nestling under the thick thatched roof looked like something from a fairytale, she'd feel compelled to write.

She thumbed through the pages until she came to the next blank one then flipped the notebook over while she poured herself a cup of tea. It was lovely not to be expected at the surgery quite so early today. She wasn't even sure Dr. Pilkington would open unless he received a dire call. Perhaps he'd ring her and say that he'd stick to house calls today. She quietly hoped so yet worried about how he'd taken her rejection the other day. The last thing she intended was to hurt him, especially when she wasn't completely sure of her own feelings.

She turned over the notebook to let her fountain pen speak for her. She shook it then checked that the nib was wet. A small drop soiled the paper, and she began writing. She couldn't understand why the words came easily this morning. Normally, she'd battle with words trying to find just the right ones, but not today. She tucked a long strand of hair behind her ear then continued. It was a spirited poem this morning, one that had a feeling of new beginnings. Maybe it was all the life around her.

Some crunching under the bushes caught her attention as two meadow pipits hopped playfully from them before flying off. But it was a tiny dragonfly sitting stock-still on the table that captivated her. Gillian wanted to be sure it wasn't dead, so she reached to the ground to find a small twig then gingerly touched its legs. With a start, the dragonfly darted up but didn't fly away. Instead, it seemed to be watching her as it hovered for ages, moving sideways then back again. Gillian sat quietly admiring it when she could almost hear a faint voice from the past saying, "Don't move." She gasped remembering that moment as though it had just happened. A breeze rushed across her skin making her hair flutter. When she looked down, tiny goose pimples rose from her forearms as she noticed that the wind had flicked the pages to the first poem she'd ever written about Christian, just after they'd met for the first time.

CHRISTIAN SILENTLY TUSSLED with the cobblestone underfoot. Though unsteadied, he took that challenge like any other. He noticed a few more boats in the harbor this morning, five of them tucked against the stone wall he'd sat on last night. The water was low against it and quietly teased the small beach at the bottom of the steps.

Barnaby Crow's wife was a character that one, but she couldn't draw a map to save a Manx cat's tail. Christian followed her scribbles confident that in a town this size everyone would know where the new doctor had set up his office. They seemed an earthy lot. If something was different, they asked about it. Christian liked that raw spirit, and everyone who passed either nodded or stopped to chat. He wondered how anyone got any work done around this place—they were too busy gabbing. On second thought, work wasn't just a *means* to live but a social way of life. He saw that first hand at a vegetable stall outside the grocers, the bookshop he'd just passed, the docks where no one grumbled but genuinely appeared happy to help others. Just like Tobermory, only bigger.

As Christian turned the corner, he noticed a small sign above a black door that read,

SEASIDE SURGERY AT PORT ST. MARY
MEDICAL PRACTICE—DR. REGINALD DEAK PILKINGTON

Christian was confused because this place looked nothing like the one in the article. This was obviously the doctor's private office and maybe the photograph was taken at the hospital—if there was one in such a small town. He rang the doorbell twice, an unmistakable buzz. He waited, but there was no answer. Even if they'd been busy, the office would have been open. Christian turned to the narrow street, wide enough for just one car. His eyes traveled the opposite walls as he wondered what he should do now. Scrambling out the neighboring door, a woman carrying a hefty basket filled with scallops stopped to chat. She knew where Gilly lived and described a simple route through the countryside that went further down the coast.

Christian sat down in a small coffee shop mulling over his choices. He could try to find a hospital or go straight to Gilly's house. He wasn't sure if the surprise, or shock, would be best in public or private. His vision floated past the backwards lettering on the shop's window. "Poppy's Coffee Shop," he could make out. As he studied the hum of the street with its one car and two bicycles wobbling along the cobblestone, a pot-bellied pig rounded the corner pulling a lanky, pasty-white owner with rusty hair. It was Gilbert, the man accused of causing Jony's bad eyesight. This wasn't an everyday sight for Christian, but not a soul passing by seemed to give it any notice. They greeted him as if it was perfectly normal to be walking a pig on a leash.

Gilbert spied Christian in the window then brought Mr.

Ballard into the coffee shop. Instead of kicking the pig out, he was greeted with a sloppy kiss from the woman who served Christian his tea. Christian smiled and asked Gilbert to join him. They got on well, somehow sensing the other was trustworthy and spun on the same ropewalk, at least in the important ways. Gilbert insisted that with a little adjustment, Christian could take his "lorry," which was parked around the corner, to Gilly's house.

GILLIAN HAD CRAFTED A SIMPLE POEM and was nearly finished when she heard the telephone ring. She laid her fountain pen between the pages and sighed feeling satisfied with the effort as she pranced up her walkway and into the cottage.

"Hello, Gillian speaking. Who's calling, please?"

"Gillian. It's Reggie. Do you mind terribly? Mrs. Hemsworth has rung and said she's gone into early labor. Can you come at once?"

"Yes, of course, doctor. I'll be there straight away."

"Now stop calling me doctor. We don't stand on ceremony in private, do we? We've tumbled down a ditch together, after all." Gillian couldn't help but notice that space of silence where she should have chuckled. "I need you here, Gillian. Hang up now and mind you don't dawdle."

WHORLS OF DIRT ROAD trailed off in the rearview mirror as Christian rounded another bend, finally bringing him to a long stretch of straight road. This one traveled along the coastline through all of those square fields he'd seen from the sky. In the distance, he could see a small patch of houses with the Irish Sea at its back. He slowed down, making way for a smattering of sheep not caring in the least that he could run them into the ditch. Or was that the other way around, he thought. When he stepped from the car to shuffle them aside, it was in glancing up that he saw it—the cottage that the woman had described. It was around the corner and slightly obscured from view, slightly anyway, from where he was standing. He felt his heart race as he turned his back to scoot one particularly stubborn ewe from the dirt road.

GILLIAN ROLLED DOWN HER DRIVE, the gravel crunching under her motorbike and sidecar tires, her helmet propped proudly on her head. Zippy little thing it was, but it couldn't go fast enough today. Though it wasn't far to the Hemsworth's farm, she was sure this was the real thing and not just another one of that woman's ploys. Gillian looked to the right to see that the way was clear then to the left but was glad not to have to go in that direction, for she didn't have time to fuss with a herd of sheep in the middle of the road. Poor sod over there had to be stuck dealing with it. She swerved onto the main road headed westward.

CHRISTIAN LOOKED OVER his shoulder when he noticed something disappear over the crest of a hill further down the road, leaving a puff of dust behind. He pushed the ornery ewe to the edge of the road then watched her finally trot off with the others. Christian slid behind the wheel, put the truck into gear then pulled ahead, slowly approaching the cottage just around the corner. He drew a deep breath before driving down the laneway where the truck sputtered to a halt.

He sat in the pick-up for a moment taking it all in. He could imagine Gilly in a place like this. It reminded him of a cottage in one of the old fairytales his mom used to read him, *Snow White* or maybe *Rumpelstiltskin*. Only this cottage wasn't tucked away in a dark forest; an open landscape with just enough trees and hedges marked the edge of the garden. It was cheerful and made him feel good just to see it. The thatch hung over the wooden front door, just enough so he'd probably have to duck, and the cladding was a milky white as though it had been freshened up at the end of the war. The front yard was green, so green he could hardly believe it, with a towering tree he couldn't recognize. It almost looked like some kind of palm, but he thought that was unusual for this part of the world.

There was a bench against the cottage just under a window with white grilles and flowers hanging in a basket next to it. A path of small stones led to the front door. Christian emerged from the truck then closed the door behind him. The place was quiet. He suspected she might not be home, otherwise she'd have been outside by now having heard the truck roll up.

Christian rapped the knocker twice then waited. When no one answered he peeked in the window, but she definitely wasn't there. He rolled his shoulders back then sighed, turning to face the yard. Even the arbor with purple clematis next to the cottage shared Gilly's smile. She'd made it welcoming even in her absence. He noticed a small table in the sunlight then wandered over to it. "She was just here," he muttered. She must have been. The cup was half full and she'd left a book. Christian picked it up, reading just a few words.

A strange confusion swept over him as though time and place were baffled, as though he shouldn't be playing with fate, as though he shouldn't be there at all. It was Gilly's handwriting. He recognized it immediately from the one and only letter she'd ever written him. The one she'd left behind when he came to her aunt and uncle's cottage to find her, never thinking for a minute that he'd never see her again. Christian lowered himself to the seat. This notebook. It wasn't his to read. His eyes glanced down, but he knew it was wrong. He turned it over then placed it face down on the table. Christian felt like an intruder; he had no right to show up like this unannounced. He was glad she wasn't here. What was he doing? She loved him once, a lifetime ago. What right did he have to flirt with the idea of being loved by her again? Who was he kidding? Just wanted to see that she'd survived the war? And he couldn't use Griffin as an excuse... could he? Every time he imagined the possibility, it was like the world was pulled out beneath him.

Even so, Christian lowered his head thinking this was just about the craziest thing he'd ever done. An ocean between them all this time. Had she wanted it to be different, she would have been knocking on *his* door. He sat for a long while, too long, when he convinced himself that it didn't matter if she still had feelings for him or not. They'd shared something once, something time could never take away. Maybe that was enough. He'd gone on with his life after all and he was happy—maybe not the kind of happy that people dream about, but the kind that brings a simple peace to life. Maybe that was enough after all.

Christian stood, no longer brooding. He put the notebook back the way he'd found it then walked to the truck. He opened the door, turning to gaze one last time at the place that suited Gilly, a pretty place filled with color and life by a town that oozed personality—just like her. As he slid behind the wheel, he heard some tires roll over the stone drive behind him. Stones crunched under foot toward him and Christian knew what that meant. He knew it was her.

"Good morning. Can I help you with something?" A candied voice signaled her approach just as he was about to turn the key in the ignition.

Before Christian could answer, a hand cupped the door where the window was opened fully. He turned to her, her green eyes dancing only for a flash. She stood there with measured concentration as though she was studying who it was, perplexed as everything silenced at once. The birds stopped chirping, the crashing surf against the cliffs froze, and a haze filled the garden framing her face. It was an instant fairy tale. He sighed feeling a smile creep into his mouth. As though she'd snapped out of a daydream, a pale, disbelieving gaze rose in her expression; Gilly's eyes fixed on his as she stepped back.

They met one sunny morning
They both played a game
Pretending they cared,
Then one day it rained!

They sheltered together
And stood hand in hand,
Her cheek on his shoulder,
Well, you'll understand!

When he whispered, my darling,
The game's at an end,
This love is for always,
No need to pretend!

And whatever life holds,
We will face without fear,
Secure in this love,
Through the passing of years!

Chapter 9

THEY HAD ARRIVED on the breeze of Dominion Day hoopla. A chilly breeze for July, according to Uncle Herbert, that swept through a maze of wooden shanties lining a small harbor in a place called Tobermory. Never would she have imagined being in such a place just a year after tapping on Beaty's door in London. Canada of all places. On its birthday.

The harbor was rather wide open in the center, like a large car park, but it was its name "Little Tub" that stole Gillian's heart. Whose brilliant idea was that? It was just how it looked, like a big fat washtub with oodles of toy boats bobbing gaily in the bath.

A smattering of barns sat on the edge of the water. Gillian imagined they housed great big boats for repair, or maybe some enormous treasure discovered from one of those sunken ships Uncle Herbert was telling her about. How could anyone not like such a place? The name alone brought back such lovely memories of a Scotland she once met. How she missed her mother sometimes.

As Gillian stepped from the car, dust kicked up her skirt, reminding her at once that she could be free here, free to do as she pleased all summer long.

Oh, the sun. The water. She could breathe here. If ever there was a place that drew you in at once, this was it. Smiles, laughter, and silly pranks from little boys whisked past her eyes. The mood was electric like a fool's tonic for the Depression. None of them could help being taken in by it as she, her auntie and uncle and Roderick stood by the car soaking it all in. Streamers made from fishing net with something sparkly dangling from them draped from porch columns to the masts of fishing boats. They made her feel light on her toes. Gillian brushed more dust off her skirt, feeling as though she could drop to the ground and roll in the dirt anyway. She didn't care. She was just so happy to be here.

As a gust of wind flew past her nose, wind chimes tinkled a summer song. Gillian tried not to notice Roderick sticking his nose up at them, the scowl no doubt meant for her. Still in a huff over their little pact! Never mind. The waft of sugared puff pastry and cinnamon, something Auntie Joyce called elephant ears, teased her mercilessly. It was well worth having to put up with her annoying cousin to be in its wake. Palmiers *were* always her favorite after all.

Oh yes, Uncle Herbert was perfectly right to fall in love with such a place. Gillian couldn't help but laugh out loud at absolutely nothing. Even her sundress was laughing in a pretty periwinkle, showing just a hint of cleavage, and her sandals already scuffed. Her hair was fluttering in the breeze, spurring a little action. Time to investigate!

As she wandered closer to the water, a ruckus coming from shore further down the way caught her attention. Children were jumping from the rocks, splashing and squealing while their mothers laid blankets by the shore, setting baskets on the corners so they wouldn't blow away. Coming from the woodland a sprinkling of men walked toward the wide, open space nearer the docks. She wondered what they were going to do with all that wood, piling it higher than the princess and the pea's eiderdown bed.

This wasn't exactly a crowd, but it certainly felt festive with fisherman displaying their catches in crates with some kind of lottery table set up next to them. Every now and again the air filled with the aroma of crackling from the roasting pig by that boathouse. In the balmy air, she could taste it on her lips already. By far what made this place sink into her bones was the fiddler standing beside the open doors of that same boathouse, playing a jig that reminded her of Ireland. Gillian closed her eyes for a moment, imagining that it was Daddy playing. Then she opened them and realized it wasn't. *But there you go*, she shrugged, still feeling light on her toes.

"Hi. You looking for someone?" a girl about her age said spritely.

"Why? Does it look like I am?"

"Well, you look a bit lost. I watched you wander to the hog roasting."

"Is that unusual?"

"Well, yeah, only the guys are ever interested in that. The set-up's kind of gruesome."

"Hmm," Gillian nodded.

"I'm Kit," she said smiling. Gillian couldn't help but notice her teeth. She'd never seen such perfect ones before. She glanced down at a sweet thing next to her wearing a flowery dress and bow in her hair. Couldn't have been more than four or five.

"Hey Kit, who's your friend?" one boy said as he crept up, grabbing her around the waist. Kit giggled while playfully hitting him in the shoulder. Suddenly feeling as though she was intruding, Gillian turned to walk away.

"Hey. How's it going?"

Was the voice addressing *her*? Gillian swiftly turned. But when she looked up, a sudden breath clenched her throat. She'd never seen anything like him. Two arms and two legs, of course, but he was beautiful. Not the kind of cinema beautiful. No, it wasn't that at all. It was something subtle, in his expression perhaps. Those eyes. They were droopy and the color of the bay just over his shoulder, a dark, mysterious blue like one of the pirates lost in the water's depth... eyes that felt as though they were looking straight through her. While all the other boys her age had stiff hair, his was a crumb shaggy, just enough to let soft whorls dance around his face. Either way, he was truly and utterly sublime. She nearly choked on him.

"Good God," she thought she muttered.

"Excuse me?"

She shook herself out of it. "I'm sorry. Were you talking to me?" she said, trying to put the onus on him. How was it that this person standing in front of her had unearthed her so briskly? He'd hardly uttered a word.

"Yes." And his lips moved, too. But he came out of nowhere it seemed. Scurried out from behind Kit's friend, either bashful or sneaky. She wasn't yet sure which.

"I'm Christian," he said, his hands tucked in his pockets.

"Gillian McAllister." She gave a pithy nod. "How do you do?" She offered her hand but suddenly felt flustered as though she'd made a near universal blunder. She felt her face instantly flush.

"Well," his smile was warm, "I *do* fine, thank you." Her brow kneaded together wondering whether or not he was teasing her.

Kit was busy now chatting with the other boy. Gillian had no idea who he was. Moreover, she wasn't sure whether to give this Christian the benefit of the doubt; Gillian certainly didn't want him to think she was keen. No. Paying attention to this peppermint next to Kit would throw him off, and she was too sweet to ignore, anyhow!

"And who is *this* little biscuit?" she added bending down. Mind you, she couldn't scrape her eyes off the background. He really was delicious, fair and tall with the most gorgeous forearms. Oh, how she loved a nice forearm. Hadn't known she liked them until now.

"I'm Romy," she whispered bashfully. Her eyes fell back on her easily now. How couldn't they? She was adorable.

"How lucky you are, Romy, to have such an unusual name."

"Do you think so?"

"Oh, I know so."

"How do you know that?"

"Because when your name is in sparkling lights at the cinema when you're all grown up, the world will remember a name like Romy and they will know exactly who it is. If your name was Sally or Margaret, you'd be forgotten... *poof...* straight away." She flicked her fingers as though blowing away a fluffy dandelion clock.

Romy threw her arms around Gillian's neck, which took her by surprise. Just a little squeeze before she dashed off. Gillian glanced up at Christian who had listened to every word, smiling in an oddly grateful way. Perhaps he knew

Romy.

"Can I help you find something or someone?" he offered.

"Well, I was rather investigating the place."

"Were you *rather* now?"

Okay, now she knew he was teasing her. "You know, there's a lovely village called Snickerfield near where I'm from. I suggest you get on a train and go there," she said, marching away at once. "And by the way, there's an ocean in between. Careful the train doesn't derail!"

"Hey!" He shouted skittering after her. "I'm sorry. I couldn't resist. It's that accent of yours."

"If my accent bothers you so, then it's best you don't hear it."

"Why do you think it bothers me?"

"Well, why else would you take the mickey out of me?"

"The what?" he smiled. "It's just that you're so formal."

"Am I?"

"I like it. I like *you.*"

"You don't know me," she said soberly.

"Maybe not. But what I know so far, I like."

"Hmm. You are a curious one aren't you, Christian...?"

"Hunter."

"Good day, Mr. Hunter," she said nodding as she walked away.

"See you tonight at the bonfire, Gilly... I hope."

She swung around, feeling the skirt of her dress whirl around her as she gazed, stunned at what he just called her. For some unknown reason, she felt a smile work its way into her cheeks, their eyes meeting one last time. She turned and walked toward Auntie Joyce, who was busy digging out the picnic basket from the boot of the car. She felt his eyes still on her, but she daren't turn again. Then he'd surely know she was keen. Her chest swelled as she breathed in deeply. "Gilly," she muttered lightly, not able to wash the smile from her face. She liked it. No... she adored it.

It had been the perfect day, though she toyed with the idea of the bonfire. Roderick wanted to go, and she was certain Christian expected her there—no doubt because he had a high opinion of himself. The way he strutted past her, more times than she had fingers to count.

No, she wouldn't think about him any more than she'd think of a varmint's sleeping habits. Instead, she'd sit back on this lovely porch step of her auntie and uncle's summerhouse and admire the rippling water not far from her toes—that is until the mosquitoes would begin to eat her alive. She scurried quickly to the gazebo at the end of the dock then closed the door in a snap.

The water was serene. She'd never seen such blackness before and so many stars. They made her feel tiny. At the end of the harbor, the bonfire was blazing wildly as cheers erupted, energy pulsating along the water all the way to her.

Gillian wondered if he was there now. As mini flutters inside her danced on the heels of excitement, she considered his behavior earlier. He was sweet really, not as cheeky as she made out. Maybe he'd never met anyone with an Irish accent before. It threw him, that was all. She remembered a boy in grammar school who was too shy to express his affections toward her best friend, Tilly. So instead he teased her horribly, pulling her hair and even once closing his desktop on it so when she stood up in front, she was pulled back like a bucking mare. If she recalled correctly, they were married now. She hadn't seen Tilly in dogs' years. Wouldn't that have been something had they been called Gilly and

Tilly. But no one had ever called her Gilly... until now.

Roderick shuffled his feet outside the door, making her heart skip. "Are you coming?" he said.

"I thought you'd never ask."

THE BLAZE UP CLOSE was even more spectacular. Although she and Roderick had come together, Gillian hoped he would set off quickly to scout for fun. That way, she could spy the brew of Canadians without being coddled. Besides, Roderick didn't deserve her company. After all, no wink... no cousinly coterie! She'd hold that grudge later though. For now, it served her well arriving on the arm of such a good-looking fellow.

Gillian was wearing her wide-legged trousers. Although she had decided to pay no attention whatsoever to her clothing, she had changed, fearing those flying leeches they called mosquitoes. They were even worse here than the midges back home. But these trousers would whack them off with every step, making her feel bold. Perhaps she should buy Roderick a pair.

Her little sailor top cut across the shoulders and she could feel her clavicle attracting attention. Where was that Christian? Her eyes shifted in all directions, though they weren't *woggly* in the least. Who would ever say woggly wasn't a word? She once knew a boy who could only be described as having woggly eyes. They were nearly dangling from the sockets.

"Come!" Roderick shouted, pulling her hand. "People are roasting hot dogs in the fire with long sticks."

"Good Lord! That's awful!"

"No, silly! They're sausages," he said laughing. Roderick set one up then handed it to her. Gillian's head was whirling with all the activity. Even the nans and granddads were out, some sipping on hot toddies no doubt, keeping their bones warm in the night air. Although it wasn't the least bit chilly, especially with the fiery cocktail in front of her.

The flames were high, and the fiddler was back, she noticed. Oh, how it made her long for Ireland, this music. She sighed, her chest swelling again when suddenly she saw *him* through the flames. He was watching her. She made doubly certain it was true by spying those around, but *those* eyes were most definitely planted on *her*! Didn't even bother to shift them—nervy creature! Gillian felt her brow knit together; she didn't know why, but somehow he infuriated her. He was so obvious—brash. Or perhaps it was simply that he found her electrifying. She couldn't blame him for that. Though he might well have been dishy, not every girl was going to drool at the very sight of him. In fact, she didn't see a single female melting by his side.

Good God, he was coming this way. Even the throng of people didn't faze him. He *was* lovely in this firelight, the way he walked, the ease about him, the way his shirt was rolled up to the elbow, loosely hanging over his trousers with a simple undershirt to keep warm. His shaggy hair ruffled even more as he combed his fringe with his fingers before reaching her. Before her next breath, he was standing in front of her.

"Here, you can have mine," he said.

"Pardon me?"

"Go on."

"I have my own thank you."

"Not any more," he said looking into the flames.

"NO!" she gasped, half amused at the sausage sizzling below. "I didn't notice it had fallen off. I can cook another."

"Oh, stop being a pain," he said. "If someone offers you something, just take it and say thank you." She felt her brow actually crocheting. "Come, I want to show you something."

"Where to?"

"That's a surprise."

"I'd be mad to go off with you. You're a stranger."

Christian smiled and offered his hand, "Please. It's just by the rocks here."

Clambering over the rugged shoreline wasn't easy with wide-legged trousers, but Gillian felt like a star in them anyhow. She adored the tingling of adventure and liked it even more knowing how her auntie and uncle, and Daddy for that matter, would disapprove. They reached a small cove with some sort of stream wriggling off the end— at least it looked that way. It was hard to tell in this dark. Only the tip of the bonfire was visible now, and the hum of the crowd had faded.

"Where are you taking me?"

"Shh…" Christian hushed, drawing his index finger to his lips. The dark was blinding, but there was a stream of moonlight cutting across the water and a few boathouse lights on the other side of Little Tub, which helped. Christian reached for her hand, "Here we are." Trying to shuffle into a comfortable position on a very hard rock, she wasn't quite sure what she was supposed to be looking at. Christian leaned into her, their shoulders touching. A chorus of shivers tingled inside her, not sure whether it was a chill or him. "Do you see that tall tree over there?" he said, pointing.

"Yes," she whispered back.

"Let your eyes follow down its trunk if you can." She did as he said, coming to a jumble of sorts. "Do you see it?"

"I see something, but no idea what."

"It's a beaver dam."

She felt her breath catch at the thought. "Really? I've never seen one before."

"I know it's dark, and with the bonfire over there I'm not sure they'll come out tonight. They're stubborn, but when they don't feel threatened, they just get down to business."

"How many are there?" she asked curiously.

"Five. Two adults and three kits."

"Is a kit a baby?"

"Yeah, it's a family. Beavers mate for life." Christian caught her smile and offered one back. "They're amazing animals. Their lodge is on the other side of the dam."

"You mean they don't live in their dam?"

"No, no," he shook his head. "They build it to make a pond for their home. The dam protects them and makes it easy to get food."

"I'd love to see one, but I daren't say it's possible in this dark."

"If you keep an eye on that strip of light across the water, you might just see a head moving along the surface."

"Just a head? I hope there's a body attached to it," she said, feeling flirty until she felt an elbow in her side.

Quiet filled the air, but she felt relaxed and safe. She pulled her knees up to her chest, wrapping her arms around them. A few distant sounds crept into the background—crickets chirping, and she knew the sound of frogs when she heard them. Beaty thought they made a terrible racket, but Gillian thought their harmony was exquisite.

"About Romy today," Christian said picking up a stick then trailing it in the dirt next to him. "Thank you for what you said to her."

"What do you mean?"

"Well, hardly anyone can get a word out of her, and you managed in a snap." Gillian smiled. "It's what you said."

"But she's a darling, and I adore her name. I can actually see it in lights, can't you?"

Christian gazed at her softly. "She gets teased by some of the kids."

"Why?"

"She can't say her own name, has trouble with her *R's*."

"Nonsense. She said it perfectly fine."

"No... she didn't. But somehow you knew exactly what she was saying." Christian drew in a breath. "If she could only get others to hear what you hear."

"Oh, for goodness sake, it's nothing. I bet I could help with that. The Irish have always been masters at *R's*."

Christian chuckled.

"Perhaps I can spend some time with her—no joking," Gillian said. "It wouldn't do any harm."

"How long will you be here?"

"All summer," she replied with hidden hopes. "I'm not leaving Canada until the end of September."

"Well, we can see then. She doesn't live far from me. Kit's her older sister." Gillian nodded then drew a breath while pretending to look elsewhere. "Are you cold?" he asked.

"Just a little."

"Maybe we should get back then."

"Oh, no," she begged. "Just a minute longer."

NO BEAVERS TONIGHT. But Gillian wasn't disappointed. She had all summer and fully intended to meet one face to face! All in good time. She and Christian strolled back the long way around toward a dwindling flame when Kit approached them with some friends. She finally introduced her to that boy she'd been friendly with earlier, a Matthew Dunsbury.

"Hey," he said nodding. "This is my cousin, Angus Pugsley. Angus *Stanley Spencer* Pugsley."

Janey, what a name! she thought. It threw her off kilter. A name like that would make anyone lean to one side. His face didn't match it apart from that mole on his cheek. The cousin had elbowed this Matthew Dunsbury, clearly annoyed for taking the mickey out of him. Such a quiet thing standing behind his cousin's shoulder like that. Yet he stared at her so. She wasn't sure what to make of it. Her attention quickly ruffled back to Christian, wanting him all to herself.

They wandered back to the bonfire, just the two of them, then sat for ages talking. She could see Roderick through the flames chatting with some fellow. He seemed happy enough, but no wink. The cinders and white ash in front were drawing the night to a close. Smoke had sewn its way into their clothes and hair as a wonderful reminder of a most perfect day.

"Can I walk you home?" Christian offered.

"I'm afraid my cousin there will have a conniption if I leave with a boy I've just met."

He rubbed the back of his neck, letting nothing faze him, "Yeah, of course. No problem." Suddenly she felt self-conscious. She was never lost for words, but he just stood there gazing into the smoldering remains. "I'd have a conniption, too, if you walked off with me," he said grinning easily.

"Why?"

"Because your cousin's right; you shouldn't trust someone you've just met."

"Are you saying I can't trust you?"

"I'm saying you *shouldn't*—yet."

"And once you have earned my trust? What then?"

His eyes were suddenly penetrating. Christian slid his hand around her waist, drawing her close—his hand pressed against the small of her back, his fingers against her skin. She felt her chest rocket and wasn't sure whether he was as nervous as she was. Their eyes surrendered to a long moment before he slowly brought his cheek to hers.

"You're extraordinary. Do you know that?" he whispered into her ear, then pulled away, leaving her numb. "Goodnight, Gilly."

As she watched him saunter towards the dirt road away from the last of the idlers, Roderick was by her side in a flash wondering what "that" was all about. He didn't press her though, instead leaving Gillian to her thoughts as they walked back to her auntie and uncle's house, her arm coiled in his. She glanced up at her cousin, stiff hair like the others, and smiled. She liked Roderick. He'd make some fellow happy one day. She was sure of it.

GILLIAN SAT BY THE MOONLIGHT in her auntie and uncle's conservatory with a small kerosene lamp next to her. She had written loads of short stories before. But for some reason she couldn't explain, her fountain pen tonight whirled into words in a way she'd never known them before... into her very first poem.

They met one sunny morning
They both played a game
Pretending they cared
Then one day it rained...

She gazed up at the white marble in the sky and for a

moment, she was quite sure it smiled down at her. *It was you, wasn't it, Christian Hunter? You were the one looking at the same moon, the same stars that night at the maharaja's. You were here in this small town on a big lake somewhere in God's country, and you were looking for me.* The marble rolled closer now, nearly filling the sky as she folded her arms to keep warm in the cooling night air, her thoughts not leaving him for a moment. She couldn't escape this feeling that she would love him for the rest of her days.

Gillian's eyes were drawn to the water speaking softly in ripples and echoing the eeriest, most romantic birdsong she'd ever heard. "The Great Lakes," she muttered, feeling lucky to be here. Now she finally understood what was so great about them. Gillian pulled her auntie's afghan over her shoulders as she lay back on the settee. Yes, quite sleepy indeed. A smile sneaked into her cheeks, and she could smell the smoke on her fingertips as she ran them down her lips. "So, I'm extraordinary am I, Mr. Christian Hunter?"

When I was young
I had a gift bestowed
Of such great happiness,
But was it really mine?
Or could there be a day
It would no longer shine?

When that day came
I was bereaved, bereft
With empty hands.
This gift was never mine,
Just lent to me
For a short spell of time.

I found heaven on Earth
Then swift as lightning strikes a tree
The joy was dashed from me.
And like the tree, my life was blighted,
For evermore, for evermore.

Chapter 10

1946

"Hello Gilly," Christian said, remembering to tread carefully. Gilly stood there at a loss for words. He thought he had prepared himself for this look, one he'd expected. But it came crashing in on him, making him feel as though he'd done something terribly wrong. "Listen… I'm sorry. I shouldn't have stopped by like this, unannounced." He was already feeling intrusive, but her silence made it worse.

When she took off her helmet, her hair fell in waves to her shoulder, her green eyes standing out against its nutty brown color. There she was as beautiful as the day they'd first met.

"Christian." That's all she said for a long moment. He lowered his eyes to his lap then hastily decided to put the pick-up into gear. "Wait!" she chirped. "Please don't go. I'll be back in two shakes."

Of a lambs tail, his lips finished her sentence without a sound, remembering the funny phrase she'd used time and time again. Old-fashioned. Yes, that's how it sounded. He liked that she didn't seem to care. She spoke the way she spoke with an air of grit about her. He found that sultry. Even now from this rundown old truck, all he wanted to do was take her in his arms as though no time had passed.

Gilly ran into the house, leaving him there to wonder what was so urgent, more urgent than meeting her long lost love after fourteen years, including a Depression and a World War. He opened the car door, sliding away awkwardly from the seat, then stepped out of the truck.

GILLIAN SKITTERED THROUGH the cottage, flipping over books and leaving papers strewn across the dining table she'd used for churning out stories and articles and poems whilst picking at her meals on coolish, drippy evenings year after year. It was only in her off time that she was able to write, otherwise her days were filled with community work. But she couldn't find it anywhere—something she'd treasured, something she had to show him.

As she was digging about, paying no mind to a man who could easily dash off in a fit of ill-patience, the telephone decided—yes, decided on its own—to muffle up her immediate quest. She tried to ignore it, but the darned thing wouldn't stop ringing.

"Yes, hello. Gillian speaking," she said drawing the receiver to her ear while peeking through the kitchen window at the lorry sitting in the drive. She couldn't make out Christian. Was he hiding in there?

"Thank God you're alive, but you sound agitated, my dear. Have I caught you in a twist?"

"Oh, Beaty! I can't talk now, I'm afraid."

"Just tell me if you've received my letter. I've been trying to reach you by telephone but it's been impossible."

"Yes, I got your letter. But I really must dash."

"No further explanation needed. Do ring me when you have a moment to spare, won't you, dear?"

"Yes, of course. I've just returned from a false alarm, that's all."

"You mean Mrs. Hemsworth? The way she churns out the little dumplings, one would think she had a conveyor belt on that trough of hers!"

"Beaty!"

"Well perhaps she should engage in a little restraint. Lock her up in that loft of hers a few nights a week! Right. No worries, but do ring me back. Love love."

The telephone clicked on the other end. "The loft! That's it." Gillian muttered to herself, grateful to her sister.

She dashed up the creaky steps to her own loft where she kept a smattering of old boxes, some frayed, some damp from the testy, harsh sea air. There was just enough light coming through the tiny window tucked into the thatch at the back of the cottage. Gillian slid one box she'd marked *1932* to the stream of light. She peeled the top open then rummaged through a few articles of clothing she thought would be considered heirlooms one day: her wide-legged trousers from that summer and a pretty muff she'd used in the cool evenings when she'd returned to the British Isles.

At the bottom of the box, she spied a Waterford dish she'd inherited from her mother wrapped in a blue velveteen cloth. A mini gasp reached her throat knowing she'd found it. She gingerly lifted it out then wiped the silver lid. Gillian remembered that she had tucked it away in this dish and box for all time after writing a spritely poem in her notebook about Christian. Though she had used it for some time, the constant reminder became too much. Eventually, keeping it at bay and forcing herself to forget its whereabouts was the only solution.

Though the poem was lovely, it made her long for a man she'd never see again. Moreover, this keepsake was an even greater reminder, greater than the words that filled the notebook's pages. "Indeed," she muttered to herself. But he was here... now... in her garden. She had to see it again, the one constant reminder that good fortune and luck or fate or whatever the heavens wanted to call it could be rendered again, if only for a moment on this sunny day on this tiny island.

She lifted the silver lid and there it was. It wasn't worth a single penny, but it was more valuable than anything Gillian had ever known. She shot a glance out the window and noticed that Christian had wandered to the back of the cottage that overlooked the moody sea, waves smacking madly against the bluff, rocks tumbling into the water. Gillian tucked the keepsake into her pocket and whisked down the narrow staircase past a small mirror framed in shells. A speedy inspection with the lick of her finger to flatten some unruly strands of hair. She decided quite frankly that he would have to accept her precisely the way she was.

He was gorgeous even now, more astonishing than her failing memory allowed. She glanced in the mirror again for one final check, but in its reflection, she noticed something leaning against Christian's lorry. Curious, she went to her kitchen window for a better look. Her hands pressed hard on its sill as though they'd been instantly glued down. She felt a gasp seize her when she saw what it was.

She hastened to the rear door then stood at the threshold for a moment to calm herself, door open wide. Gillian had learned long ago to shield her emotions when faced with another's plight, to see only the ways that would make her useful, ways that would turn an unfair and dare she say horrid reality into something beautiful and meaningful. She held her head poised and confident, although she was sure her legs would buckle underneath at any moment. How could it be? Was it really *him*? She snatched a breath in disbelief, feeling a wave of shivers flood her skin.

Gillian reached into her pocket and felt soothed by the trinket or lucky charm, as he would have called it. And it was just that, a lucky charm. It had filled even her worst moments with pieces of joy, sometimes in the oddest of circumstance. Gillian had learned over the years to see things in a different way, to see through the obvious. Perhaps everything had been in preparation for this moment, to test her resilience, her belief that a greater good could prevail.

Or was the trinket meant to be a constant reminder of a decision she should have regretted but didn't, a conflict inside her for all eternity? She had comforted herself in the thought that Christian, being in Canada, was far-removed from the immediate dangers of the war. She gazed at him now, feeling her eyes begin to well with tears, controlled. It was what she had learned to do. Her lucky charm; it was one they both had needed. Although now, she couldn't be certain why she needed it more by *her* side. She only knew that she did.

Maybe it had been irrational to dart off like that, but nothing made sense these days, so why should her behavior be any different? Her eyes remained glued to Christian, his back to her as he faced the sea, the lush green at his feet. He looked different somehow, stood in a way that felt odd. She turned her head 'round seeing the lorry in the drive and knew why. Her brow pinched together wondering what had happened, wondering why he chose now to come to her. It *was* him… Christian Hunter… the only man she'd ever loved. And that same thought, the one she couldn't dismiss the day she met him in the summer of 1932, spiraled through her veins like a German buzz bomb out of control—she would love him for the rest of her days.

"CHRISTIAN." His name sounded sweetly behind him, calm now. Just one turn, and he would know. Her eyes would say it all. There was no going back.

"Gilly," he said as his eyes left the sea and fell on hers. There she stood, just a touch away. She looked the same, only more beautiful with age. He could see that even hard times hadn't robbed her of smiling, for the lines at the sides of her mouth were beginning to deepen, adding to her character. *In her prime*, he thought. Her hair rested on her shoulders, still with its natural wave. He would never be able to remember what she was wearing. He saw only her.

He'd expected a short gasp or sudden dip of her eyes, but he wasn't even sure she noticed. How? How could she not see he was different? Before he could say another word, her eyes never leaving his, she slid her arms around his waist, slowly, earnestly, then rested her head in the cradle of his neck. He could feel her breath against his skin. It was warm and made him forget the distance that had been between them for so long. He relaxed and wrapped his arms around her.

Not a word was spoken between them. Neither had any idea how long it lasted. This was a moment Christian would remember. That much he knew. As he ran his hands over her hair, feeling coarser than he remembered, Gilly suddenly pulled away.

"How marvelous to see you! I can hardly believe it's you," she said now with an air of formality. "You could have tipped me over with a guinea pig's whiskers—honestly!" her brow now arched high as though he shouldn't believe her.

"I'd say I scared you off more than anything," he said flitting his eyes toward the cottage. She turned, following them as she calmly explained herself.

"Yes, well," her eyes full of tales but her lips sincere. She offered no excuses. "It's true I've been known to scurry off like that. Must be something in the feet." *There... there* was the mini gasp he'd expected as she bit her lower lip perhaps annoyed with herself for mentioning such a forbidden word as "feet." A smile erased her blunder. She relaxed and looped her arm in his. "Come, I have something to show you. It's why I whisked myself away so impetuously." She led Christian, who was already amused by her expressions. They never did fail to entertain. He'd never known anyone who spoke that way.

With the sea at their back and the skies turning ugly, Gilly led Christian to her small patio outlined with tall lavender, out in full bloom. Its scent hung in the air, even overpowering the tang of the salty sea. Clay pots in various sizes were home to at least a dozen green tomatoes, not ready for picking. Thyme and chives and parsley and God-knows-what filled the others and hinted that this was a home for the long haul.

"Do have a seat, won't you?" Rather than putting up a fight with her courtesies, he decided this must have been Gilly's way of dealing with the shock. She was probably rendered numb through her curtain of pleasantries. He had ages to prepare for this moment, after all; she'd had only a breath.

"Thanks." He pulled out a small wrought-iron chair from a matching table, café size, nothing fancy. "So... I could have knocked you over with... what did you say? A guinea pig's whiskers?"

"Well, I suppose I could have said a mouse's whiskers but that would have made me sound frightfully frail, don't you think?"

"Yes of course, and I'd never want to think of you as frail," Christian said grinning. "What is it you wanted to show me?"

"Do you remember that summer—you gave me something."

"I remember giving you a lot of things."

"I'm quite sure you do!" She raised her eyebrows, but those eyes of hers told him very sternly to tread with caution. "I'll wager that you'll get further in this meeting if you don't mock me."

"Is that what I'm doing?"

"Perhaps."

Some squawking above from a pair of seagulls seemed to be on Gilly's side. He was out-numbered, so he backed off.

"Still feisty, I see," he added.

"Is that your idea of acquiescing?"

"I didn't come here to start a fight," Christian said, holding his hands up in surrender.

"Why did you come?" Her voice sounded sincere.

Christian lowered his elbow to his knee and cupped his chin with his fingers. His eyes traveled to hers. "I don't know." A long pause rested between them as he suddenly couldn't recall why he'd actually come. "I suppose I just wanted to see you."

He could see Gilly swallow with a quick tilt forward, in

a way to accept such a simple truth. And it was the truth. He didn't really know despite his self-analysis time and time again. Gilly reached into her pocket.

"This is what I wanted to show you."

Gillian could see straight away how affected Christian was. Age made that even more beautiful. The lines on his forehead had deepened, and his face had filled out in a rugged sort of way. Even time had etched small lines around his eyes. He was much fitter than he'd been as a younger man, as though he'd been made to pull his weight in more ways than one. Of course, it was hard to tell through his clothing but she could see it in his forearms and in the opening of his shirt just under the hollow of his neck. His eyes still drooped, although now there was an air of sadness in them like he'd been lost for these fourteen years.

She took his hand and placed her lucky charm in his palm, curling his fingers around it.

"My pocket watch," he said, his breath shortened in surprise.

"I've kept it all these years. It's seen me through times I wouldn't wish on anyone."

He gazed at her then turned it over.

"I can't believe it. It never worked properly. Why did you bother?"

"It worked brilliantly for your information—as a bookmark."

He chuckled, "Yes, that's right. Did you really use it for that?"

"Of course, silly. Why not? The chain is perfect for reserving pages. And you know I'm never without a book in hand." She glanced down at her empty hands. "Well, almost never."

"Knowing you, it's held pages in hundreds of books."

"At least!" She smiled back.

The watch hadn't changed. It was as tarnished as the day he'd given it to her. She'd considered cleaning it on occasion and restoring the silver to it's original beauty but stopped short every time fearing that it would no longer feel the same, no longer have Christian's stamp on it. Somehow she'd always felt as though this watch was on loan to her even though he'd given it to her with all the love possible in this world. She felt as though she was safekeeping it until it was in its rightful owner's hands once again.

CHRISTIAN HELD THE WATCH, understanding now why she'd dashed off the way she had. He felt touched that Gilly had kept it all these years. No, not touched. Something much greater, but he didn't have the words or even the emotions to define it. The dirty gray was maybe a little darker, but otherwise it felt the same. The weight in his palm felt the same, too, and he smiled looking at Gilly, knowing that she'd taken care of something that meant so much to him. True, it wasn't worth a penny—that was for sure. He didn't even think for a minute he'd get a dime if they melted it down. But he was glad she knew what it had meant to him and where it came from.

Christian had found the watch along the shoreline just outside Tobermory when he was on the hunt for more pirate bones. He'd just laid Snarky Cutter beside the captain in his wooden box and would label the new bone later. The storm the night before had churned up the shoreline, leaving fallen tree trunks for Christian to clamber over. He'd overheard some fishermen saying that the winds had reached over sixty knots in Lake Huron and all they wanted to do was get the heck out of there. Christian treasured the calm after a storm like that, the way things sat heavily on the beach, the way the thick air held them down. He reveled in the array of findings on a shore littered with storm debris. As Christian balanced himself along a shaky log, pretending he was lost at sea, something shimmery had caught his eye just at the edge of the water. Christian remembered he jumped down into the spongy grass and bulrushes. He liked the velvety sausages and tried to grab one in mid air. His mom always insisted they weren't rushes at all but reeds and everyone else got it wrong. Didn't matter to him what they were called. The only thing that mattered to Christian as a young boy was finding treasures.

Christian shuffled his feet into the shallow water, following the dull sort of glitter that came from the sun falling behind a cloud. Christian curled down into a ball, not caring that his bottom was now soaked, then lifted a stone that was holding the treasure in place. Nothing could have prepared him for the thrill of finding a real treasure, one that maybe even Captain Ripper St. John had used. Something this marvelous had to have been his. Tarnished, aged from years of sitting at the bottom of Georgian Bay, then churned and twisted by the storm, and finally set free. No businessman here on summer holiday would let something like that go unpolished. No way! No, to a nine-year-old, this had definitely been owned by a pirate!

Christian could have jumped out of his pants. He'd run back to the house, the watch in one hand and his bones box in the other. He sat behind some crates in his dad's fishing shed and rubbed that watch till his hands nearly bled. Almost silver-looking. Silver enough to give to his dad for his birthday the following week. He spent ages trying to get it to work but couldn't quite manage even a tick. But it didn't matter. His dad could fix it. His dad could fix anything. Christian had knots in his stomach all week imagining the great surprise, the great reveal. He knew his dad would never forget such a present.

When the day came and went, Christian knew it was one *he'd* never forget either. His dad smiled and patted him on the back—a genuine smile he thought. Then he tossed the watch onto a chair, Christian's eyes following it, where it bounced onto the rug then rolled behind the couch. His dad left the room, and the watch stayed exactly where it had landed, behind the couch, until the day he'd left and never come back.

On his father's birthday, seasons later, Christian took the watch and kept it for himself, a watch that Griffin explained was known in the great legend of his very own Ripper St. John's nemesis, Captain Sardinious Scum. They had battled for the glory and title of Ruler of the Great Lakes—the greatest lakes on Earth, and it was Scum's pocket watch, one that was without a doubt looted from a ménage of commoners, that was drawn when all fell silent in the trembling swells beneath both ships. Nothing stirred apart from the moving hand... *tick... tick... tick* until it fell upon the third hour when Scum signaled, hooks and ropes in hand and canons at the ready. Oh yes, the element of surprise, Griffin cautioned, was of the utmost importance.

Ever since, Christian carried that watch on him like the prize-find it was meant to be. And when he'd tasted love for the first time, he couldn't think of anyone more deserving of a treasure than Gilly.

"It's yours Christian. It was never truly mine. You know

that."

"But I gave it to you. I wanted you to have it." He gazed quizzically. "Do you remember that day?"

"How could I forget?" she said while reaching for the watch in his palm. She opened it gingerly, not wanting to crush into tiny flakes the treasure that did, in fact, belong to her.

"God, Gilly, you still have it?" She flinched at the sound of his name for her. She hadn't heard *Gilly* for fourteen years and now twice in the last five minutes.

She carefully lifted the stem of a now brittle four-leaf clover. "Yes." A soft smile merged into her cheeks, making her feel more relaxed. "I haven't opened the watch in all these years, but I knew it was there. My lucky charm," she shrugged, her brow arched high.

Drips fell from the sky, tiny ones from brooding, indecisive skies. Gillian couldn't decide herself. She felt odd, thrown into a mix of then and now. It wasn't right. Her life had changed in a myriad of ways. Was it the rain gods up there who were toying with her now? Or her God, a God she'd learned to trust, one that she'd believed had her best interest at heart. No, she decided quite frankly, the moody sky came out of nowhere!

"So much for the morning sun," she said, trying to find a reason to quibble. But she couldn't. It was lovely to see him again, rain or shine, watch or not. It didn't matter whether it was his or hers. All she knew was that he gave it to her with all the love he had to offer. A sunny day in Tobermory, a flowery meadow, a copy of *Gulliver's Travels* in hand with Lilliput soaking her in, her head on his lap and a patch of clover sitting next to him.

"This is for you," he said. She remembered feeling a light

gasp when she saw it had four leaves. "It's good luck, you know."

"Yes, I know. Daddy found one for me years ago when I was just a tot. We had been strolling on the knoll but I remember letting it slip from my fingertips and sobbing till my eyes were like little puffed sausage rolls as I scrambled about trying to find it. I never managed and haven't found one since." She knew how earnest her expression must have appeared to him and felt a sigh overcome her. "Thank you for this. I shall treasure it always." She opened her book intending to lay the four leaf clover between the conditions of the contract for Gulliver's freedom—that nasty Skyresh Bolgolam—perhaps the clover would be a bit of a good luck charm for Gulliver? She had a feeling it would serve anyone who had good intentions when Christian snapped the book shut.

"Here. Use this instead. You'll never find your page like that, and besides the clover will crumble and get lost in those words forever." He opened his pocket watch then carefully set the four-leaf clover inside the case cover. Gently closing it, he let the chain dangle from his finger as the watch swung like a pendulum. "There. Now you have a bookmark."

Gillian gazed up at Christian, feeling such an intense love it was almost painful. "A good luck bookmark," she sighed.

I used to long for riches
The key—or so I thought –
To all the things the world has got,
To smooth life's tortuous road.

But passing time has proved to me,
The things I value most,
Are yours, or mine and have no price,
Though priceless in their worth.

A kiss of love, the smile of a friend,
The clouds are silver lined.
And whether to castle or cottage they come,
Each brings something no riches can buy.

Chapter 11

2003

SATURDAY MORNING is proving to be optimistic here at the farm. I woke up after all and that's something poor old Angus couldn't do the morning I found him next to me, motionless. He hadn't even twitched in his sleep, but it was his time and I was grateful he hadn't suffered the way I've been. Quite frankly, I'm pleased I have another day. I refuse to let damp socks ruin the attire.

Though the doctors may well be annoyed with me, insisting that I reconsider at once being admitted sooner than later, that remains their problem. As a matter of fact, I think I've stumped them that I'm not already packed and shipped away to the heavens. Granted, I refuse to leave this world being told what to do in my final hours; I will dawdle as much as possible. I know it's only a matter of days before I must say good-bye to this lovely horse farm forever, but until they drag me away, I want to feel the countryside in me. If that means falling dead in the neighbor's cornfield, causing a swarm of locusts in the flat cold of late November, gnawing on me till there's nothing left, then so be it. At least

I will have left this world in the open air.

"Grandma?" A tapping at the door pleases me. I always like to have a bit of company. "May I come in?"

"Yes, of course," I say, trying to turn up the volume, but I'm afraid low is the only setting I have these days. Gilly pokes her head in, looking concerned that she's taken me from sleep. "Don't worry, dear, you didn't wake me."

"Kate said you were napping, but I really wanted to talk to you."

"About your book?" I ask curiously.

"Well …" she says as her eyes turn away from me, "maybe, but not now. Actually, I wanted to take you somewhere."

"That's getting more difficult, I'm afraid, and I'd like to avoid a stroll through the cornfield across the road."

Gilly's brow pinches together. "There's no corn this time of year, Grandma," she says patting my hand as though I've lost my mind.

"Where do you want to take me then?"

"That's a surprise," she smiles with a naughty gleam. I can see it in her eyes even behind those dark rims. "You don't need to worry about anything. If you're going to the hospital soon, there's no way I'm going to let this opportunity pass."

Opportunity? I've always loved that juncture somewhere between surprise and freedom, and goodness knows opportunity is freedom.

"Well, you don't need to twist *my* arm. If I know you, taking me out in this state," I mumble, eyes whisking over my boney limbs, "it must be for good reason."

"Of course it is, Grandma, and what state?" she lies skillfully, "You're still a vision. I know Grandpa would agree if he was still here." We both smile at the thought of him.

"Have you told Kate?" I ask, worried she might dissuade

my granddaughter especially with the weather being what it is.

"Yup, all covered."

SECRETLY ANXIOUS that Gilly would be taking me to a crowded place when I can hardly stand let alone focus on more than one voice at a time, she surprises me by helping me into a snowsuit... I repeat, a snowsuit, of all things! If her plan is to *plonk* me on that old splintered toboggan—I still prefer that word to *sledge* no matter where my loyalties might lie. I sigh, suddenly feeling dozy. Losing my train of thought irritates me. Where was I? Right... the toboggan... on which we used to sail through the winter many moons ago... she is either conspiring to end my misery with this glob of cancer or she's forgotten that I'm eighty-nine years old.

I look at her as she rounds the driveway and out onto the main road, as confident as *I* used to be behind the wheel. Snow is piled at the sides but the road seems clear enough after the ice storm the other day. It's unusual for late November. Reminds me of the seventies when Angus and I had to cross-country ski just to pick up a carton of milk at Mac's. I always loved the feeling of being snowed-in, and London never disappointed in those days. But ice storms are only beautiful from the quiet of one's lair.

As I look out the car window, trees snapped in half lay fruitless on the ground. Yet the one car that's passed us barreled through with an edgy confidence. It makes me want to pull the collar of my snowsuit high around my neck like a guardrail. Admittedly, gazing out the window I wonder what on earth my granddaughter is thinking taking me out in this. Though the alternative leaves me dry. Anyhow, she's bundled me up like a furry banana, so tightly I'm not sure I can breathe, but she's certainly snatched my attention.

JUST WHEN I THINK we're out for a long drive, it turns out we've only gone 'round the property to the far end. Gilly swings off the main road onto my son's old dirt trail that's blocked by a long steel netted gate. Perhaps it was put there to contain the sheep that used to graze on the property before my son bought it. At any rate, Gilly darts out of the car to open it. She looks like a real country girl when I see her do things like that, a furry sort of wellington to her knees, rubbery and warm-looking, a long parka to keep the bottom toasty, and a tuque pulled over her ears. She jumps back into the car then rolls along the trail that's just two strips of dirt, wide enough for a tractor. Today it's covered in a thick layer of snow as it winds through a wooded area filled with white trilliums in the springtime. I used to come here with Angus just to see the forest floor waving hello in the breeze. And if I squint my eyes now, the white of the snow could almost pass for them.

"Where are you taking me?" I ask curiously.

"Shhh, no questions, Grandma. But you'll have to do a little bit of walking," she sighs. "Don't worry, though, just hold onto me nice and tight."

For the first time in too long, I feel that kick of excitement.

NARNIA. That's the only word that comes to mind as I walk with my arm coiled in my granddaughter's. She's nearly sewn into me she's gripped so hard. But a path of hay has been laid down just for me, I think. And with boots that could easily be mistaken for snowshoes, I manage well enough. I don't know why the hospitals keep patients pinned to their rooms when just a breath of this icy air is like a shot of whiskey. Wakes you up! The proof is in the puffs of air billowing from your mouth—a glorious reminder that you're still alive.

The path has straightened and though I've seen the woodland much like this before—a gaggle of trees heavy with snow and the sky as blue as blue—I suspect there's something else brewing.

"We're almost there, Grandma," Gilly says trying to hide that tingle in her voice that comes with surprising someone you love. I remember feeling it the day we gave Ballerina her new home. Such a sweet feeling! So much more delicious than doing something for yourself. Of course, I've always got back ten times what I've given. But I do feel that jolt of excitement again as I hear the crunch of snow under my feet. The hay has fallen away as we reach a cluster of branches wrapped in thick ice.

"I don't think we can go any further, dear," I mumble.

"Just wait," she says as she pushes apart a slew of branches that have wound themselves like grapevine, whorls of icy sculpture.

As the crackling sound of ice breaking rings in the air, Gilly makes an opening just wide enough for the two of us to slip through.

As I MOVE FORWARD, it feels as though I'm going from one world into an entirely new one, stepping into a book. The frigid air suddenly warms me though it's colder in here than all my winters put together. Only a few, select times in life have left me as astonished as this moment. Even Gilly stands beside me without a word leaving her lips.

The heavy snowfall yesterday has left this place nearly

untouched as icy branches have woven into a canopy above us, like a glassy cage of spun sugar. Specks of blue sky try to fight through but lose out to skinny rays of sunshine. The crackling in the opening behind me is quiet now and all I can hear is my breath. Small clouds puff from my mouth. *I'm alive!*

Has the brush of the woodland now traced in ice, all gathered here to make this hideaway for me? I glance at my granddaughter thinking, *yes but with a little magic from Gilly, I'm sure.*

As a fat starling slips through an opening, curious to see who's joined in on the fun, I watch like an excited child. It hops along the white floor, the room curtained in glittery ice, as my gaze follows it to two garden lounge chairs placed in the center. Both are draped in sheepskin and sleeping bags with blankets propped at the ends. Between them sits a small table with a thermos and two mugs. And between those, "My poems!" I gasp.

"What do you think, Grandma?" Gilly sighs.

I don't have words. All I can feel is the welling up of tears in my eyes as one finally splashes down my cheek, nearly turning into a tiny icicle. I can't believe she's done this for me, and in the same breath, I can. "Here, let me help you," she says, supporting my arm as we approach the chairs.

"How did you find this place?" I eventually ask.

"Sebastian and I found it yesterday when we were out walking."

"Oh, how is he?" I say, fond of her newish boyfriend. "Why don't you bring him 'round to see me?"

"He's fine, and I will, I promise. I've just been so busy."

"I know you have."

"He helped with all this," she says motioning to the lounge chairs and blankets.

"How kind of him. He's a real dish that one."

"You think so?" she asks, feigning surprise by my comment. She can't fool me.

"My dear, I'm old, not blind! You need to keep that one, I'm telling you. There's more in those eyes of his than simply wanting a good roll in the hay."

"Grandma! You're terrible!"

I take my granddaughter's hand. "It's true, Gilly. That boy's in love with you, I know it."

Gilly's grin widens and I can see that she feels the same. "Ask me anything and I'll tell you the truth," I say pointedly.

"Okay, why did you really leave Christian?"

"I meant about you and Sebastian and using your feminine wiles on him to good effect."

"You promised," she snaps.

"I lied," I say pursing my lips and brow into a good scowl.

"Okay. As recompense, you have to name ten lies you've told me over the years."

"Oh, a challenge! I do like those!" I say biting my lip with my horsey dentures. "Let's see. Do you remember I plucked your eyebrows for the first time and said that that bald spot had already been there?" I say with my now hairless brow arched as high as my scalp and a cheeky, furtive glare to go with it.

"I plucked yours, too, and I said the same!" She scowls back.

"Indeed. Now look at me." A giggle almost gives me away. "Let's see, another one. I haven't defeated you at ping pong fifty-two times either," I say. "It was only forty-three. But who's counting?"

"And I let you win," my granddaughter spits.

"I never liked that boy who took you to your high school graduation dance."

"Neither did I."

"You look silly when you dance."

"So do you!"

"I like you best when you tell stories of malfunctioning, Montezuma's revenge-ridden bowels no matter how many times I tell you it's unladylike."

"I knew it!" she bellows, nearly bursting.

A moment of silence eases our laughter as we nestle in our den, steam curling up from our cups.

"Isn't it wonderful when your cheeks ache from smiling?" I add.

"Even better when they ache just at the thought of someone," Gilly says, squeezing my hand.

Silence now whirls around our wintery cage—our cups now empty. I can feel the silence nudging my granddaughter until finally she asks me something I have been expecting.

"Grandma, I've been wondering something."

"What is it?"

"I hope it won't upset you but ..." she hesitates. "Are you afraid to die?"

I glance away trying to sort out my thoughts. "Well, I try to think of it like this. Even in my darkest moments, even when I've been angry with the Lord, I've never actually doubted Him. I know you feel quite differently, dear, about all that. But for me, it's comforting to believe that He is there waiting for me. If I'm not afraid of Him, then I'm not afraid to die."

"Is it really that simple?"

"Yes, I suppose it is. And even if you never feel the same

about the church as I do, you can at least be comforted knowing that *I* will be there waiting for you," I say, smiling easily.

Gilly turns away for a moment. Perhaps she's trying to gather some strength, not wanting to flood the cage with tears. Yet her movement draws my attention to the table between us. I can avoid it all I want but it's not going to skitter into the bushes with that starling. I glance at my leather folder tucked inside a Ziploc bag.

"You want me to read those, don't you?" I ask.

Gilly wraps her hands around the mug, warming them. "I need to hear the words from you."

"Why?"

"Because I'm afraid this novel is coming too easily, that I'm missing something between the lines. I haven't even written a plan, Grandma. What kind of novel starts without a plan?"

"Perhaps one coming from the heart."

"But I'm writing like a fiend. I can't stop, and I don't even know what I'm writing until it's on the screen in front of me."

It's true. She stays up writing until the wolves go to sleep. I see her by that window every night. I crunch what's left of my brow together, baffled. It's such a strange phenomenon with writers, the way a story starts to breathe life, the way the characters become real, the way a writer becomes a servant to the story as much as its creator. Writing a story becomes no different than trying to sort out the structure and details of our own lives. If I go to the shop now, how will that affect my child who is needing to be fetched at noon, all while trying to keep secret a surprise party we've planned for him for that very afternoon. These problems need to be carefully solved, arranged, and shaped. And that's what's happening to Gilly; I know it.

"And you think my voice will make a difference?" I ask, partly afraid that she's on to something, that my voice will shake out the real meaning behind my words, the truth that I don't want her to hear, not even from myself. It's a battle that I continue to fight because underneath it all, I want her to know everything. And she will when the time is right.

My granddaughter smiles lightly. "Maybe, but of course you don't need to read them to me if you don't want. It's just…" She stops, momentarily tucking a strand of hair into her tuque. "Sometimes I wish you could get into my head, not so much because of the book but because I'm afraid you may never know what you've meant to my life."

"But I do know. That's the one beautiful thing about growing old. You slowly come to realize the important things in life. You begin to see the truth in people, what makes them worthy of your devotion. With you, it's been different. Perhaps it's something impossible to articulate, but I've felt our connection since the first time I saw your tiny face."

Gilly reaches out to my hand wrapped in a down mitten. I like being cocooned in this sleeping bag. It makes me feel the tang of childhood again when I used to sleep under the stars on warm summer nights with my siblings. I think we only did it once, in all honesty, but it was enough to remember the honeyed feeling of summer. Now it's far too cold for a dying woman; the stars have been replaced by glittery ice. But I'm still living. I wouldn't want to be anywhere other than where I am at this very moment. And there's no one I'd rather be with.

I sigh, the icy air very nearly clearing my lungs. "Kate

doesn't really know you've taken me here, does she?"

"No," Gilly admits.

"I thought so."

"She'd never have let me take you in your condition, not somewhere like this."

"I'm glad you didn't tell her the truth. Sometimes the truth can be more upsetting than a small white lie, especially when you're trying to protect the ones you love. It's our little secret, dear," I say now patting her hand.

I reach for my leather folder then begin to read from the blue notebook inside, my glasses propped on my nose. Turning the pages proves painful not only to my stiff arthritic fingers, but with each poem come memories that even cancer can't eat up. Even through the pain it feels right to read the poems aloud. It's something I hadn't expected— three surprises in one day. And it's good, I suppose, if my voice shakes out the truth. Perhaps it will ease Gilly's mind about my story. After all, she's never written a novel before, and I'm proud to bits she's taken it on. Of course she's got the time now to do it before starting with a career that will swallow up her days. And I know it's stealing time from her new relationship. Despite that, I know she wouldn't do it unless she was driven, unless it was in her blood. Moreover, it's fantastic training for her destined career as a journalist.

OH MY GIDDY AUNT! *What was I thinking?* I feel my poufy mitten cup my mouth in felicity—sheer, utter joy. *Of course... it's time!* After reading these poems, after years of waiting, it really has come. Angus is gone, after all. Biting my nails to protect the snug love he always shared with our son is quite simply foolish now. Even good ol' Angus will understand from the pearly gates—and if he doesn't, we can have a delicious row when I come knocking. Waiting any longer would simply be a ruse to keeping my sights on life when it is the dark of death that I must soon face. No, I'm right. It's time for my granddaughter to soak in the mood of the places I lived as a young woman, then all those stringy bits will somehow weave together more easily. It's always made perfect sense.

"Gilly," I say, feeling the words like satin on my tongue. I was sure when the time came, they would stumble clumsily from my mouth, but now I know that everything in life has its timing, its place.

"What?" she buzzes.

"I'm going to ask you to do something, dear, but I don't want you to answer until you've had time to bathe in the possibilities of my request."

"You sound so serious," she adds, trying to temper my mood.

"Maybe so, but I can assure you, the invitation is as curly as it is fruitful."

"Curly?" Gilly's brow darts up. "You do have a way with words, Grandma. Haven't a clue what could be curly about an invitation. But I would love one."

"I thought you might." To be doubly sure of the moment, I want to savor it with the last drip of this gorgeous hot chocolate. Gilly's fidgeting in her chair as though I am making her suffer while I pour.

"Grandma!"

"You're like a squirrel, my dear."

"A squirrel?"

"Yes, darting around me, wagging tail and all, trying to get whatever morsel you can."

"Oh, you make me crazy!" she says wavering between a

smile and a scowl. "The invitation?"

"Yes, right." I scowl back. "Quite simply, when I am dead and buried …"

"Grandma!"

"Well, there's no point in dipping death into lemon curd. It is what it is. *When I am gone*, if that makes you feel better, darling, I would like you to step into my past. Go to England; visit your Auntie Beaty. She won't disappoint, I promise. Then I would like you to go to the Isle of Man. Treat it like a pilgrimage if you prefer. I want you to breathe the air there. I want you to feel the cobblestone under your toes, get drunk on the sweet olivy scent of primrose, and grow tipsy with the delicious coconut from gorse blossom. It will make you wild with curiosity. Sadly, I had a neighbor there who lacked severely in nasal faculty. Good Lord, I thought at the time, she'll be in need of a support group. Just imagine not having a smeller to nose around even the innocent bouquets that sweep across the meadows. A tragedy, I tell you." A grin weaves into my wrinkled mouth as my granddaughter waits breathless for my next thought. "But nothing will escape *you*, Gilly. Leave nothing unturned. My little cottage waits for you with answers that lie spent beneath its thatch."

A long moment lingers between us. I'm not sure what I had expected. I've played this moment out in my mind a hundred different ways since Gilly was born. But here it is.

"I'm not sure I want to talk about this now," she mutters. "I don't want to think about you being gone."

"Don't be a fool child," I say, putting my granddaughter in her place. "Even when I'm dead and buried, I'll still be walking beside you every step through your life, so much so we'll be tripping over each other. I'll wind up spending half the after-life with bruises on my feathery wings."

Gilly giggles. "You must be mad, Grandma."

"No, far from it. I've never been saner. I have nothing better to do with my money than buy you a ticket. Sebastian can go with you if you like. Everything will be paid for."

As cold creeps between my layers, a lovely quiet fills the air. I think Gilly's lost in my proposal. As a matter of fact, she looks at me with a misty eye, like a long-lost Brigadoon anxious to materialize, yet full of mystery in its own right.

"It's settled," I say. "Speak to Sebastian about it. And Gilly," I say reaching out to her hand, "don't wait for me to sweeten the earth; go as soon as you've said your good-byes."

It's LATE WHEN WE RETURN, and I can hear Kate's snippety whisper outside my door, likely questioning why the mounds of winter clothing. She's very protective of me, which is sweet. I think Gilly's tale has worked as Kate's voice has now simmered.

"Grandma," Gilly says popping her head in. "The coast is clear. We got away with it."

"Come, dear." My granddaughter walks over to the bed. "Look!" I say, pointing to the window as a single fat snowflake falls past the windowpane. Her eyes travel back to me.

"Thank you for today, Grandma. I'll never forget it."

"My darling," I say as a rush of emotion hijacks me. "Today was magical. Thank *you*."

"I didn't expect a trip out of it," she says.

"It doesn't matter what you expected. It's what the day has brought. Make all the arrangements as soon as possible. I don't think I can hold on for much longer, but you needn't worry about money. Just go when I've turned to fairy dust and find your answers."

Why am I so fearful?
Why am I so sad?
With my life full of promise,
Now I am beloved.

What is this feeling
Which fills me with fear?
When I have in full measure
The things I hold dear.

I blame the truant thought
Of deserting melodies,
One will leave the other
With naught but memories.

To fill the days with endless pain
And longing for what has been,
What, alas, can never
Never, never be again!

Chapter 12

1946

THE TINY DRIPS had swelled into globs, pattering down on the flagstone patio. They plopped on Christian's shoulder as though they were trying to awaken them both to reality, bringing them back to 1946.

"I'm not sure how much longer we're going to last out here?" Christian questioned.

"Right you are! On the other hand, it's only water!" Gilly laughed. "Here, let me help you."

Christian pulled away, a sliver suddenly embedded in his voice, "It's fine. I can manage." He drew in a deep breath realizing at once what he had done and couldn't tell whether the streams of water running down Gilly's face were tears or rain, as she stood shell-shocked. Yes, the clouds had opened up in one fell sloppy swoop and already he had to clean up a mess. In all this time, he'd never reacted that way. Why now? Why with Gilly? He softened his voice instantly, feeling guilty for the tone. She'd only wanted to help—he knew that. But why hadn't she asked about it? Why all this skirting around the issue? Or was it an issue? He felt his brow pinch together at the thought.

"Won't you please come indoors?" she said with a trace of a smile, a forgiving one at that. Of course she hadn't a tear, Gilly was too stout for that. "I can see you manage very well on your own. I didn't mean…"

Christian placed his index finger on her lips. He didn't want to make her feel awkward or force her to say something she didn't quite mean.

"I'd like that… thank you."

GILLIAN RUMMAGED THROUGH her kitchen cabinet trying to find the tea. It seemed to have grown legs on it the way she kept her cupboard these days. She'd traded her neighbor just last week a loaf of bread for tea coupons. At one shilling three pence, it wasn't exactly a bargain. But with tea in such short supply even now after the war had ended, Gillian was grateful to have some at all. Still, after all these years, when she'd sniff the severe lack of aroma of Typhoo tea, the one and only brand available from coast to coast here and on the mainland, she'd imagine the musky spiciness of the Darjeeling tea she had sipped and savored in the maharani's kitchen after the children had gone to bed. Sometimes the maharani would join her—two women from vastly different cultures appreciating such a simple luxury.

Found some. Gillian opened the packet, and as she scooped up some tea leaves, she felt slightly unraveled and could see her hand shaking—nerves, that's all. It wasn't every day her first love wandered about her sitting room picking up photographs and glancing at books she'd read just last evening. He looked terribly tall, just shy of the old timber beams that cut across the ceiling. All these cottages had low ceilings. And she was glad, too. Nothing worse than trying to heat a room filled with unnecessary space. She could see him making the rounds as she spied over her shoulder. Yes, he managed perfectly well on his own! She struck a match, lighting the gas cooker, then filled a pot with water. Another breath as she turned—now facing him while she patted her hair dry with a dish towel. She wandered toward Christian whose eyes were fixed on a photograph of her father.

"He looks stern, don't you think?" Gillian tilted her head toward the posed headshot showing off that long, curled mustache of her father's.

Christian threw her a glance. "Yeah. Sure does."

"It's all a facade really. He's the gentlest man I know."

"Is this your father?"

Gillian sighed, "Yes." The room grew silent as she collected her thoughts. She sat down on the hearth of her stone fireplace and looked up at Christian. "He's gone now. As Beaty would say, he's in our Lord's arms."

"Do you believe that?" Christian asked.

"I believe that in some way Daddy is still watching over me."

Christian nodded but left it at that.

"You have an amazing place here," he said, changing the subject.

"Thank you." Gillian furrowed her brow, still wondering why he hadn't asked more about her father or expressed his sympathies. "I've been here for some time now. When I'd first arrived in Port St. Mary, I stayed in a pint-sized loft above a cow house of all places, just outside town. I can't tell you how the smell nearly toppled me over each evening I came home. In the beginning, I was quite worried I'd never wake up from a night's sleep. Surely all those dung fumes affect the brain, don't you think? Thought they'd render me witless in some way. But I survived it and truth was, the cows were rarely brought indoors, and there were only two in fact. Darling creatures. Elspeth and Bernie they were called. Bernie was a female. Don't know why they called her that. But she was quite well behaved compared to Elspeth. That one was a right so and so, always nudging up to people, no doubt trying to pass along the flies that irritated her so. Couldn't blame her, really. Every time I'd sit down under my favorite tree with a good book, she'd wander up to me and whack me incessantly with that tail of hers as though she was green with envy over my book getting all the attention."

"You haven't changed a bit, have you?" Christian said grinning.

"What do you mean?"

"I like your stories, that's all."

"Well, I have plenty of those if I do say so myself." Gillian could hear the water boiling on the cooker and invited Christian to join her at the kitchen table. "I'm afraid all I have is tea to offer," knowing full well he never cared for tea, at least not in those days.

"Perfect," he said.

Gillian turned to the table, motioning to the chair opposite her.

"Do sit down,"

"Thank you. But you know, you don't need to be so formal with me," he added. "We go back a long way."

"We do. But I don't know any other way to be. Am I really being formal?"

They both sat down. Christian reached across the small, square table sitting next to the window and placed his hand on hers.

"Relax. It's only me."

She studied him—he thought she was likely wondering about his intentions. Then she poured him a cup of tea. It was strange this feeling, as though he had just met someone for the first time, yet she was just the same as he remembered, only a blink older. He pulled his hand away and smiled.

"So tell me, what's with the motorcycle and sidekick?" he said motioning out the window toward the driveway.

"Oh, do you like it?"

"It suits you."

"Well, I got it for a steal. It was also how I came to find this cottage. Nearly three years ago come November there was a terrible crash near town. A Halifax bomber came down on one of the farms of a well-known family here." Gilly gazed out the window, a serious tone reaching her breath. "I remember it was a Saturday because I worked at the infirmary at the Ballaqueeney Hotel those mornings and I had just finished seeing the last internee that day. She had a terrible ear infection, that one. I remember because she was crying so. I tried to comfort her the best I could, but her English was rather broken. Most internees spoke fluent English, but not this one. Apparently, she hadn't been in the UK very long before they collected everyone and billeted her here. She was Austrian—*that* I do remember. Nonetheless, I was on my way out through the protected gate." Christian gazed at her curiously wondering what she meant. "The noise from the airplane rendered me useless—crippled I'd say—but only for a moment. Honestly, I thought we were under attack. I dashed to the top of the lane where I could see over the bay. A trail of smoke looking more like swirling spun sugar gone rabid disappeared behind the cloud, and a moment later there was a bang I'll never forget. Pieces of airplane fell from the sky, some fluttering in the air, and the fuselage came straight down like a torpedo into the ground, leaving nothing except a veil of smoke.

I can't tell you the urgency I felt. As I ran in that direction, I noticed Port St. Mary's fire tender was well on its way. I was foolish to think I could help in any way, not being a qualified nurse, but so be it. I went anyway. To my surprise Dr. Pilkington, the hopeful town doctor at that time whom I had never actually met before, pulled up next to me on his motorbike. No cajoling was necessary. I jumped into the sidecar and off we went. He was so impressed with my determination that he promised me his motorbike if the day ever came that he could afford a proper car befitting a town doctor." Christian noticed her chest swell with pride. "It was on that ride out to the farm that I saw my little cottage for the first time. You wouldn't think I'd notice something so lovely being in such a tizzy as I was, but I did. I noticed enough for my heart to skip. It was mine nearly two years later. But that's a whole other story," she said grinning.

"So what happened to the plane?" Christian asked drawing the teacup to his lips.

"Well, the whole brigade was there, naturally."

"Naturally," he added with a slight mock in his expression. Gilly kneaded her brow just a little, enough to warn him, he figured.

"As I was saying, the whole brigade was there. It was a good thing, too, as several haystacks went up in flames upon impact. There was a silly man, known as Gilbert Brody, with a pot-bellied pig on a leash standing in the way of everyone. The pig was making a terrible din, squealing, nearly ripping everyone's ears right off their heads! Dr. Pilkington had to step in and give that pig a sedative."

"Did they find the pilots?"

"As far as I remember, only the rear gunner was found," Gilly lowered her chin. "Such a horrid thing... war. Even now I avoid the hotel. It looks so austere to me, standing on its own at the end of the promenade, like a big... cold... square institution."

"Then why did you work there?"

"I came for *them*."

He gazed quizzically, "What do you mean? I know there were internment camps on the island, but here in Port St. Mary?"

"Well yes, just until the size of the Rushen Camp was reduced. Remaining internees were moved to Port Erin. Hundreds of women were housed between here and there. They are the reason I moved to the Isle of Man. I came for them, to help in any way I could. Beaty was dead-set against it. Worried for me. But I never agreed with such an atrocity. Many of them had been living in the UK for years, some of them were even born on this very island. Just because they had German or Austrian blood, or spoke Italian or were Jewish, non-allied blood, they were made to feel like the enemy. But what surprised me most was that the women themselves created a divide and made *each other* feel like the enemy. There was a vicious war within the confines of the boarding house, I can tell you that! The government simply provided the playing field." Gilly dropped her shoulders clearly in exasperation, "Thank the good Lord, shortly after I'd been working there—I think it was in the spring a year later—Ballaqueeney became a married camp. One hundred and seventy families! You can imagine the workload. The camp ran all the way down the promenade really, but that hotel was like the mother ship!"

Gilly took a moment, sipping her tea, ghostly swirls of

steam still rising from the cup. "Though the memories of that camp sadden me to this day, I was proud to walk away from it all knowing that I had done my best to treat each woman with respect. Of course, in my heart I didn't always succeed. Things improved greatly when the husbands were brought to Port St. Mary, a chirp I hadn't heard in their wives' voices until then. Before the husbands arrived, it was difficult not to judge the women's venomous tongues. How could they treat each other with such insolence and cruelty? The women were far worse than the men, you know. Though I couldn't possibly imagine what they had been feeling, caged in the way they were. They may have had schools, a club room, and even a cinema, but they were caged in nonetheless." She drew a deep, unsavory breath, "I can tell you, the number of times I felt like socking one right smack across the head. Some of them were horrible. The things they'd say. I heard with my very own ears one woman who was a proclaimed Nazi degrade a Jewish teenage girl who'd been forced to share a bed with that evil creature. Telling everyone that she smelled bad, Jewish bad, and that that was the very reason the tyrant refused to attend service at the local Methodist Church on Sundays. Wasn't hard to put the puzzle pieces together, even with her broken English. The reverend was a sweet, old man and invited anyone of any faith to join in his service.

That same tyrant was the Austrian with the ear infection three years later. I would never forget her face. It was then that I felt sorry for her. Not because of the pain but because she'd been fooled like the rest of them. Brainwashed! That's why I felt sorry for her. I really did do my best not to judge. I'd read the camp's journal, *Rushen Outlook*, whenever I could get my hands on a copy. And there I came to realize how even a minority of National Socialists could cause such distress among a group of women who should instead be enjoying life and caring for their families. Oh, what a mess it all was! That's why I was so happy to see Port St. Mary become a married, family camp. At least then these women could have a semblance of a normal life."

Christian sat silently taking in her words, realizing that open wounds came in all shapes and sizes. That the innocent, maybe even spoiled, girl he'd met fourteen years earlier had seen more than she should have.

"If you weren't a nurse, why were you working in the infirmary?"

"I was in training; Dr. Pilkington had eyed me on occasion when he'd visited Ballaqueeney during his internship."

"Eyed-you?" Christian said raising his eyebrows.

"For purely professional reasons, thank you very much," Gillian said as flatly as she could, not wanting him to suspect that she'd imagined kissing the doctor, let alone considered a relationship with him.

"Right! Professional."

"You still like to take the mickey out of me, don't you?"

"I never quite knew what that meant."

"Oh, I think you do now, Mr. Hunter," she said with a sliver of a grin.

"I guess this Dr. Pilkington got the job after all, since the motorcycle is sitting in your driveway?"

"How clever of you."

"Now who's taking the mickey?"

They both smiled, letting go of any leftover tension between them.

"Dr. Pilkington is now my employer."

"I know."

Gillian looked curiously at Christian.

"I went looking for you at his office."

"The surgery?"

"Yeah. But it was closed."

"How did you know to find me there?" she asked with a bewildering gaze.

"It's a small town, Gilly."

"But how did you know where I was at all?"

A sudden ring of the telephone snapped the conversation in two. He could see she tried to ignore it and was irritated at the timing.

"Excuse me while I answer this. Probably Beaty ringing back."

"Of course," he said.

Gilly rose from her chair and reached for the telephone on the wall. "Hello, Gillian speaking. Who's calling, please?"

"It's Reggie. No false alarm this time. I'm already at the Hemsworth farm and it doesn't look good."

"I'll be there straight away!"

Christian could hear a definite urgency in her voice and was already up collecting the teacups and saucers.

"I'm sorry. Do you mind?"

"Of course not. Is everything okay?" Christian asked.

"I hope so. But I really must dash." She grabbed her helmet and propped it on her head with a guilty expression.

"Don't wait for me. Just go," he said.

"Right. Okay." She hastened down the gravel driveway as Christian closed the door behind him. As she approached the pick-up truck, she stopped... staring at what he'd propped up against it earlier, then threw a glance his way. He stood still watching, wondering. Gilly picked it up, running her hand along it as though she was getting acquainted with it then brought it to him slowly. If ever time had stood still, it was then. He couldn't know what she was thinking, but in that moment he needed to know more than anything. Holding it in both her hands, she handed him his walking stick. Not a word left her lips; what he saw in her eyes said it all. There wasn't a drop of sympathy. And if there really were a god up there then he'd thank him for that. It was a different look, one that he hoped she'd define one day soon.

"Your pocket watch," she said with a sudden jolt as she turned toward the cottage.

"No. It's a bookmark. Thank you for showing it to me, but it's yours." Gilly nodded with a soft smile, understanding that somehow it was theirs together.

She sprinted down the driveway then threw her leg over the motorcycle. He noticed she was wearing a skirt as she pulled it high up on her thighs. He felt dazed by her beauty. When Gilly revved the engine, it spluttered excitedly.

"Tomorrow?" she shouted over the noise. "Shall we meet again?"

"Where?"

"By the lighthouse. You can't miss it!"

"Which one? There are two!"

"The bullet, of course!"

"When?"

"No idea," she shouted, laughing. "This house call may take a while!"

"I'm staying at an inn beside the Manx's Tail. Do you know it?"

"Everyone knows that pub! Manx cats don't have tails!" she cheered with a thumb's up and the prettiest smile he'd ever seen. Gilly rounded her motorcycle on the driveway, crunching the stones as she rolled off, her hand throwing a jaunty salute.

Christian's eyes followed her to the end of the gravel, and as Gilly traveled in the opposite direction, he noticed the herd of sheep was back.

Yesterday my heart was breaking;
We quarreled bitterly and long.
Today the angry mood is over;
I wonder how to say I was wrong.

I pray he will forgive me,
When I tell of tears I shed.
Which wiped away all bitterness,
Leaving with me instead.

A longing to be near him,
His dear hand clasping mine.
While we kiss in silent gratitude,
A lesson we have learned in time

To err is very human,
But to forgive divine!

Chapter 13

1932

A LETTER FROM BOMBAY, INDIA.

Her Highness Maharani Sonali Raje Shrimant Sethi

A secret voice inside Gillian twittered like little waves of shock as she held the envelope in her palm. She couldn't believe the maharani had written to her. Wary of its contents, she tore the wax seal gingerly then slid out the sheet of veined papyrus. The maharani's handwriting was exquisite, like a moving sonata for the eyes.

1st of August 1932

Gillian,

I hope this letter finds you well. I am sending it to your sister's address but expect that it will work its way into your hands.

I have been pestered, as the English would say, by my daughter each and every day since we returned to India to write to her favorite nanny. Of course, I have explained to her that playing favorites is a dangerous game as someone is bound to get hurt eventually, and in this case I fear that may be her. We are all very fond of you and were disappointed that you were unable to follow us back to India. If I had been your father, I would have done exactly the same, so I quite understand his position.

It is Shashi who wanted to write of her adventure back to our homeland, so I shall leave you here and pass my fountain pen to this little girl sitting next to me. She feels quite grown-up with a real fountain pen and insists that I give her privacy. A slight warning—I have promised not to check her spellings.

Do take good care of yourself in these troubling times, and please know that we are all well.

My best to your family,
Sonali

Hello Gillian,

I hope you are having a nls time. I went on a big bot. I playd with my bruther but he made me cry. One nite I was very, very fritend. There was a angry monster in the sky and the bot was tippy and I cryd so I runned to you but you were not there. I went to the bech with my frend and she made me laf. Just like you. I meat her many times. It is funny to be in India agen but I miss you very mush.

Wen will you come to see me?
I love you Gillian.
Shashi

23rd of August 1932

My sweet Shashi,
Oh, how your letter brought tears to my eyes. I

cannot tell you how happy you made me. What a big girl you have become to write your own letters and to do all of your own spellings, which I might add, were excellent. I do like the way you sound out your words. It's the best way, you know. English is a funny language. I'm still working on it myself! I especially liked the way you described the sky. The next time there is an angry monster in it, I want you to show him that you can grumble even louder than he. Be sure to have some pots and pans at the ready. You and Samir can dance around in circles banging and clanging. You mark my word—you'll scare those monsters away in no time. Good thing you have such a large home in India, otherwise you might scare off the neighbors, too.

I am so glad that you are happy to be home again. There's not a day that goes by that I don't think of you and your brother. My life is a better one having had you in it. I learned all of my sillies from you, and I can't thank you enough!

Though I am not living in England at the moment, I am happy. I am staying in a far-off land called Canada, at least for the summer. It is a very big country. I think you would like it. There are mazy lakes and forests of pine trees by the bushel-full and windswept fields of wheat and corn as far as the eye can see. It is a marvel, I promise.

Do you remember when you asked me how I would know Mr. Right when I saw him? Well, I saw him at Canada's birthday party, and I was right—he has a very good pair of hands. Between you and me, I have a feeling that one day he'll build me that mushroom to live in.

Shall we make a pact, just as we did with our stories? If you send me one letter, then I shall send you two in return. That's double the pleasure for me. So if I find myself on the other side of the world and you happen to be back in England, then you shall send me two letters and I one. A letter can take any form, even a photograph so it needn't be work to write to your dear ol' nanny or shall I say friend?

My love to you and Samir,

Always,

Gillian

Post Script – Do thank your mommy for me, won't you, darling? It was so kind of her to write to me personally.

GILLIAN HAD TO BE SURE to thank Beaty for forwarding Shashi's letter, and Uncle Herbert of course for bringing it safely from the postbox in Rosedale. She missed the little muffet. Imagine the maharani writing to her personally. That really was something for the books! But she refused to let the joy of this letter spoil her disdain for one Christian Hunter. Their quarrel yesterday was quite justified, the way he ogled that wretched Janine Southerby next door. Nearly ten years his senior and wearing a come-hither blouse like that. Gillian should have pulled those droopy eyes right out of their sockets! But he wanted to make it up to Gillian tomorrow, a special place in store for her he said. Well… she thought everyone deserved a second chance.

Auntie Joyce and Uncle Herbert were sound asleep already—must have been the country air. She felt sorry for her uncle having to go back to the city for the workweek, but how lovely he was able to come back here each weekend.

As Gillian sat at her dressing table, brushing her hair and wearing a long cotton nightgown, she couldn't help but think she was unfair with Christian. How could anyone have avoided those beasts in that blouse? Even her eyes were glued to them if she was dead honest. She glanced down her nightgown at her smallish breasts feeling slightly inadequate. Then she peeked again. On second thought, they were really quite an ideal size, a no-nonsense size. Just as she tied the ribbon at the neckline, a tap at her window startled Gillian.

Roderick!

She drew up the window wondering what he was up to. "What are you doing out there? It's nearly midnight?" she said with a disapproving glare.

"Midnight is two hours away."

"Yes… well… it will be midnight soon and you're up to no good. I can smell it."

"I've been out. Come," he said flicking his dark fringe to the side. "I want to talk to you."

"What's so urgent that it can't wait until morning?" she asked, curious as a bee in a wildflower meadow.

Roderick didn't say another word. Instead he stretched his left eye wide open then shut it in a tight squeeze. Then repeated it. Gillian wasn't quite sure whether he'd developed an awkward tick or he was winking. But a gasp darted to her chest as she bit her bottom lip in sheer glee, nearly drawing blood! *If I dare say so myself, I do believe it's a wink,* she thought.

"Oh, Roderick!" She flew out the window and over the sill as though she had sprouted wings.

"Here let me help you," he said.

"Don't be silly, it's the first floor."

Gillian braided her arm through his, squeezing him around his waist as they walked toward the gazebo, frogs in full harmony—undoubtedly singing their praises for Roderick.

"Now tell me all about it—every detail."

"If I asked you to tell me everything you've been up to with Christian over these past two months, would you?"

"Well, not *everything*."

"Exactly," Roderick responded with a tilt of his head.

Gillian felt her spine start to stand on end like an angry cat.

"Well, why did you ask me here at this late hour if you hadn't intended on spilling the beans?"

He returned her glare, a seething one at that. Yet she wasn't sure whether Roderick would foam at the mouth before she had time to apologize. Regardless, he really was callow in his ways, dangling the proverbial carrot that way then casting it aside, causing a deplorable overuse of similes, metaphors, clichés and those delightful idioms that Gillian wished she had invented herself. Even she was out of breath with her long sentences!

She twisted her own mouth conceding that he had a point.

"Can't you give me just a crumb?" she asked pleadingly.

The cousins strolled to the end of the dock but decided not to go into the gazebo. The mosquitos weren't too bad tonight so they sat down on the wooden planks, letting their legs dangle above the water, the black sky hovering on top of them.

"All I can say for sure is that it's not love, but I know it's right."

"Is it that shy-looking fellow you were chatting with at

the bonfire the night we arrived in Tobermory?"

"He's the one," Roderick replied, turning the mischievous lines around his mouth into a grin. "But he's not all that shy. Not when you get to know him."

"I'm so pleased, Roderick." The crickets making a terrible racket in the forest squealed with delight, too. Gillian wondered if he noticed. "I hope you're beginning to see that you *can* have the life you want if you simply choose it."

"You're still as naïve as ever Gillian, but I like your optimism."

"I may well be naïve, but there's one thing I will not compromise and that's my dignity. If I believe in something, if I know without a shadow of a doubt that something is right for me, I will stand by it at all costs."

"Is that how you feel about Christian?"

Gillian threw back her head breathing in the misty, cool air, knowing how she felt but not wanting to admit it… to herself at least. "Time will tell," she said soberly.

Roderick put his arm around her. "Does this mean you're talking to me again?"

Gillian laid her head on his shoulder and coiled her arm in his. "I never really stopped."

24th of August 1932

Dear Maharani Sonali,

I hope this letter also finds you well. I would like to thank you ever so much for sending me Shashi's letter. If it is appropriate, I would like to maintain contact with her through letters as she always manages to bring a smile to my day, and I do feel that I have much to learn from such an open-minded child as yours. Before I begin, I have a request. Since I am about to dribble on and write words that may be challenging for a six year old's sensibility, perhaps you can do me the favor of reading my letters to Shashi before she goes to sleep at night or in a hammock on a sunny day if you have one in India—a hammock that is, not a sunny day as I am quite sure you have plenty of those. Shashi loves hammocks. Perhaps you can do this until she is old enough to read them on her own? Do forgive me if I am being forward in asking such a favor, but it would mean very much to me.

Most sincerely,

Gillian

Dearest Shashi,

My little buttercup, the moon has gone to sleep and the sun is smiling today. I promised you two letters as per our agreement—be it one-sided at this point since I only wrote to you last evening. But I shan't waste any time. A good, meaty letter you shall have.

Today, I have a surprise awaiting me. I don't know what, otherwise I would tell you. What I do know is that I will be taken somewhere very special. Don't you just love surprises? It is with Mr. Right, and when he says something is special, it is completely out of the ordinary. Never a jewel or fancy cloth in sight. No, it will be something adventurous. One time he took me to see a pirate ship under the water. Yes, you can let out that breath! It's true, a real pirate ship! If you drained all the water from the bay, you'd have a village of pirate boats, I'm quite sure about that.

We rowed a small boat to just the right spot and both had a mask so we could see properly under the water.

I had never worn such a thing before. How thrilling it was to see life as a fish would do. I am very good at holding my breath. I had plenty of practice growing up with seven siblings and all those nappies to change. I quite surprised myself, in fact, but Christian— that's Mr. Right's Christian name, Christian—isn't that funny? Well, he was very protective and stayed by my side. The water is as clear as a bell here in the bay. (Yes a bell! It doesn't always have to refer to sound now does it?) Back to the clear water. You wouldn't expect so in such a mystifying country as Canada, but it's true. The question I keep asking myself is why so many boats would sink in such water? If you ask me, I don't think it has anything to do with the rough tides but everything to do with those pirates!

Well, on that day I could see something lingering below, like a mysterious shadow. Everything around it was clear, even the speckled trout shimmered like tiny diamonds wriggling through the water. Not the boat. I thought I should cripple with fear; it was electrifying. The ship was too far down, but I could see its shape as it was lying on its side, and I have traced that image in my head for all time. I could see the rusted railing where Captain Ripper St. John himself stood as he went down with his ship. That's what Mr. Right told me, and the fantasy burning inside me can't bear to think it any different.

It's been a summer of unexpected wonders, Shashi. Every evening when all has settled down, we take Mr. Right's boat to a small inlet and watch for beavers. Do you know what a beaver is, darling? To me they are like wise, old, furry philosophers with flat tails and great big front teeth. Not teeth that would hurt you, but teeth that would make you stand at attention. A very noble animal. The French call it "castor." But for you, my sweet, you can think of them as gentle, sturdy animals that love to swim and build big houses with sticks.

I'll never forget my first sighting. The boat was lolling on the water. The air stood still. Even the birds stopped calling out to their loved ones, just so I could see, at long last, what I had been waiting for. A minute lasted for hours until I heard a paddling. I scanned the water's edge with my heart in a tight squeeze. The animal wasn't anywhere near the shoreline. It was then that Mr. Right had signaled to me to follow the stream of moonlight cutting across the water. My eyes travelled the spotlight and as they drew nearer the boat, something dark glided through the water toward me. I didn't move a single muscle as a huge, portly beaver grazed the side of our boat. I don't think he even noticed me. He was as relaxed as when you and I would pick daisies along the wooded path after school. Well, he swayed leisurely to shore. I didn't quite know what to expect until he clambered over the rocks, padding with great self-confidence. You could see that straight away. I think every one of us could learn a little something from him. I was very touched when he stood erect on his hind legs turning to us and rubbing his nose, as if to wave goodnight. Oh yes! He noticed us in no uncertain terms. It was then that Christian looked at me and smiled. That was the second time that I knew he was Mr. Right.

I dare say there are many more adventures to tell

but I shall spare you from pages and pages of nanny-talk. I look forward to hearing of your next adventure, Shashi. Even the smallest pea-sized adventure is great indeed. Life would be so dull without them.

My best to your parents and a little cuddle in this envelope for Samir.

Always,

Gillian

Some folk call it luck,
Some folk call it fate.
I call it destiny,
Because all too late
I found myself lost,
On a long, lonely road,
My love betrayed,
My happiness flown!

What have I done
To have earned such a cross?
Where did I fail
And so suffer this loss?
Can one find an answer
To such endless pain?
Can one go on living
Emptied and maimed?

Chapter 14

1946

THE BULLET. Gilly was right. It really did look like one. It was the first thing Christian noticed, too, when he'd seen the newspaper photograph for the first time—white, octagonal, cylindrical masonry with a dome lid and red band around its middle as though it could be shot into the sky at any moment. Just the sight of it wrung out memories of Big Tub Lighthouse, different shape of course, but where he and Gilly had bridled their passion under the starry Georgian Bay skies. He swallowed the lump lodged in his throat and shook his memories clean. *Different time, different place.*

Christian sat on the wall looking out toward the Inner Pierhead lighthouse, the same wall he'd sat on the night before finding Gilly again. A ribbon of sand curled along the edge of the water in the distance, just past the rocky shores. The inner harbor was bustling with small boats this morning. He liked that; the activity meant something to him, and the salty air was tasty. He reached into his pocket and gently took out the article. Unfolding it, he suddenly became curious if it would be possible to map out exactly where and from which angle the photograph had been taken.

Christian studied the photo, intermittently letting his eyes travel the harbor's edge, the town's edge, the houses that wrapped around the dazzling scenery, then back to the photo. His curiosity grew the more he thought about it, the more he examined the details of the photo. He held it at arm's length in front of him. From what he could tell, the photo had been taken from the northeast. He scanned further along the rocky shoreline, past the ribbon to the wide saucer-shaped beach at the far edge of town when a sudden jolt hung heavy in his chest. The hotel Gilly had mentioned, the one where she'd worked in the infirmary, the one that was for all intents and purposes, a prison for women born with the wrong nationality, stood like a suit of armor… imposing… just as she had described.

Christian considered walking toward the hotel, but it was a trek that could too easily be foiled in his… he glanced down, *condition*. What would have been a simple hike now took twice as long and three times the effort. Although that didn't usually deter him, he knew he'd be seeing Gilly soon and nothing would tear him away from that. Christian was glad she had phoned the inn and left a message with the owner when he was out returning Gilbert's truck. Same place he borrowed it, around the corner from Poppy's Coffee Shop. Mr. Ballard was there on his leash, too. That pig looked off-color this morning, though. Christian could imagine Gilly thinking Mr. Ballard was a pig of spirit anyway. A grin slipped into Christian's cheek, just the right side, when he realized he thought the same.

Christian sighed thinking of her. A part of him had felt dubious all night whether Gilly would contact him at all.

Maybe by dawn reality would have kicked in and she'd shy away from trudging up memories she'd sooner forget. He glanced at his wristwatch. Eleven o'clock. She'd soon be here.

Christian folded the article and slid it back into his trouser pocket. He had intended on showing her the article yesterday but never got the chance. That Dr. Pilkington. *Professional, my ass* he thought. *Just look at Gilly!* If she took *his* breath away, he knew darn well that doctor would take plenty of notice. But he knew he had no right to be leery of a man he'd never met. And truth was, Christian should be grateful to this doctor. He'd obviously given Gilly the opportunity to do what she'd always been amazing at: making others feel good about themselves and helping in any way she could.

He glanced up noticing a pair of white terns coasting on a gust of wind above the sea. They looked playful, reminding him not to take the day so seriously. He brushed crumbs off his shirt from a scone he'd picked up at Poppy's then headed toward the lighthouse with his walking stick in hand.

GILLIAN COULD SEE THE BULLET at the end of the pier as she rounded the corner. As she drove her motorbike onto the quay, sudden nerves engulfed her. All night, she hadn't a chance to think about yesterday and what had taken place. Mrs. Hemsworth saw to that. Had Christian Hunter *really* shown up after all these years? Gillian trickled her motorbike to a halt not halfway down the quay. The sudden flutter in her chest was dizzying and she feared a terrible sweat would follow. Had she really rung the inn this very morning to arrange a time? Gillian McAllister, the woman disguising herself as temperate and cool. Hardly. Yes, she did ring and she did say half past eleven at the agreed upon location. Had he received her message... she wondered. Gillian took a moment to gain some composure. She glanced down at her dress, a pretty blue one with small flowers. A light breeze from the sea swept up its skirt making it balloon out. The wind tickled her legs, hatching a smile on her face that felt familiar until the dress dropped flat against her thighs again. "Christian Hunter," she murmured to herself, "have you come all this way for me?"

CHRISTIAN CAUGHT A GLIMPSE of Gilly's motorcycle and sidecar. Nobody could miss that sidecar. He grinned, still thinking it suited her. Christian stood next to the lighthouse as it towered high above him gracing the end of the pier. Gilly waved when she pulled to a stop at the side of the quay. She took her helmet off, shaking her hair free, giving in to the breeze that played with it. Christian could see it was routine for her; she felt comfortable and sweetly pleased with her mode of transportation. His eyes followed her as she walked the rest of the way. This time he couldn't help but notice her dress and how she carried herself in it, the confidence in her gait. She was even prettier than yesterday.

"Hello," he chimed.

"Good morning," she said with a layer of reservation in her tone. "I'm pleased to see you received my message. I wasn't sure whether I had dreamed any of this."

"You dream about me?" he said, sliding a grin into his expression.

"I'm sure you'd be delighted if that were true."

"Are you saying it's not?"

"I'm saying good morning... and *only* good morning."

A silence fell into the conversation making Christian feel

awkward. He gazed at the lazy swells off shore, too lazy even to make waves.

Drawing a deep breath, he asked, "So why did you choose this place to meet?"

"Because I like it here. I like to watch the boats coming and going. It's a lively place, don't you think?" She gazed up at him, squinting from the sun in her eyes. The sun today shone on his skin differently. Tiny lines etched into it, by his eyes, on his neck, made him seem more real today. He hadn't shaved, and a light bristle was working its way into his jaw. But it was his eyes, even now, that made her weak—the way they drooped like her neighbor's St. Bernard puppy's.

"Yeah, there's something about this place, this island." Christian hesitated as he scanned the shoreline. "I like it."

"Then you wouldn't mind if I showed you more?" she said with her eyebrows arched with impulse.

"No. Not at all. But are you sure you have time? I mean, Dr. Pilkington might need your services. Your *professional* services," he said feigning a very serious expression.

"Now, now, Mr. Hunter. If you're not careful, I might be inclined to think you were indeed jealous—as green as an avocado."

"This conversation could go many ways."

"Oh, you *are* a cheeky blighter aren't you? Haven't changed a bit."

Christian relaxed in their banter with one another. Except for the hidden tone threading their words together, the conversation felt almost natural, as if no time had passed. But time had passed. So much was yet unspoken, and they both knew it.

CHRISTIAN FOUND BLISS in being chauffeured by a beautiful,

fiery woman. Although he'd offered to drive, he suspected Gilly was uncertain of how he could. She hadn't yet broached the subject with him, so he went along for the ride until she was ready.

The promenade hugged the edge of the saucer-shaped beach Christian had noticed earlier. Through a whistling voice tempered by the buzz of the motorcycle, Gilly explained that the townhouses following the line of the curve had been home to a slew of prisoners. It had all been part of the camp. In the distance at the end of the promenade, there it stood, the Ballaqueeney Hotel, even more severe than Gilly had described. Christian could understand why they chose it. The structure was perfect for a prison: stiff lines with towers like guards on each corner stared out to sea, and arched windows, no less than eyes, watched every move. The fence surrounding the building hadn't yet been torn down. Although internees had relative freedom during the war, Gilly explained that there was a perimeter wire keeping them in check, but no barbed wire. Sometimes, she said, the police wardens carrying truncheons and revolvers had made her more nervous than the internees themselves.

A weightlessness rose in her expression when they drove past Cowley's Café, then again when they took a moment by the sea. Sitting on a bench that faced the water, just outside the white hotel that housed a lifetime-to-come of troubling memories, Gilly had told him of the one joy she'd seen every day. Cowley's Café had been requisitioned and equipped with everything needed for a school. On her way to an elderly patient's home (a civilian who could afford to pay her a small salary in exchange for home aid and a little companionship) she'd pass children on their way to school—child prisoners—laughing and forgetting about a war they couldn't understand. At least *that* piece of childhood hadn't been taken from them. Children always found a way to laugh, Gillian said, and Christian knew that would have meant the world to her.

"Shall we stop by the grocers and make ourselves a picnic lunch?" Gilly asked eagerly. "I know the perfect place where we can sit and talk. I think you'll like it."

Christian mulled over her suggestion, wondering if she'd cleared her schedule just for him. "Are you free from work today?" he asked, worried about monopolizing her time.

"I've just come off work. Mrs. Hemsworth's baby was as stubborn as an alfalfa sprout working its way through concrete. I like the name alfalfa, don't you? Didn't have a clue what it was until my Uncle Herbert in Canada told me it was a de facto term for lucerne, simply lucerne." Christian darted up one eyebrow, curious as ever about the mechanics behind that beautiful face. "You know, like the town in Switzerland," she added unable to suppress a grin. "I didn't get home till nearly half eight."

"You mean you haven't slept at all?"

"I had precisely forty-one-and-a-half winks. It's more than I sometimes get," Gillian said ruefully with a shimmer of playfulness.

"Sounds great—the place you want to take me, I mean. But now that I know the truth," he said glaringly, "I'm driving!"

As Christian straddled the motorcycle, he could feel her eyes on him.

"So what's this place called again?" Christian asked, pulling off the dirt road.

"Cregneash is the village we just passed. But this place

here can be called a *piece of heaven* perhaps." Gilly clambered from the sidecar giddy as a schoolgirl, grabbing the cloth bag the grocer had loaned them. "Come! I'll show you!"

She sat on a partially tumbled stonewall, swinging her legs over it, then scampered through a pasture filled with tufts of stunted grass, clumpy to the step and greener than Christian had ever seen before. The grass rolled off the cliff, cascading into a sea the color of ripened Ontario blueberries, the islands opposite girdled in softened green, white foam churned up from the crashing waves. Christian stood for a moment drinking in the view, not quite believing he was standing here and now beside the girl he'd fallen in love with all those years ago.

"Come!" Gilly shouted, waving him toward her. The breeze had already begun dancing in her hair and dress. It was the second time today he'd noticed how it played with her figure.

Christian lumbered through the pasture, the tufts of grass at odds with him, but he could make it if he took his time. He was swift on flat ground; with Gilly standing there, he did everything he could not to fall. He'd mastered most things. Rowing his boat and pulling it to shore had been at the top of his list when he'd first gone home. But there were still challenges and some things he hadn't a hope in a month of Sundays to manage; climbing down a cliff side was one of them. When he looked up, Gilly had swept the blanket from the sidecar into the air like a billowing parachute as she shimmied it down to the ground. He gazed at the staggering scenery around her, not a house or person in sight except Gilly McAllister, and she was even more staggering.

GILLIAN COULD SEE straight away that Christian was as

taken with this place as she was. She hadn't known any pirate ships having sunk in these waters, and there were undeniably no beavers anywhere near this island. Yet it still felt adventurous, being here with him on this beautiful day. She'd expected rain or at least drizzle, but it was as though the gods blew the skies clear in one great puff just for them.

Their picnic spread was simple, four slices of Hovis bread cut on the diagonal as a favor to Gillian. She was certain the proprietor had eyes for her, as he would often slip a recipe into her produce bag that she was sure he'd copied by hand from *Florence Greenberg's Cookery Book*. The best by far was, "How to Make a Meatless Meat Pie." She'd nearly considered acknowledging his affections after that meal until her eyes met his lips again. Beaty had always said that you couldn't trust a man with thin lips, and for whatever reason Gillian could never seem to shake that insight away. From then on, every man she'd encountered unfortunate enough to be unhallowed with such a deformity as thin lips began to look deceitful, even downright ornery in some cases. The latter wasn't such a worry, it was the crafty creatures she needed to armor herself against.

Spread out on the blanket were a rather large wedge of cheese, hardly tasting of anything—more like rubber Gillian entertained—and some beetroot, neither of which were rationed now nor during the war on the Isle of Man. She never liked queuing up for the meager supplies in the grocers, but for the second time today, the gods up there had puffed away even the drizzle in the shops. She normally loathed beetroot and cheese sandwiches, but today they tasted gorgeous. Treacle scones were dessert. She wasn't sure if Christian would like them, but she'd brought two wedges from home in the off chance they may wish for a snack. There *was* one little dazzle in their picnic lunch: some Cadbury's chocolate.

"So tell me," Christian said biting into his square of milky, brown delight. She could see the satisfaction on his full lips now, something the grocer would never be able to proffer. "Why didn't you ever return to Ireland?"

The question startled her, though she wasn't certain why. After all, it was a perfectly reasonable question. Ireland was her home, where she grew up, where all her siblings lived, except Beaty, of course. But the longer she had lived away, the more she realized that nowhere became home... though everywhere had. Gillian had a strange mix of belonging while simultaneously feeling distant, detached, sometimes utterly severed from the culture or the people, even on this tiny island in these bizarre times. Even so, she was drawn to it, living in the unfamiliar while feeling completely at ease with herself and the life she had nurtured.

"Well," she thought for a moment, remembering her good-bye letter to Christian all those years ago. "I returned to Longford as my father had expected, but only briefly. I feared that although home had likely stayed very much the same, *I* had likely changed without knowing how. I was afraid to be trapped like a caterpillar in its shelly skin, not knowing if it was dying. Can you imagine the torment of not being able to spread those wings? To be hemmed in so ruthlessly? I'd rather have been squashed flat by that pot-bellied pig I keep running into in the streets. Sublime beast he is. Don't know if you've had the pleasure yet. At any rate, Daddy was furious when I had arranged with Beaty to return to London having spent only weeks back in Ireland. I'm quite sure that my father wished he'd allowed me to go to India after all. At least there I'd have been safe, he thought at the time. He hadn't expected a war to erupt. None of us had. London of all places? In the heart of Hitler's seething nemesis? He thought I was mad and demanded that both Beaty and I return to Ireland at once. Beaty was in love… a curious, slightly odd man called Horatio. The poor thing had hardly any neck at all, but Beaty's heartstrings were playing a tug of war with Daddy. In the end, neck or no neck, she was staying put and there wasn't a darned thing he could do about it."

"I don't think your sister was the only one in love at the time," Christian said as dispassionately as any man who'd been cast aside. At least that's how Gillian imagined he'd have seen it. She sensed, however, that he didn't want to harp on why she hadn't stayed longer in Ireland. Her reasons were truthful and she could see that he understood.

"Perhaps not," she agreed soberly while patting down a corner of the picnic blanket that had been kicked up by the breeze. "But that's not the only reason I didn't stay in Ireland. It felt too easy. I knew if I had stayed, I'd have been taken care of, coddled if you will, and I couldn't have that."

"The butterfly imagery again?"

"Yes, I suppose so."

"The thing about *you*," Christian said leaning into her as if to whisper in her ear, "you need to be the one taking care of people—not the other way around. I saw that right away with Romy, the way you dived into that challenge. No one had been able to help her until you came along. Within weeks, her speech had improved enough to make the kids on the peninsula sit up and notice, all the while picking up your Irish *R's*. And no one would mess with that!"

Gillian couldn't bridle her wide grin. "How *is* Romy? She must be nearly twenty now."

"Nineteen," Christian sighed. "She's great. A regular spark plug! First one in her family to go to university."

Gillian gasped, "How thrilling! I knew she'd make something of herself. I'm just waiting to see her name in lights."

"Not a chance. She's set her sights on politics."

"Good Lord!"

A silence fell around them, relaxed, untethered. It felt comfortable, as though they were getting to know each other again and not only catching up. Gillian had always imagined that Christian would harbor ill feelings toward her for all time but was deeply thankful for his sobriety and good nature.

"So tell me," Christian said brushing his hand against hers on the blanket, "what happened to your father?" Gillian gazed at a patch of wild flowers nestled among the tufts of grass as she considered his question. They were pretty, the flowers, white like the breaking waves below. She glanced at Christian, pleased that he had asked about him.

"He died in his sleep—an aneurysm, the doctors say. One day he was here, the next he was gone. Just like that," she said, her eyes travelling back toward the blue sea. "It was all very uneventful as far as deaths go—a plain, naked sort of death. I suppose I thought that when it was his time, he'd go in a blasphemous rage directed toward his disobedient daughters with a theatrical fall to the ground. At least *I* would have driven him to that, I'm afraid. But no, he wasn't that sort, no pummeling on a desktop, just a quiet, soulful man masked by a firm tone. Others saw him as unyielding, I think. But he was never that way with me, not once… well, apart from India." She gazed at Christian, unable to wash the sadness from her eyes. She knew it.

"Don't you know how affecting you are?" he said. "You have such a way of looking at people. Makes them want to do the right thing, makes them believe in the impossible. Your father was that way with you because he trusted your instincts."

"I do fear he left this world disappointed in me, never having returned to the land he loved so deeply, the land where my dear mommy was buried."

Christian's voice sharpened enough to make Gillian feel unsteadied. "You could never have disappointed your father. Just the opposite. I may never have met him, but I would bet these legs," he said glancing down at his awkward position, "that your father was more proud of you than just about anything in his life. The way you talked about him. Don't you see? It didn't matter how far you were from him; you could have lived in Timbuktu and it wouldn't have driven a wedge between you. He got his way with India, but you got your way in the end. You're where you were meant to be, on a small island in the Irish Sea helping others, and I bet he beamed when he talked about that." Christian drew a liberal breath. "Do you remember all those monarch butterflies by the cove back home, fluttering around the milkweed laying their eggs?"

"How could I forget? It felt like a fairytale, as though they were waving me into their story."

"Well, that's how I saw you, still see you, like one of them. There's your caterpillar tale again, only yours is an epic. You got to spread your wings after all, and your father has flown in their shadow ever since, making sure you get where you need to go."

Gillian felt touched by the sentiment, letting herself drift into reverie for a moment to her earliest memory of her father, a memory so vivid that she was certain the images came out in words to a man she never thought she'd see again.

GILLIAN HAD TAKEN A STROLL into the meadow just on the edge of her back garden, slipping away undetected from Beaty's watchful eye. At nearly five years old and soon to be a fully-fledged primary school girl she paid no mind to her older sister. The heather was in full bloom. As purple as purple can be. And the sun was happy that day. She couldn't forget that. Gillian scooped out her favorite book that she had kept wrapped in cheesecloth and nestled in the hollow of a log. She couldn't yet read the words, but she would follow along line by line and create her own version of a story she knew by heart. She revelled in the small changes, making the story her own.

As she knelt down in the rough to shuffle into a comfortable position, Gillian saw a figure approaching. She couldn't make it out with the sun grinning so. It haloed the figure in a shadowy streak of light. Stiff shoulders and a stiff cap was all she could discern. She crossed her little legs with the book cradled in her skirt. And in the moment it took to breathe just a single breath, the figure stood directly above her. She sagely lifted her chin as it moved from the sun's blinding glare.

"Daddy!" she squealed.

"Gillian! Oh, my sweet girl. It really *is* you!" He knelt down on one knee as she tossed his officer's cap into the stinging nettle where it belonged.

"Is it you? Is it truly you?" she gasped. "Are you back for good? Is the war over? Does Mommy know you're here?"

"My sweet girl, yes, I'm back. I'm back for always," her

father sighed stroking her velvety cheek.

Gillian threw her arms around her father whom she adored above any other creature that walked the earth. Barrelling him over with a flurry of questions, he was overwhelmed.

"All in good time, Gillian," his voice quivered as he patted her shoulder. "What are you reading?"

"*Five Little Peppers and How They Grew*. Do you know it? It's American, Mommy says."

"Yes. That's a good one. Shall we read together?"

"Oh yes, I'd like that," she exhaled.

She and her father curled up against her hideaway log with the sun warm against their skin in a blanket of violet spread across the knoll. He gazed lovingly into her eyes whilst drawing his index finger to his lips.

"Shhh. If you listen carefully Gillian you'll hear the breeze's aria."

"What's it singing?" she asked.

"Why… 'It's a Long Way to Tipperary,' of course." Gillian smiled. That moment rolled into hours and now into years.

"He fought in the Great War?" Christian asked.

"Yes. But we walked away from that cap of his, and I never saw it again." Gilly said placidly. "By the time Britain declared war on Nazi Germany the second time 'round, my father wanted nothing to do with it and was satisfied that Ireland had taken the stance it did."

Gilly turned away as though carried by the breeze. Christian could sense she'd had enough of the military, enough of this conversation. Yet he couldn't help but wonder when she was going to ask about the obvious. It was as though she was trying to evade even the subtlest hint to his legs.

"So what were you doing before you came to this island?" he asked, steering the conversation in a more pleasant direction.

Gilly eased off the blanket then stood up donning a cardigan that had been stored with the blanket. She resembled a moving painting as her dress and hair rippled in the wind against a crisp, blue sky, long grass at her feet. Just behind her, a pair of seagulls floated on the wind, hovering nearby to catch any scraps of treacle, he thought.

"I was living in London for a time but rather quickly moved to Ascot further south. It reminded me of such happy times with the Maharaja's family at their home in Wentworth Estate. So I thought I'd give it a go myself."

"And how was it?"

"Busy mostly. I was working as an auxiliary nurse both privately and at Hogweed Home, a very small sanatorium. Beaty called it a madhouse filled with loose brains. There was only the one ward that you needed to be wary of. I remember one day I was up on the third floor chatting with an orderly. Well, he wasn't really an orderly, though he liked to pretend. Perhaps he should have been admitted himself. Anyhow, he was sweeping the floor when he glanced out the window and said in wonder, 'Funny, but I don't ever remember there being a statue in the front garden.' Well, I took heed of his query and followed his gaze when I threw down the bedpan I had been holding and shouted 'That's because there isn't!' I sprinted down the staircase. Not a soul walking by Hogweed even noticed. Imagine that. A grown man stark naked, stock still with his legs spread and holding a broomstick like a trident, as though he was Poseidon. God knows how long he had been stiff. I nearly broke my back dragging him off that birdbath."

Christian couldn't suppress his laughter, banishing everything serious in this world. He relished Gilly's stories then and relished them now. A war hadn't really changed her—at least not in any of the important ways. He was starting to see that now.

When the crocus spreads a carpet
Of purple and white and gold,
I know such perfect beauty
Is a gift from the Lord.

The daffodils, the tulips
The velvet wallflowers, too,
The chestnuts lighted candles
And bluebells in the wood.

Pale pink of apple blossom
White bloom on a cherry tree,
The lilacs scented pyramids
The laburnum's golden sheen.

All offerings of the springtime
For old and young to see,
And every year when winter dies
This miracle revives.

Chapter 15

1946

THE AIR WAS COOLING OFF NOW and the seagulls long gone. Calf of Man across the sound was beginning to look lonely with all the cloud-cover building up.

"You know this place has a way of creating moods just for me," Gilly said as she turned to look down at Christian, still sitting on the blanket. She folded her arms, rubbing them to keep warm.

"In what way?"

"If you look there," she motioned with her chin, "at the Calf of Man when the sun is shining, I'd wager it's as far as the horizon. The green looks more like a happy chartreuse. Sometimes I reach out trying to touch it. Other times, I feel as though I could skip across Kitterland," Gilly said pointing to the islet just off shore, "like in a game of hopscotch. Silly I know," she added studying the island. "But when the sky sinks down, feeling heavy with dew like it's starting to now, the island saddens me somehow. The green darkens to match the sky. It's rather affecting don't you think? I take on the mood of the sky or the sea and with it something stirs inside—sometimes memories, sometimes forecasts of the future. I like it best when the skies make me feel like dancing. Unless I'm already in a foul mood and want to wallow in it for full effect; then I come here. There are times this place fights back and I walk away spirited once again."

"I think anyone coming here would be at its mercy," Christian said, his eyes traveling the wide-open landscape. "And you're right, the mood is changing quickly up there. I'm not sure how long we'll last out here." A silence hung in the air between them with a faint whistling beginning to pick up in the streams of wind. "Shall we take a stroll before we're forced away," he asked, feeling restless.

"Yes, I'd like that… but…"

"It's no problem if you wouldn't mind…" he said reaching up to her, deliberately not finishing his sentence. *Still nothing, not a word*, he thought. She held his arm, supporting him as he stood. "Thank you." Their eyes met for a long moment as his arm remained cradled in hers. He wanted nothing more than to run his fingers through her wavy tresses. The breeze robbed him of that pleasure. Her arm remained coiled in his as they walked, which surprised him. He couldn't yet decide if Gilly was uncomfortable with any of this. She'd always had a magical way of making others feel at ease, but truth was he didn't quite know how he felt. In many ways it had been the perfect day with the perfect woman, yet he had to slice through thoughts of doubt. It wasn't pragmatic. Nothing about this was. She was still living a different life here. He couldn't pretend as though the last fourteen years hadn't happened for her. They had, and he hadn't been part of them.

As Christian teetered along the grassy edge overlooking the bluff, he wondered how Gilly had managed to stay the positive, spirited person he met all those years ago given the plight on this side of the Atlantic.

"Tell me what it was like before you moved to the Isle of Man, just after the war was declared. That is," he hesitated, a lump forming in his throat, "if you don't mind talking about it."

"Mind?" Gillian said, her brow springing up, "I've done nothing but talk about myself. I haven't asked you anything about Tobermory or…" She hesitated before saying his name, "Griffin or even the elephant ears at Dominion Day." She stopped with her feet planted firmly in the grass then took hold of his hand.

"I *want* to know about those things. I really do, but not yet, not now." She could see in Christian's droopy eyes that he wondered why. But she couldn't explain… not even to herself. Gillian could feel the wind nip at her through the cardigan she'd knitted from clews of rustic yarn from a flock of Manx Loaghtan just down the way. It was a dreary cardigan she always felt, brown and dull and ill fitting at the best of times. But it did the job most days, and it was all she could afford.

"So, after the war was declared?" she repeated his question.

"Yeah. I'd really like to know. We were sheltered in ways back home. It seemed from Canada we were fighting a war indirectly though it quickly became real for anyone joining up and then a blow for those who didn't want to but had no choice. Not sure if anyone over here even knew we had stepped up to the plate."

"You must be joking. How do you think the phrase floating around our parts 'The good ol' Canadians' came about? Every time I heard it, I'd think of you," she said, her eyes peering up into that dubious expression of his. "Great Britain was in the war only seven days longer than Canada. You think I don't know this? I read every word coming from the Allies, every word printed about your efforts. I'm quite sure you felt the sting of it back in God's country." Gillian could feel her heart begin to race and wasn't ready for where the conversation was headed. She broke loose, stretching her woolen sleeves over her palms, her fingers fastening them to keep warm. One might think she'd be well accustomed to the sudden drop in temperature the moment a chain of cloud hovered above. But no, at least not on this day, a day that had begun by fooling outsiders with a mask of sunlight to warm the skin.

Gillian picked up her pace; she felt a sudden need for distance between them, just enough to calm her angst.

"The worst part was the constant fear the moment the skies began to rumble with engines. Beaty loathed that I lived between two great targets, London and Southampton. It was bad enough in London, she said, but being somewhere in the middle was like having your arms bound to two horses running in opposite directions. 'A gruesome dismemberment' she'd say. I'm not sure if she quite understood how that image lingered every night I found myself curled up in my wellies and stuffed inside that tin can they called a shelter. Ours was an Anderson. The thing never stopped leaking. But thank God for it. At least the air raid shelters were a semblance of protection, dug well into the ground in the garden. I shared with the family from whom I hired a room. They were kindly enough, but I never felt so alone as I did watching them nuzzle up to each other with terror sinking into the children's faces, then buried into their mommy's chest as German planes flew overhead. We always knew which were their planes even in the dark, for they made a terrible throbbing noise. Ours had a steady hum, though far from soothing. The dogfights above us made the children crumple into tiny balls. There were two, a little boy and girl. Reminded me of two very special children who've turned me into a gooey meringue over the years." Christian smiled as she continued.

"I had no arms around me for comfort, although Mr. Baxter would pat my knee when he'd notice I was shaking. I'm not one to feel sorry for myself, but in those moments I longed for my father... for Beaty. My brother and other sisters were safe in Longford, but oh, how I wanted Daddy to drop everything and come to me at that very moment so I could bury my eyes in *his* chest."

Christian didn't breathe a word.

"I'd still take the heavy rains and puddles at my feet in that time capsule we called 'Billy Bunk' over those incendiaries any day. I imagined the sky raining with fireballs, but fortunately the fire brigade dealt with those expeditiously. The worst part was the gas masks we were issued at the primary school in the event of gas warfare. Tried to swindle the children into believing they were funny by pasting a red nose on them like a cartoon character. Didn't work, you know. I watched one little girl nearly asphyxiated by hers. And the adults weren't much different. They terrified me—the gas masks. I'm sure you've seen more than your fair share." Christian nodded. "Made me feel as though I was right down in that Nautilus with Captain Nemo himself."

"You mean in *Twenty Thousand Leagues Under the Sea?*" Christian asked, puzzled.

"Well, what other?"

"They weren't actually gas masks," he added, hatching a

smile.

"And your point?"

That smile grew so large, it flashed happy memories of a time when neither of them had been able to wipe away their grin.

"When did you start reading Verne?" Christian wondered.

"After having a summer of pirate dreams at Georgian Bay," she replied with narrowed eyes. "By sheer grit I was able to get through its narrative. How I loathe reading in first person, yet you couldn't have peeled my eyes away. I have since read every work of both Verne and Wells. My sister thinks I'm mad to read such an abomination with creatures under the sea and warmongers from space coming to Earth. She's never bothered to hide her repugnance and still can't resolve how they'd get past the gates of heaven."

Christian's smile finally broke into laughter. "I would like to meet this notorious sister of yours."

"She isn't *completely* mad, I promise!"

Gillian's gaze sailed across the sky, noticing that the clouds had darkened, growing heavy in the distance as though someone had scratched gray streaks down to the horizon. Rain. She didn't want this moment to end; maybe the storm would bypass them.

"Should we head back to your motorcycle?" Christian said. "I'm not sure I can outrun that sheet coming toward us."

"Yes, of course, but we needn't run. It's still only water," she said braiding her arm in his for support. They walked back to the blanket where Gillian whisked it into the air then rolled it. She scooped up the grocery bag then reached for his arm again.

"So who were these other children you were talking

about? The ones who were special?"

"*Are* special actually."

"Are they yours?"

"Goodness, no. I told you about them when we'd first met. The little Indian children I took care of before I was sent to your wild place of birth," she said ribbing. A mole poked his head from its nest as they approached a series of raised ridges in the meadow, no doubt trampling over their tunnels. Worried Christian might topple over, she held on tightly. "I don't know what I would have done without them during these past years. Perhaps you don't remember, but I had received a letter from their mother, the maharani, during my stay in Tobermory. Inside, there was a short letter from Shashi. We've been writing ever since. I've followed both of them, really, right through childhood but more intimately with Shashi as she is the one who writes. I hear of her brother's antics through her."

"That's wonderful," Christian said as they reached the stone wall. He sat on it then laboriously lifted his legs over. He'd left his walking stick in the sidecar, and although she'd had the urge earlier to offer it to him, she suspected he'd refuse it. They stood on opposite sides of the wall.

"I remember one time Samir, I think he was perhaps ten years old at the time," she said looking into nothingness, "decided it would be amusing to coat the bottom of a laundry basket with a handful of vine snakes—seven to be precise. He placed a bath towel over top then waited behind a tree. When the servant returned to fold the remaining washing, he muscled up the courage to run to her and confess his crime. But she was called away again by her superior before he had reached her, leaving him to tend to those snakes. To his dismay, there were only six in the basket. Before he had time to breathe, a scream ripped through the palace walls all the way into the garden. Apparently, he was so afraid to face the maharaja that he went missing overnight. Everyone thought the worst—that he had been taken by some hooligans for ransom, perhaps. They even drained the palace pond for fear he had drowned. But there was one place they hadn't looked: a secret burrow that Shashi knew her brother went as a tot when he was frightened. In the carriage house among all the beautiful palkis, some carved in elaborate design and draped in the richest jewel-toned silks, was a very small, sad palki stuffed in the corner. It hadn't carried royalty in decades."

"What's a palki exactly?"

"I didn't know myself until I found a book at the library called *A Breath of Bombay*. A palki is simply a carriage, mostly for females when they go out and about, carried on the shoulders of two or more men. The ornate ones are for processions, I suppose."

Christian reached for Gillian's hand as she clambered over the wall. The sky began to rumble with surly, whirling clouds above threatening to teem down on them at any moment.

"We best be getting on," she insisted.

"Not until you tell me what happened in the carriage house."

Gillian furrowed her brow remembering the details of the letter. "Shashi peeked into the darkness through spider nets and dust, and there was Samir, shivering in the corner of the palki. The carriage house was like an icebox during the night, she said. But she had brought a blanket and a pocket full of potato *bhajji* for his starving little body and climbed in, nuzzling up to her brother, warming him." A soft smile weaved into Gillian's mouth remembering the spicy chili bhajji she had tried with the maharani on a rainy night in Virginia Water. She insisted that piping hot tea accompany bhajji just as they used to drink in India's monsoon season. But drips from the sky tapped Gillian back to the present.

"Please..." she said motioning for Christian to climb into the sidecar.

"I don't think so, not with your sleeping record," he said presumptuously straddling her motorbike. "Would you mind?"

"You're not looking for an answer, are you?"

"No," he said.

Christian's voice fell flat in that one syllable as he wore an expression of great disappointment, rain now trickling down his cheeks. "What?"

"You still haven't told me what happened to the boy." Gillian hardly heard his words when she noticed how his shirt clung to his skin, wet, revealing his lovely form as he sat propped up above her.

"Right," she said, peeling her eyes away. "I suppose the rain pooling up in my eyes distracted me," Gillian answered in a saucy tone.

"Well?"

"Shashi never revealed Samir's hiding place but brought him back to their parents, wrapped like a cocoon. Not a word was spoken about those snakes, but Shashi said the laundry maid was never seen again hanging the bedclothes."

"You really like this girl, don't you?"

"Oh..." Gillian gave a wide, toothy smile, the rain cascading down her and into the sidecar. "She makes my heels click!"

THE COTTAGE STOOD LIMP in the rain, gray sea and gray skies dragging it down. All the green seemed to be syphoned from the garden and the chill was bone snagging. The smell of worms soaked the air, reminding Christian of Tobermory and wet days by the docks hauling in friendly-sized northern pikes and the odd giant musky. Now it felt like a different season altogether from the morning. Gilly's front door seemed miles away down that gravel path, and Christian didn't want to walk it. He didn't want the day to end. They reached the door anyway and stood under the thatch overhang. He could feel a steady stream of rain skimming his back as Gilly stood pressed against the door fumbling to open it behind her.

"Don't," Christian said taking her hand. He gazed into her eyes, his chest pressed against her. She stared up at him, her mouth slightly open with the sound of the rain tapping the window next to them. He wanted nothing more than to kiss her, but her silence nudged him to walk away. A woman who never found it difficult to strike up a conversation, a woman who talked so much that he'd kiss her just for a little peace that summer at Little Tub Harbour. And with all that chatter, not one question about what happened to him. *Why?* he asked himself as she stood there looking as if she wanted to be kissed, needed to be kissed.

GILLIAN COULD FEEL her heart begin to race. She'd almost forgotten how disheveled she must have looked, her hair wet as a mop and her brown cardy sagging and smelling like the soggy Manx sheep that wore the wool in the first place. She tried straightening the strands of hair at the sides of her face.

"Stop," he said taking her hands away. "You're lovely just the way you are."

She could feel her chest rise suddenly, unsure of the moments to follow. Knowing she wanted to be kissed but knowing it was madness to fall for a man from her past, the one man she could never erase from her heart... the same conflict she'd fought under the Georgian Bay moon.

"Why did you take me home first?" she asked, a tiny piece of her wanting him to say, *Where else would I spend the night?*

"Haven't you noticed it's pissing down rain?" he said instead.

"Well, I wouldn't have put it quite like that but yes... I noticed." His eyes drew closer as he lifted her chin. Her heart had left the starting gates the moment the rain splashed all over him, leaving his skin gleaming, teasing from underneath his soaked shirt.

"You should be home in this weather," he said soberly. "I'll walk."

"The inn's too far."

"For someone like me?"

Horrified at such a rebuttal, Gillian refused to feel her pulse any longer. "That's not fair."

Christian smiled, but it wasn't condescending. It was humble. "Thank you for today. It was perfect," he said, a hint of shiver to his skin.

As he turned his back to leave, a desperate gasp reached her lips, "How long will you be here... on the Isle of Man?"

"Till I know."

Gillian swallowed, her pursed shoulders suddenly relaxed as she felt her own shiver fly away. She stood under the thatch, and through a screen of rain she watched Christian walk unsteadily down her drive, his walking stick now in hand. "Good-bye," was all she managed to mutter through empty lips.

The autumn has a beauty, no other season knows,
It gently turns the leaves from green to brown and bronze and
gold.

The smoke of garden fires, prepare the earth to sleep,
In winter's storms, it's snug yet free, and never calls to weep.

The leaves are gone, the scene will change, as it likes to do,
The distant fence thro' naked trees and hills beyond stay true.

As swirling mist, their beauty veils, silence reigns again,
As evening fades and peace descends, it brings the close of day.

Chapter 16

1933

My dearest Shashi,

It has been a long while since I last took pen to paper. Such a hiatus (your mommy can explain) was necessary given my raw state of mind. You are too young to understand, but you can know that I have been nursing a broken heart. I have left Canada and Mr. Right to return to a familiar place, one you know well, where there's a pond swimming with stories of India and Ireland. There is a weeping willow in the garden, do you remember? I can only see its top over the stone wall surrounding the residence, but if I close my eyes, I get a perfect view. I have bought myself a small motorbike, which I take to Wentworth Estate on Sundays. You should see me on it—free as the wind. My kit bag and a good pair of goggles and I'm off. I once had a Mayfly sail into my ear. I thought they must only come out in May, but I was wrong. You can't imagine the panic I was in when I quickly realized the poor creature must have been in shock himself, the way I tried to dig him out. My advice to you is to don an exceptional pair of earmuffs in the event you take to the roads at high speed. Do you have a bicycle, darling? (I would have loved to teach you to ride.) If not, perhaps you can hint to Mommy while she reads you my letter.

I hope you have been busy stirring up all sorts of adventure in my absence. My surprise last summer was by far the most exquisite adventure of all. Do forgive me for waiting so long to tell you about it. My heart has finally mended, or at least stitched together in layman quality.

Now on to the juicy bits! Mr. Right had taken me to a very special island, so wild they had to name it Bear's Rump. Apparently, those living on the peninsula rarely take a rowboat out so far—but we did! Remember, these are the same treacherous waters as those swallowing up pirate ships. Was I frightened you ask? Terrified. But Christian, that's Mr. Right if you recall, assured me that the bay was as smooth as a baby's bottom. Try not to giggle now!

I felt as though I was in the middle of the sea although it oddly lacked that tangy sea air that seems to go hand in hand with such a place. It's all fresh water, Shashi, have I told you that? I could drink the whole basin clean and wouldn't get a sore tummy. Of course, there was a fishy odor wafting past every so often, so I chose not to drink even a thimble full.

We stopped at Flowerpot Island to rest our weary fingers from gripping those oars. I managed to pull my weight on occasion, but I much preferred the view when I rested—though we dared not tarry longer than was necessary, otherwise our fate might have mirrored those pirates! (If you brave the seas with Samir, do take a pair of gloves. I sported three terrible blisters after that feat.)

The bluffs of Bear's Rump were waiting for us. You should have seen them, as high as the heavens and peppered in tall pine trees. Even my tongue was dazed at the very sight. I couldn't utter a sound. It's quite a feeling to be put in your place when you meet something so daunting. (That's big and scary to you, my sweet.) I wished for your courage that moment. The beach was white with small stones, and the water a surreal mix of green and blue, like something you imagine in the South Pacific or Indian Ocean near where you live, darling. Although I've never seen photographs, my mind paints a beautiful picture. Have you ever seen a colored photograph? I've heard about them, but I won't believe they exist until I see one myself. Be that as it may, if you tell me it's true, then I shall trust your word.

I'm rambling as usual. A terrible habit I've picked up from my sister since returning to the United Kingdom. Where was I?

Yes, Bear's Rump. Christian had prepared a lovely picnic that he had hidden in the bow of the boat under a blanket. We hiked like two barbarians through the forest and up to the very top of the mountain. By the time we reached its crest, the sun was beginning to whisper "goodnight" through swirls of tangerine and violet. It hung in the sky threatening to leave the bay for just one more night, soon to return in a playful daybreak. I remember smiling as I thought the sun and moon are friends, like you and me, never truly leaving each other. If you close your eyes now, Shashi, I think you'll be able to see our sunset.

The smell of pine brought a sweetness to the air and with it memories of Sunday morning boxty (Irish potato cakes), to which my father lovingly added far too much sugar and a whole tablespoon of my mother's homemade gooseberry jam. I can taste it now as I write. And it was there that I saw it with my own eyes, tucked into the wood overlooking the mural in front… the mushroom I knew Mr. Right would build me one day. It was large enough for two and made from the trees right there on the island. There was a door and a big screen window to keep out mosquitoes and a fire pit just outside for warmth and late evening chatter while staring into the flames.

We stayed until the hours would have us no more. I don't even remember time passing, yet I shall never forget a single moment of our lovely adventure.

I shall write again soon—two letters as promised—but for this night, my mended heart needs rest.

If you look closely into these inky pages, Shashi, you'll find a squeezy hug just for you.

My love to you and Samir,
Gillian

7th of July 1933

Dear Gillian,

I know about broken harts. One day I went butterfly cetching with my father in the medow. I cetched the prettiest butterfly I had seen in my hole life. It was the color of your sunset. My father said, No Shashi. Butterflys need to be free. But I begged my father to let me take him for just one day. He showed me his home so I wanted to show him my home. My father said yes but I must set him free when the sun comes on the morrow. But when I was sitting by my pond I wanted to show my butterfly how I could read so well now. I lifted the top to my jar and he flyed out and onto my page. I was so happy becus he liked my story. But my brother Samir came like a snake behind me, to quiet for my ears and snapped my book shut. He runned away laffing but did not know that when I opened the pages to my book, my butterfly was dead. I cryd and I cryd.

Me and my father went to the medow the next day. Samir came to. We brot my butterfly to his home and set him on a big rock like a reel maharaja looking at his kingdum. I was suprised to see a tear fall down my brothers face. I think his hart was broken to.

That was not my favrit adventure. I think saying goodby to Mr. Right was not your favrit to. But I like to think that life is like a bumblebee flying from flower to flower. It takes all the sweet it can. It flys to the next flower and shares what it taked from the first then a new flower grows. The old flower does not die you know, it wates for the next bee.

I would like to see Bears Rump Island but I think the name Flowerpot Island sounds much prettyer. What is a rump? And why is there a S in island? I cannot here the S. I have been working very hard on my spellings. Can you tell?

I also have a hug in my inky words for you but it is

a maze to find it.

Love,
Shashi

7th of July 1933

Dearest Shashi,

I'm so sorry to hear of your butterfly's demise though your bumblebee analogy has given me great food for thought. What a wise old soul you are!

A rump is your bottom. A bear needs something to sit on, too, after all. Island has an "S" because English makes no sense at all, and no I can't hear it either. And yes, I can see you've been hard at work on your spellings—a remarkable improvement, my dear. Everything about your writing is improving. You are a pure pleasure to read.

My next adventure you ask? A new job! I am the new auxiliary nurse at Hogweed Home. I will clean bedpans and take temperatures and change dressings and tell wild, adventurous stories of little girls from Ireland to make patients forget all about their illness, and when given permission, I'll include a few stories from little Indian maharanis.

Must dash my sweet. Until next.

Love and cuddles,
Gillian

I swore I would forget you
The day that you broke faith,
I'd quickly find another love
To fill your vacant place.

Love doesn't work that way.
My grief wouldn't die,
And to others who came
I soon said 'Good-bye'.

Now I am left
In a world of gray,
My heart in the past
My future astray.

With nothing to hope for
As night follows day,
But another tomorrow
Seeking solace in vain.

Chapter 17

1946

MONSOON SEASON. Or so it seemed in the Irish Sea. The rain hadn't rested its weary drops since Christian disappeared behind Gillian's hedgerow—until now. A timely break in the clouds let her breathe some fresh air as she sat nestled in tufts of grass high on the bluff. She hadn't a clue how long it had been since Christian left—hours, days perhaps. She knew it had all been her doing. Not having once asked about him and how he'd suffered all this time, all these years. No, she couldn't bring herself to ask. She knew it hurt him and no picnic by Cregneash would take that sting away.

Gillian hadn't returned Beaty's call, and she had walked away from the telephone ringing a tumbler full of times since. She didn't know what to say after having read her sister's letter. She tried to brush it aside, pretend she hadn't read the article, never for a moment thinking he'd actually appear in her garden. No, she couldn't face Beaty right now. She'd know instantly from her voice that she had forecast correctly, that Christian was... Gillian felt a lump swelling in her throat... "here," she muttered.

Gillian held the letter snug in her hand, having read it a dozen times in the two days before Christian had shown up and a dozen more since he walked away. Had she missed something obvious, something that Christian hadn't mentioned? After all, why had he really come? Gillian glanced down at the letter, unfolding it yet again.

10th of July 1946

Gillian,

I haven't time to mess about with pleasantries. I've been trying to reach you on the telephone for three whole days but have had no success. Now I am at the mercy of the post. I would send a telegram but I'm afraid that for what I have to say, I haven't enough shillings in my purse. You worry me sick, my dear, when you don't bother to keep me informed as to your whereabouts. These darned telephones! Mine has been giving me nothing but trouble. Horatio says it's all my twaddle that strains it so. And I am quite aware of how finicky your telephone can be, having no doubt that you've trained it somehow to screen my calls. There is method to my madness, dear. I'd be on your front doorstep if it weren't for Horatio's bad chest. There's no reason at this time of year that he should bark in lieu of speaking like a normal human being. I'll ring the doctor if he worsens.

Now, do you remember at the start of the war there was a curious fellow asking all sorts of questions down in Cuckfield? You remember our weekend away after the scare of that first blitz, surely. We were by that lovely Elizabethan manor house. You know the one, down that pretty little lane where we were thieves shifting our eyes in all directions before taking a sprig each of that gorgeous English lavender for our pillows. Ockenden Manor, it was called. We both assumed it was still a Jewish boys' school after Horatio had told us so. Why I bother listening to that man when he only lived there as a small child, I'll never know. Things change, I tell him.

Now brace yourself, my dear. Did you know that Ockenden Manor housed Canadian soldiers at the very time we stood at the gate's threshold? You would think it would have been obvious, a quiet lane like that and not a menorah in sight. And don't think for a moment that I'm not fully aware of when those twinkling charms are lit each year. Mr. Adler, not two doors down, made a point of luring in even Horatio by baking his caramelized pear bread pudding then setting it outside his kitchen window, right next to his menorah to see which badger would come watering at the mouth. Needless-to-say it was Horatio, who was meant to be looping garland around the bannister outside on the occasion of our annual Christmas do. Both caught with crumbs sprinkled around their lips! Sadly our dos came to an abrupt end the moment fate decided it was fair game to drop a Jerry bomb on Harrow. My point being, though it wasn't winter with twinkling menorahs shining up the streets, one would expect to see at least one Jewish boy running about the grounds. And what were the chances we would run into a Canadian in a small village like Cuckfield?

Suddenly it occurred to me when I was rummaging through some papers just days ago that you didn't meet this man at all, this soldier. You had turned back in the direction of the inn to rest your weary mind from all of those loose brains up at Hogweed. I was telling you about him, that I had tuned out his atrocious dialect in favor of focusing on his dishy good looks. I thought I might feast on him, if he'd only kept his mouth closed. The Canadians are something, you know—not as pasty as our homegrown men, but they know it. You can see it in their eyes. You do remember this conversation, don't you? It was only months before you left your dear sister in harm's way to move to that island you now call home.

I do recall asking him to hand me down the moon. He was rather tall, you know, but his personality rather inveigling. Do you like that word? I thought you might.

My point you ask? Well, I now believe it was him, the man you've tried all these years to forget. The man you've kept locked in your past. The man that Roderick once wrote to me about so that I may watch over you and care for you silently in your healing. You weren't privy to that, were you? What a dear cousin to safeguard you so. It never bothered me that you chose not to include me in your secret. I knew it was your first love and that you needed to deal with it in your own time, in your own way. I know his name was Christian and the soldier I met that day in Cuckfield was also Christian. I didn't think to mention his name at the time. I suppose in the back of my mind, I had concluded there was more than one Christian in Canada. Honestly, what would be the chances that it would be your Christian? In any case, I know I'm right because I am staring at a photograph of him now...

of wounded Canadian soldiers stationed at Cuckfield. The clipping was from *The Star*, a Toronto newspaper and sent to me by Roderick just days ago. Roderick was the only one who knew about him, wasn't he? I also have a feeling that you may have shared this tidbit with the little pixie from India. Even so, I'm glad you shared in Roderick's confidence. He informed me that you, too, were a source of great comfort to him in his time of need and that he is proud of who he is. Told me to give you two winks for him. Had no idea what all his prattle was about. So be it.

Hold onto your snood! There's more. According to Roderick, who wisely chose to do a little detective work on your part whilst vacationing in that wild place you called the Bruce Peninsula (how vulgar to borrow a proud Scottish name like Tobermory by the way) walked straight over to an old hillbilly named Griffin and asked flat out, "Would you kindly tell me of Christian Hunter's whereabouts?" The only reply the man would give was, and I note with gruff humor according to Roderick, "He's crossed the big one." What kind of response is that? Our university-trained cousin put two and two together and realized he meant the Atlantic Ocean.

Don't you see, Gillian? I would wager Horatio's prizewinning foxgloves that that fellow from your past is crossing the seas to see YOU. Of course we have no proof, but you cannot say that you haven't been forewarned. It's my duty as your oldest sister. I wonder what his wound was? The article didn't say. And he looks fit as a fiddle in the photograph, don't you think? The lad behind him could have used a drop of dreamy tonic himself, I'd say. You can peruse the article at will as I have enclosed it in this envelope.

Now about that Griffin fellow. Don't you abhor those select few who are dreadfully quiet, who answer questions with a "yes" or "no"? For God's sake, don't they know how uncomfortable they make others feel? How difficult can it be to drum up a two-way conversation? It merely requires a little effort on one's part to put two or three words together or half a dozen if they're up to it. I don't know how you ever managed with all that Hindi going on around you at the maharaja's all those years ago. They may as well have been silent. You would never have known if the maid of root vegetables had been blatantly insulting you in front of the scullery maid.

Now very briefly, I should enlighten you to Winnie's latest antics. Barclays was strumming with clients not one week ago and, as usual, she was weaving about looking busy, not doing a bloody thing, if you ask me. (I've already asked for the Good Lord's pardon regarding any foul language I may use in this letter. I believe I've slipped up twice now.) Well, it was precisely half ten when that succubus (one cannot ignore the way she eyes Mr. Tyler, and right in front of his wife, too!) stood in the center of the reception for bank loans and dropped to the ground, showing signs of an epileptic fit. No doubt to get attention from Barclays' most prestigious clients. Everyone just stared. I didn't know what to do, so I picked up a newspaper, the *Catholic Herald* mind you. I've already given penance for that one! And slapped her face silly. It must have worked because she came to and there

I was on top of her like some sort of sumo wrestler. I think the wooden butter knife she'd kept hidden behind the counter was too blunt for the job, but she threatened to cut my head off anyway!

There you have it—the latest news. Now be wary of any visitors from the colonies. And if by chance your sister here was right, then I shall not accept anything other than full detail of events. So don't go sending me off without tea on the slightest little pretext. It won't work.

Your fairy godmother,
Beatrice

Gillian took out the article that had been tucked in the envelope. The newsprint had been smudged, likely by her sister's appetite for tea. It looked as though vanilla teardrops had fallen then dried. But in the foreground, sitting on the edge of a hospital bed, was a man who could never escape her memory. The man she'd just spent a day getting to know all over again, yet she hadn't learned a thing.

Gillian stroked his silhouette, the murky gray of the article. His features weren't clear, but he stared into the camera as if staring right through her with a sedate expression. The loose curls of his hair fighting their way through a modest military cut and Brylcreem—something she knew he never liked. She could feel her cheek rise and fall at the bittersweet memory of a man she once loved. So much had happened since then. At moments, she felt as though the world had tumbled into bits at the bottom of a canyon, the weight of sorrow too heavy even for her.

Hard times were wrung from even the best of families. The lad standing behind Christian was probably just another example of a boy torn from his family to fight in a war he never wanted to be a part of. Suddenly, a tiny gasp sounded from her lips as she squeezed her brow together, drawing the photograph closer. "That man?" she mumbled. She hadn't noticed him the way Beaty had. He was dressed in everyday military garb. Gillian nearly dismissed it as RAF when she noticed a badge on the shoulder, which she was sure read *Canada*. Gillian studied his face when it occurred to her that she'd seen him before. She was sure of it... but where? She couldn't place him.

This letter, this article had taken all that she'd worked for over these years and scattered her life like confetti in the wind.

Gillian tried to focus on the sea instead. It was raging now, clouds swelling again, ready to burst at any moment. She glanced behind her when she heard the wind smacking her back door. Her cottage, a place that had become home, was never more at odds with the stubborn Irish Sea as it was now, fighting for her attention. If she could just loosen her grip on the article, the wind would slip it from her fingers and carry it out to sea. Perhaps then she'd be able to forget Christian. Maybe she should have heeded Beaty's warning and taken a long trip to anywhere.

Instead, Gillian sprinted to the cottage under the rain. She ignored the telephone as she closed the door behind her, not ready to speak to Beaty. If it were Dr. Pilkington, she'd have to give an excuse as to why she hadn't come into the surgery today. But he *had* help and she wasn't up to seeing him, not with everything that had been going on. *Oh Reggie, you'd have been much simpler,* Gillian thought as the web with Christian was tangling itself into the tiniest of knots. If Christian had only given her more time, she could have been married to the doctor and all her guessing would have been pointless. But no, he had to show up when he did.

Wind shifted the rain as it now slapped her front door with a curtain of water falling from the thatched roof. As Gillian sat huddled at the kitchen table, tea in hand, beads of water slithered down the leaded beveled glass window just inches from her nose. A constant tapping on the tin barrel outside caused Christian's words to trickle back. *'Till I know'* grew rampant in her head. She tried to stamp them out and instead dissected every possibility. What exactly did he mean? Till he knew what? That what he'd hoped to find wasn't there anymore? That he still loved her? That he was finally over her? That what they'd had in Canada was nothing more than a youthful infatuation tied with a string of sundry emotions? Why had he returned?

Suddenly it occurred to her. "Griffin." The name wheezed between her teeth like a frightened child. Could he know? Was it possible?

She whisked her teacup to the lounge then set it on the hearth—cold slate lintel slabs that made the chill rise to her bones even in summer—then reached for the hand bellows to make the smoldering fire swell into something more… "tempting," she muttered. Gillian plopped into the overstuffed armchair, her mind whirling into the past.

ALL DAY, GEORGIAN BAY had been glittering like a bath of diamonds. Gillian and Christian soaked in the sun while sprawling across his rickety old dock watching the butterflies he'd promised dance around them. The bulrushes were as high as she was, and the Blue Jays just as greedy. She wanted every morsel of sun to soak into her bones. If there had been a drop left, she'd probably have stolen that, too.

Of course she loved what it did to Christian's skin, the way it shimmered against his tan, teasing her. But it was the dip he'd take every so often when the sun became too much that freed him like a little boy who'd just learned how to ride a bicycle. After having spent nearly every moment of the summer together, it was the first time Christian had shared more than two sentences about his family.

"You know, my mom always liked days like this," Christian said. "The kind of day that lasts forever."

"Mmm. I know what she means." Gillian looked at him. "You must miss her terribly though you don't talk much about her."

"That's because there's not much to say."

Gillian laughed, "What do mean? There's always oodles to say about a family. Mine drains me, but I wouldn't change any of it."

"You're lucky then," he sighed. "Gilly, I haven't told you about my family because I've moved on."

"What does that mean, you've moved on? No one just moves on from their family."

"I haven't had much choice."

"Okay, so you're one great mystery. Is that it?" she snipped.

Christian smiled, "I like when you get scrappy."

"Scrappy? What are you talking about? I'm not scrappy. I don't even know what you mean by the word."

"Oh, I think you do. And yes, you are. It's the one thing about you that my mom never was."

"Scrappy?"

"Right." His smiled widened.

"Well, what about your father, was *he* scrappy?"

"I don't know. I never saw much of him. Except when

he had to fix things or when he had deliveries to make in Toronto. He'd always invite me along." Christian shrugged, "I guess he wanted some help when I got big enough. But I was a kid then, and I haven't seen my dad in over eight years. He left a week before my twelfth birthday." Christian sighed, "It wasn't his fault. He needed work and the nickel and copper ore mines up in Sudbury offered something regular. Trouble is, he went up north and never came back."

Gillian was already seething, sure Christian could see smoke coming from her ears. How could a father do that? It was one thing going off to war like Daddy did, but never coming back... on purpose?

"How did you and your mother manage?" was the only thing she could think to ask.

"I don't know; we just did. But it was hard on her. She never really got over losing my brother."

Gillian felt her chest sink. "You had a brother?"

"Yeah. He'd gone ahead and found himself under the wheel of a threshing machine one day when he was doing some work over at the Dewey's farm. I was only six at the time, but I remember that day like it was stitched in my brain." Christian sighed then dropped his shoulders. "Like I said, it was hard on her. Burying your own child just isn't right. No," he said. "You never get over something like that. And then she got sick."

"When did she pass away?"

"Two years ago."

"How awful, Christian," she said coiling her fingers in his as they dangled their feet in the water.

"It was the toughest time I can remember. You would've liked my mom. She taught me how to handle live-wires like you," he said winking. Gillian smiled, understanding the serious tone beneath his words. "If I'm patient, it's only because of her. She appreciated all the things that most people over-looked. *Busy* was an evil word to her." Christian smiled when he said it. "A word for people who didn't know how to enjoy this," he said motioning across the cove. "People who didn't know how to slow down." Gillian could tell that he felt sorry for people like that, and she admired his way of looking at life. To him, breathing just felt better, he explained, when he'd wait quietly for those wild lightning strikes of inspiration. "Even igniting a clump of tinder had this way of triggering ideas. They came when they were darn well ready to come." Christian put his arm around Gillian, and somehow she felt it was his way of saying, "I'm glad I've finally told you."

The sun was already sneaking behind the treetops with shadows smearing the cove. The monarch butterflies had settled onto their velvety sausages and the chipmunks stopped darting in and out of the dock's planks. Evening was starting to fall.

"Speaking of tinder," Christian said, "I thought we could have a fire on the beach further down. One of the fishing boats came in late last night, and I saw some nice musky I could get for a fair price."

"I'd like that, but I shouldn't be late this evening. Auntie Joyce keeps asking all sorts of questions, and I'm not ready to tell her about you. I just know she'd be concerned and would wire my father. I know that sounds awful but…"

"It's okay. I'm not bothered. But I'm sure she already knows. We spend so much time together and it's not like Tobermory's big. There's almost nothing here." His lips turned up at the corners. "I know you'll tell people when you're ready."

"Well, Roderick knows, of course, and Shashi in India. Truth is, I like having you as my little secret. With six sisters and a brother, secrets are hard to come by in my family. Just this once, I want something special all to myself."

"I feel that way, too," he said, giving her a kiss on the cheek. "Why don't we take the pick-up into town quickly then rustle up a fire."

"Don't be silly. You go into town. I'll stay here and start the fire." Christian glared at her. "What? I *can* start a fire you know."

GILLIAN COULD HEAR THE TIRES of Christian's lorry roll away toward town. It was that time of day when the light felt odd and she teetered back and forth trying to decide whether or not it was getting cool enough for a cardy. She needed to change her clothes anyway. No good wearing bathers well into the evening. And since she needed kindling from the woodshed, it was as good a place as any to change into something warmer. She knew Griffin wouldn't mind her fetching what she needed. She'd seen Christian do it a hundred times, and he was probably out front whittling away at his engine anyhow.

The door screeched like a Siamese cat when she opened it. A window at the other end let in just enough light to see what she was doing. It surprised her how large the woodshed seemed inside. A stack of crates in the center funneled light to the sidewalls covered in pine and birch logs. Some freshly cut cedar smelled curiously like a hamster's cage. Gillian leaned down to sniff it. No, it was bang on the smell of Daddy's cedar chest, the one in which he kept all of his grouse hunting clothes. She inhaled a little more, trying to make the memory last.

Closer to the window, there were sheaves of kindling and bits of old newspaper to start a fire. *Perfect*, Gillian thought. An old workbench at the end would serve as good a place as any to set her clothing down while she changed. She stood there for a moment taking it all in, not quite sure if she wanted to be there after all. There was something raw about the shed, something that made her feel uncomfortable. It was cold nestled in this patch of trees, and she could feel a shiver rise in her skin. No. She was being silly, that's all.

There wasn't a curtain on the window, but since it didn't face the house she decided she'd be fine. Gillian's brow crinkled together, still not feeling quite right about it. As she lowered the straps to her swimsuit then pulled it down to her waist, she turned quickly away from the window. A creak in the floorboards made her jump. *Surely it was nothing.* Must have been *her* shifting weight.

When Gillian looked up, she noticed a hummingbird fluttering just outside the window feeding on some nectar. Such tiny things they were. That's when she noticed a photograph of a woman pinned to the wall hidden slightly by an animal trap. The photo had yellowed and was stained around the edges. Gillian looked closely and marveled at how alike she was to this person. Her hair was dark and wavy just like hers, and there was something confident about how she stood, as though she knew she was something a little bit special with one of those smiles people always remember.

Gillian slipped her blouse over her head then changed quickly into her knickers and skirt. When she sat down on a crate to put on her shoes, another creak sounded. This time it couldn't have been her. Gillian's eyes widened, trying to see past the stack of crates, pins suddenly pricking her fingertips. She felt trapped as though she had been caught in one of the spider webs dangling across the low trusses.

"Is someone there?" she called out.

Gillian felt a pinch in her throat when she heard the door bang shut.

"Christian, is that you?" He didn't answer. "Please stop teasing, I don't think I like it." A grumble sounded behind the crates. The walk was clunky, uneven, and it occurred to her when the floorboards fought to hold his weight, that it wasn't Christian at all. "Griffin!" she gasped holding her chest as he stepped into the light. "You gave me a scare. You know you shouldn't do things like that."

"Didn't mean to spook ya, dear," he mumbled. Griffin looked more like a troll in the woodshed, lines of years marked across his face. He was unshaven and grubby; he barely skimmed the wooden beams that held dusty baskets and rusty tools. He was wearing a discolored shirt with braces on his trousers that held up his huge belly, and he coughed a cough that shook the earth.

"You know, you really should see a doctor about that," Gillian said.

"I know, Bugsy," he chuckled. "You've told me so many times it's gone thick in your throat." Gillian kneaded her brow. *Bugsy?* she thought. She tried to recall but was certain she'd never told him to see a doctor... ever.

"I hope you don't mind that I'm in here. I needed some kindling," she said.

"Why would I mind? It's not the first fire you've started."

What a strange comment. How would he know if she'd ever started a fire? Perhaps she hadn't heard him correctly. His mumbling was terrible and she found herself having to concentrate harder, the more she got to know him. Gillian leaned down to tie her shoelaces, thinking it best to leave at once. Although she liked Griffin very much, such a mellow man, she'd never actually been alone with him until now.

"Here, let me help," Griffin said as he awkwardly lowered to one knee. He pawed at the laces, unable to pick them up with his fingers that looked like bloated sausages. She noticed how deformed his knuckles were in this light and suddenly felt an urge to knee him. Of course, she wouldn't. He was only trying to help after all. But she didn't need help.

"I can do that!" Gillian said sharply. The sting of her words instantly sketched hurt into Griffin's eyes. "I'm sorry, Griffin. It's only that I don't need help," she said as her gaze shifted to the kindling at his back. "I need to start a fire."

"So do I," he said with a throaty voice. He seemed nervous, almost vulnerable. Gillian could see his hand shaking and didn't know what to make of it. He must have been a hundred years older than her, she thought. As she started to rise from the crate, Griffin cupped her hips with his hands, preventing her from getting up.

"What are you doing?" she asked, feeling her voice tremble.

"You're so beautiful, Shelby, and it's been a coon's age."

"What are you talking about?" Gillian spat, feeling pinned to the slats.

"I saw you changing," he mumbled through a mouth that reminded her of a ventriloquist's dummy, only his expression was strangely tender... there was love in his eyes. "Somehow you still make me feel like whistling, but you steal my breath every time."

Before Gillian could react, she felt Griffin's hand like a thick club, slide up her thigh slowly between her legs as far as her knickers, her skirt like an accordion at her waist. She could feel him trying to arouse her with his gritty hand...

a hand calloused... a hand that made her feel dirty. She glanced up at the photograph, the woman smiling down at her, then shifted back to what was happening. For a moment Gillian froze, unable to think as his eyes peered at her breasts through a shapely blouse meant for Christian, meant for young love. As the stubby fingers from his other hand moved to her breast, Gillian's repulsion made her gag, waking up that strayed instinct all because she trusted someone she didn't really know—an instinct she was born to follow.

Her heart seized at once as blood shot through Gillian's body bringing her foot to his chest. She barreled through him as if he was the dummy she'd imagined, splinters everywhere. He had been teetering on one knee and toppled over easily... this big man. But the thrust gave her enough energy to break free and run. No steps followed, only the sobbing of a broken old man with words that muffled into nothingness. "I love you, Bugs. I'm sorry... I won't do it again." Tears streamed down Gillian's face as she ran and swore she'd never return.

GILLIAN GLANCED OUTSIDE AGAIN, the garden looking smudged with rain still pattering the drive and the dewy air seeping through cracks in the window's jamb. The misery outdoors was keeping most people by their wood stoves, apart from the postman who'd just put something in her postbox. The memory of that day felt as though she'd read it in a book somewhere. She remembered all the details, the smells and the feelings, yet it was in the pages of the past. She later recalled Christian referring to Shelby once as Griffin's wife and how he'd lost her in a slow, painful death. "Griffin," Gillian sighed with a sadness running through her even now.

Gillian had always prided herself on being able to brush off the dusty bits of life. Right now at this moment she felt deflated, missing a man who fluttered into her life again for only a moment. "Christian," she sighed this time. It had been such a lovely day before the rain. Why did she spoil it by ignoring the obvious? To him, it must have appeared as though she didn't care. Truthfully, she didn't care, but not in the way one might think.

Friendship is a flower
You cannot force,
It grows unfettered
Asking no reward.
A burden shared,
A heavy load is halved,
Hope and faith
Return to try once more.

For friendship true,
Ne'er seeks to know
Who was to blame.
It strives to renew
Trust and love.

Thank God
For giving me my friend!

Chapter 18

1946

THE POSTMAN ROUNDED the corner on his way back to town, his bicycle tires spitting up water and grit from the road. Had Gillian felt more spirited, she would have offered him a cup of hot mulled wine to warm the bones. She debated for a moment whether or not to brave the elements to fetch the post then decided that it might do her good. After all, stewing in her own gloom wasn't serving any purpose whatsoever. Christian did nothing wrong; he said nothing wrong. He'd been nothing but a gentleman. He came to see her, a curiosity that, for whatever reason, sailed him across the Atlantic. Perhaps it was simply what it was, a lovely picnic with an old friend. She didn't know if he had checked out of the inn, but she did know that he wouldn't have come all this way without saying goodbye.

Gillian threw on her wellies and grabbed the umbrella from the stand next to the door. The rain was turning to drizzle when she reached the postbox and opened it. Inside was a small, well-stuffed envelope and one lettercard from Berkshire—her sister, Beaty, hunting her down, no doubt!

Gillian immediately tore off the perforated selvages, the drizzle dancing down her umbrella as though siding with her sister.

Date = forever and a day!

Dearest little sister,

The Good Lord put me here on this Earth for two reasons, one to be "fruitful and multiply," at which I'm afraid I have failed miserably. Perhaps Horatio needs a good licking—and stop being vulgar, you! And two, to carry out His duties and mind my scatterbrained siblings. Why on this blessed Earth have you not answered my calls? And don't for a second try to pretend nothing is going on. My dear, you are like tumbleweed wafting through the desert with your aging sister skittering after you, butterfly net in hand. You wear me out. Though you are not in peril, thank heavens. I know this for I rang this very morning Dr. Pilkington's surgery and Mrs. Hemsworth herself picked up the receiver. (I hope she was there for a hysterectomy.) She told me that she spied my little sister off gallivanting in her sidecar with a strapping young swain. It was him, wasn't it? I was right. Christian Hunter is there on the Isle of Man. I can feel it.

Do you see how my penmanship turns to mud when I have to squeeze all of my frustrations on this tiny lettercard? Time for a cup of tea. I dare say, if you dried me out, I could be brewed!

Lovingly,

Beatrice

Post Script—In two days time, it shall be my

birthday. I will become very, very, VERY old according to my husband who likes to remind me that I am nearly a senior at forty-two. I'm not sure what planet he lives on. But if that's so then why do I still feel like an awkward teenager? You wouldn't forget my birthday, would you, dear, despite your hairy footing?

GILLIAN EXPECTED AS MUCH. She planned to ring Beaty and tell her every detail, but what she really wanted was to fly to her now and curl in her arms, not a word spoken. "Silence is bliss," she used to say when Gillian would skin her knee then come to Beaty for mending. She would hold her, patting her head till every tear dried just as Mommy had done before she died. Despite Beaty's shortcomings, it was lovely having a sister like her.

As Gillian stuffed Beaty's lettercard into her cardigan's pocket, she recognized immediately the maharani's handwriting on the plump envelope now in her fingers. A sudden pang of curiosity or worry, she couldn't decide which, made her hand twitch uncontrollably. After all, the maharani hadn't written her since Shashi's debut letter over fourteen years ago. Gillian doubted she could count the number of adventures she'd received from Shashi over all this time. Through their letters, they'd been through everything together.

Every so often, Gillian would peruse her stack of letters that she kept tied with the blue ribbon Shashi had worn in her hair to school every day. "I want you to have it," Shashi had said, "because then you will think of me." That hint of curry lingered on it even now. Gillian liked to choose a letter to re-read occasionally and found that it either spiced up her mood or made her long to meet the young woman Shashi was becoming. They were friends from the start, and they would be friends till the end. Gillian was certain of that. For some reason she knew that Shashi looked up to her, saw her as a role model. But the child couldn't have got in more inside out and upside down. As Gillian stood there under her umbrella, the salty sea air sitting heavily in the drizzle, she smiled knowing that Shashi was the real role model, the one Gillian had marveled at all these years.

A dozen letters at least showed Shashi's humility. How was that possible from a princess who'd had everything at her beck and call, who'd been sheltered from the hardships of the real world? Over time, Gillian came to realize that the two of them were no different. They both saw life as a set of tiny adventures, some big—just as she had encouraged in all those stories by the pond at Wentworth Estate. Two girls who wanted to see the world differently.

The one letter that reminded her of that the most was the one on the occasion of Shashi's *ritu kala*, her formal invitation into adult society. Gillian felt aghast at the time when Shashi was only thirteen, just a toddler learning to walk on her own, really. Shashi hadn't understood why this ceremony was taking place yet feared that the fate of her friends, all getting married around that time, would be hers, too. She had spied several meetings between her father (the maharaja) and the father (a very high-ranking officer in the Royal Indian Air Force) of a boy she'd once met on vacation. She didn't like him; he had pulled her hair and teased Samir. At the *ritu kala*, Shashi was given her first sari and showered with gifts by all the women. She couldn't understand why so many of the gifts were green. She only liked green on trees and grass, not on her! Later that evening, Samir had told her that the green was to make her have scads of babies, and when *they* grew up, another cluster or two.

Terribly upset, Shashi found her way to the streets of Bombay the next morning carried in her safe palki, observing the world from the inside. It was all she could do to get away from the palace and the traditions that suddenly felt strangling. The maharani had joined her. Shashi begged her mother to show her the real Bombay, the slums she'd heard about. And she did.

"It was astonishing," Shashi had written. The slums melted into the horizon, and Shashi wept in her palki until she saw a girl about her age standing in front of a hovel holding a baby. "Hovel" was being generous, she explained. Truth be known, she stood in a breeding ground for rats, flies, and viruses. Shashi was certain that Southampton after its worst blitz paled in comparison to this place, as though every German bomb ever dropped had been dropped on this site alone.

Gillian had always been truthful about the war but never wanted to frighten Shashi either. And Southampton was a letter that even a child could read between its lines. Of course the war had stormed into the lives of everyone Shashi knew. Even the streets seemed to be cleared of young men, most of whom had enlisted, she heard her father saying. She could feel war's presence right there in the slums but this one had nothing to do with Hitler. The girl's clothing was tattered, and although she was filthy, she stood smiling softly at Shashi with a proud gleam in her expression. Shashi smiled back. It was at that moment that she understood humility.

The next fortnight was spent begging her mother not to send her into this arranged marriage that she suspected was being secretly planned. Instead, she knew there was another purpose in her life. She didn't know what exactly, but she wanted the chance to discover it. The only certainty was that she couldn't devote her life to serving one man. She was meant for something more.

A LOUD GRUNT from the Loaghtan ram down the way pulled Gillian back to the moment. She glared at him curtly, his four horns looking as though they were ready to charge her by reason of acrimony. She'd stolen his wool for that cardigan after all. Even from a distance, she could see in his eyes that that was precisely what he was thinking. Had he only understood that it was her favourite, cozy cardy.

The letter.

Gillian felt no urge to go indoors despite the squelching of her wellingtons as she shuffled her weight from one foot to the other. The maharani's wax seal hadn't changed, although it served no purpose with the glued edges to the envelope. As Gillian tore it open, the street grew quiet like a slow, melting oil painting. The smell of newly cut timber and smoldering peat from the flues atop the thatch whirled around her. Two envelopes inside, one marked *Gillian*, the other *Please read first*.

19th of June 1946

Gillian,

I hope this letter finds you and your family well.

Since the moment my daughter met you at our home in London, it has been nothing but Gillian this, Gillian that. I must confess to you that for some time, a small part of me was envious of your bond, but I soon realized what a gift you were to my daughter and eventually to me. Because of you, we have a well-used hammock in the palace garden. We had one crafted and hung between two jujube trees next to our pond. It came to be Shashi's and my favorite nook, a place where only the two of us existed. She learned to read so quickly that I became her audience. But what she liked to do most was tell her own stories, stories at times involving pirates with peg legs and hooks. I believe she got her wild imagination from you. Who is Snarky Cutter, by the way?

There were times that Shashi would wake me to watch the sun rise together. I always told her to go back to sleep, but she insisted. I wish I could put into words the beauty of an Indian sunrise, especially from our hammock. Shashi would say that all the juices from the gods float up from the sea and splash the day with happiness. We would swing gently listening to the frogs and watching our peafowl wander the gardens. Shashi named the hen "Darjeeling" but you probably already know that. By your example, Shashi learned to be her own person, to speak her mind. Though it is not always appropriate in our culture to do so, I have come to admire this about her.

The reason I am writing to you is to fulfill a promise that I made my daughter some years ago. She has kept a secret from you but for very good reason. Shashi has always wanted you to love her because you wanted to not because you bled for her. I tried to explain that you would understand, but she would not hear of it. My little girl has bloomed into a beautiful Indian wildflower, a 'datura' I like to think—a soft flower that stands tall with its trumpet shape as though playing music to the valley in the distance. It grows at will on arid wasteland, amidst rubble, by railroads and roadsides, or in the ruins of old buildings. If you dust it off, it is quite spectacular. She has become the datura of the slums of Bombay, a symbol that beauty can grow anywhere with a helping hand. From the moment I showed her the lining of India, she has spent every drop of energy helping those in need. I agreed to interrupt marriage plans, for I knew in my heart that this was Shashi's vocation in life. It is for this reason a single datura was placed on her chest during *arati* when the oil lamp was passed over her body.

Gillian, to you I must say that our Shashi died two days ago, though it is not how we see it. Her soul will go on after life. It is what we believe as Hindus and something that should not be grieved. But I will secretly tell you that I had tears raining from my eyes in private. Shashi had been ill with leukemia for some time. She asked me to tell you of her passing when the time came and to send a letter that she had written when she was still spirited and agile. She also asked me to remind you of a playwright named William Shakespeare. "It is not in the stars to hold our destiny but in ourselves." Shashi lived by this mantra.

I know that you will be saddened by my news. I close this letter saying that a world war could not take our girl, and if you look around, the datura still blooms even in Europe under the name 'Thorn Apple' and in America as 'Jimson's Weed.' Not the prettiest titles, but daring, adventurous, and hardy. You see, Shashi's trumpet has sounded the world!

Sonali

When we are young
Such trifling things,
Take the sun from our lives
As though it has wings.

To fly away
Leaving tearful mood,
Until at last
Time frees the gloom

So however big
A trifle seems,
Youth only grieves
Till new hope gleams.

Chapter 19

"GOOD MORNING, Mrs. Pugsley," the nurse chirps. I can't remember her name. Patty or Penny—something like that. "How are you feeling today? I'll just open the blinds for you." She smiles softly like it was part of her routine. She's wearing a pale blue pantsuit that contrasts her flushed cheeks. Gone are the days when you could tell the difference between an orderly and an RN. The old uniforms were lovely, I think, but even I struggle to notice such details these days. "A little sunshine never hurt anybody, did it?" I watch her weave about the room, touching this and fiddling with that until she finally settles by my bed. "Well?" she adds. "How is the pain this morning?" I mumble something but even I can't make out what I've said. "Don't you worry, dear, a little morphine will help with that." *Dear*, for goodness sake. She must be in her forties! Why does the world insist on treating the elderly like children?

"My granddaughter, has she been visiting this morning? I'm afraid if I nod off, she won't want to disturb me." My words come out lumpy. I can hear them as though they need to clamber over a grotesque Adam's apple crafted by cancer. Either that or a leftover hunk of the Garden of Eden's forbidden fruit has lodged in my throat.

"No, she hasn't been here yet, Mrs. Pugsley. But your son popped by very early when you were asleep. Said he'd be back shortly after lunch."

I nod, knowing how I don't like to inconvenience those whom I love. I'm sure my son's work is suffering because of all the time he spends here on "the ward of the wobblies." Yet I feel selfish knowing that's exactly where I want him. Likewise, Kate is a godsend. Then there is Gilly, the one who has sat in that poor excuse for a chair, holding my hand as pain strangles me. But it's the patter of her fingers on that laptop of hers when she doesn't think I notice. It sings me to sleep, hearing my story being sculpted. All the bits and pieces I've told her over the years are coming together and I know she's doing justice by them.

"I'll wake you if you like, when your granddaughter arrives," the nurse says. "I promise, I won't let her leave."

"Oh, you are a marigold in disguise, aren't you," I say through dry lips.

"I had a grandma once, too," she adds, winking.

THE WINTER SUN IS LOVELY but I miss it from the farm. I miss watching Ballerina shield flies from the other horses as she stands like a child next to her adoptive big brothers. Her wagging tail always reminded me to wave hello to others, despite any irritations I might have at the time. Quite like now, really. I need to put aside the acute pain that drills into me whenever it sees fit and smile, at least with my eyes, to my nurse who sits next to me now.

"Mrs. Pugsley, are you awake?" she says softly. "Your

granddaughter is here. She's just gone to the vending machine for some hot chocolate. She'll be with you in a few minutes."

Hot chocolate. If I look at the wintery sky outside the hospital window, there is a giant oak and if I try my hardest, I can see a hundred small thermoses dangling from its branches, all filled with piping hot chocolate. A smile should seize me, but instead a single tear falls down my cheek knowing that soon there will be no more surprises like my icy cage in the woodland with my granddaughter.

It feels strange to know how much my passing will hurt others except for the one closest to me. I don't think it will be like that for Gilly. I think she'll talk to me in those quiet moments and see me sitting at the table having a good laugh when the family gets together. She'll see me when no one else will, when to others I'll just be a passing memory.

Though she thinks I was her rock through those trying years, realizing that her own mother didn't care enough to fight for custody, that she was so easily cast aside, Gilly's got it all mixed up. That child has been *my* strength even before she came into being.

And while my marriage was easy as far as marriages tend to go, it wasn't without its moments. Even old Angus needed a watchful eye from time to time. But I couldn't blame him, those times I saw sadness in his eyes when he knew my heart still belonged to another man. It grieved me to hurt someone whom I had grown to love deeply but in a different way. On the other hand, as long as I've had my granddaughter, I've never gone without a finely carved backbone. True, I've had one my whole life, really, but not one in my twilight years with its own ally—a non-judgmental ally at that, until Gilly came along.

"GRANDMA?" I remember her words like it was yesterday. The family and every seedling it seemed from Port Stanley to Goderich had just celebrated Gilly's sixteenth birthday. I know because Angus had dipped into the one and only bottle of scotch whiskey he'd ever owned. It was aged well and could tip over a bullfighter with the aroma alone. Normally, a party like that and I'd be leading a line dance. Well, not that night. I couldn't believe my eyes when I saw Angus on the patio after dinner trying to rekindle an old man's fantasy with that creature from Clinton's tiniest book club. A membership of one if I recall correctly! Somehow, Charmaine Dipple had weaseled her way into an invitation to my only granddaughter's party. Angus couldn't say no to anybody and fell weak at the knees to that harlot. I was horrified to see her there but proud as I am, refused to let the sight of her rile me.

They had disappeared for twenty-two minutes. All the while I was growing claws, despite knowing full well there wasn't a thing he could do in that short time.

"Grandma, are you okay?" Gilly asked.

"Go back inside darling. Enjoy your party."

"I'm not going anywhere. You're upset about something," she said in a snippy sort of way. "Has Grandpa done something? I saw him here a few minutes ago with that lady. Who is she anyway?"

"Just someone not worth mentioning, I'm afraid." And with that look that said her grandpa wouldn't hurt a fly mixed with the thought of my reddened eyes, I knew what she would do.

"Where have they gone?"

"Around the house I think." And before I could say another word, Gilly had marched away ready to bulldoze anything in her path. Sixteen years old and I could almost hear the clatter of elderly bones being scrambled for a late night snack.

Needless-to-say, Angus had returned with a red mark across his cheek but it wasn't my granddaughter who had given it to him, it was Charmaine. Apparently she wouldn't have any of Angus' nonsense either. Not at eighty years old. In the end, the whiskey got the better of him and he fell asleep on the lounge chair outside.

Even though he was a fool behaving like that, it brought back the sting of him playing around all those years ago. Albeit only once, a Charmaine Dipple one never forgets! It stands to reason that Gilly would sit with me all that evening.

SHE'S ALWAYS BEEN THERE for me, and it's been through her, because of her, that I tended my garden. That I made my own datura grow inside me—a beautiful reminder that my Shashi's trumpet from so long ago is still sounding the world. And through Gilly's book, that little seed will grow inside each and every person who reads it. And though I may not be around to see it, this small world we live in will be filled with music.

So before I leave such a world, I will find the right moment with my granddaughter to scrub clean my jar of pickled truths, but only in part. The rest is yet to discover on the Isle of Man.

When I lift my eyelids, the hospital room is blurry but I see someone in the doorway. As my vision grows clearer, that pretty smile can belong to only one person... my Gilly.

We walked together
I now walk alone,
We then trod on velvet
I now tread on stone.

No blooming flower
No bird's song,
The world is silent
Now I walk alone.

We wandered together
Without thought or care,
The sunshine could vanish
And rain fill the air.

Flooding life's gladness
To leave a deep sadness,
To the end of my journey
I walk alone.

Chapter 20

1946

FOG HUNG IN THE AIR like a soggy rag, matching Christian's mood. It was the first time he'd been missing Tobermory since he left. Sure he'd thought about it, even compared it with this place. But the rain hadn't slowed since he left Gilly's doorstep three days ago—until now—and it was getting to him, the way the skies could swallow up the earth. Relentless, that's what it was.

A foghorn brayed in the distance as he stood at the threshold of the inn and looked out to sea. A ghostly calm followed it, relaxing him and burying his blurred vision of Gilly into the seabed with all those urchins and sea stars. For the first time in fourteen years, he understood that she had categorically found a life of her own. A part of him had assumed that if he found her unwed, she would have leapt into his arms. Half a grin poked its way into Christian's cheek as did clarity into his defeat.

He came here after considering it for fourteen years, weighing the risks constantly. Even his wild search during the war, which turned up nothing, left him with the cold reality that he'd probably never see her again. But Griffin—what he told him. He didn't have the heart to ask Gilly about it. If he had, maybe he would have stirred up a memory that she'd buried away all this time. He would have upset her. And it wouldn't change anything. He'd be selfish bringing it up now even if he saw her again. Maybe it was just straining his ego to think she'd left because she didn't love him. How would it benefit her? And how could Griffin do something like that? Christian rolled his shoulders back, considering it. He wouldn't. But if he did, Christian knew in his heart that he'd never have hurt her. He would have stopped himself. He would have known Gilly wasn't his wife. It broke Christian's heart to imagine how upset—how scared—she must have been, if it did in fact happen. It broke his heart even more to think she hadn't told him.

Second-guessing wouldn't help. What was more important was that he'd found her, the girl he'd adored from the moment they met at Little Tub Harbour... well and happy, living in an uncomplicated place after a grossly complicated war. Christian felt proud of her for climbing out of it on top. And though words had told her story, he'd never know what it was really like for her—to know the trepidation *she* felt while the Luftwaffe thundered above Billy Bunk, Gilly in her rubber boots curled up with a family that wasn't hers. Maybe his fear *was* the same the time those Bf 109's emerged from the clouds heading straight toward his Tiffy. They hadn't expected them. After their earlier mission, his war-weary squadron was ready for a breather, not a battle. But a terrific gun barrage in the skies it was. Fighter planes darting in and out of the clouds like a frenzy of rabid moths around a street lamp. Even when the adrenalin was choking, Gilly never left him. He wondered if he'd crossed her mind in Billy Bunk. He wondered what the morrow held in store.

As the clanging of masts sung their evening lullaby, Christian decided it was time to leave. The Isle of Man was home to Gilly McAllister, not his Gilly anymore, but its Gilly. It deserved an impassioned, relentless woman like her. Christian glanced over at a couple who'd just sat down outside the pub, a frothy pint each and the sweet laughter that only comes with a new relationship. He nodded at them but wasn't sure if they'd even noticed until Roland came out to take down the remaining chairs shouting, "Hi ya! Ya doin' alright?"

"Yeah, thanks."

"The weather's the craps, eh? First time in days anyone's wanted to sit out here."

Christian smirked, attesting to his insight, "Brave souls!" he said, waving as he headed to his room.

The inn was about as quiet as an inn could get. If he could, he'd stock it up with every fisherman from here to Georgian Bay for the next season or two. He liked the old man behind the counter. Didn't do much. Just sat there on his bench whittling away at some piece of wood, churning out at least half a dozen nutcrackers just in the time Christian had been there. When the innkeeper wasn't whittling, he was tying fishing flies—some real beauties, too. Gave them magical names like "Silver Doctor" and "Machete Moon." Even Griffin could learn a thing or two from this clam digger. He was always friendly, but business wasn't exactly booming.

CHRISTIAN SIGHED when he opened the door and saw his backpack next to the wardrobe. He'd spent one gloomy day wondering if he should go by Gilly's again or not, then two days seeing Castletown and Douglas, the island's capital. Truth be known, he wasn't all that interested in seeing anywhere without her and had even considered asking her along. But something wasn't sitting right, and he supposed he knew why. Christian glanced down as he hobbled to the backpack, tired from his bus trip back.

He rolled up his shirts and the only other pair of trousers he'd brought with him, digging them down in the backpack as far as he could, saving room for the three-legged Manx flag Gilbert had dropped off at the pub for him. Apparently Mr. Ballard had worn it as a cape into the pub while snorting some God-awful pig version of "Tuxedo Junction." Christian couldn't have been more disappointed to miss that. He stretched his back and glanced around the room to see if he'd missed anything. It was time to leave. He stuffed his toiletry bag in the front pocket of his backpack then picked up his walking stick. Though he didn't use it much of the time, it helped with a heavy load on his back. Christian bid his farewell to the innkeeper and to Roland at the pub then got on his way, knowing what he had to do next.

GILLIAN HELD THE MAHARANI'S LETTER but couldn't feel it in her fingertips. She couldn't feel anything but the wet drizzle now trickling down her face. For a moment, she considered letting the ink run, washing away the maharani's words. However, instinct ruled as she tucked it in her pocket. Her gaze fell to the gravel beneath her wellingtons, the umbrella lying in a puddle made of tears as much as raindrops.

The smudged canvas of gorse and heather stretching across the mead and squared-off paddocks closer to the villages slowly exuded the rancid stench of death.

"Shashi," she gasped. In disbelief, Gillian crisscrossed the road like a drunken vagabond, a panic building inside her. How could this be? Was it a terrible prank, a trick to get her on a boat to India? Was it Samir impersonating his mother, thinking it mildly amusing? But she knew this exquisite handwriting could never be forged. A trace of Samir would have been left behind.

A gust of wind whirled past throwing Gillian into an awful state. Images of Shashi and all they'd learned about one another over the years flooded her heart. She'd just been talking about her, telling Christian all about Samir's secret palki.

"Christian," she muttered. His name felt sweet on her lips, taking away that sting of death. As her brow furrowed and her eyes traveled behind her shoulder to the Irish Sea, she realized that she had to see him. He was the only signpost ahead no matter what he was thinking about her. Had he left the Isle of Man, she would have unearthed him. It wouldn't matter how or where. None of it mattered—only Shashi— and only Christian's lips could sound her words. "Please let him be there," she whispered as she headed toward town, toward the inn.

ONCE OUT OF TOWN, Christian slogged along a heavily rutted bridle path before reaching the main road. Pockets of trodden hay padded underfoot made the hike easier. Christian was feeling okay, just okay, resigned to the fact that he'd be heading to Ronaldsway as soon as he said good-bye. It was the right thing to leave this way, even though there remained unanswered questions. Why had she really left him fourteen years ago? Maybe it was true. Maybe her father would have preferred her back in Ireland with an Irishman. But the way Gilly talked about him, Christian knew he wanted her to be happy even if that meant settling in a far off land. And Griffin? "No," he sighed heavily. He couldn't bring himself to imagine it was true. He'd never do anything like that. Griffin had a heart of gold. Christian resigned himself to never knowing the truth. Seeing the life Gilly had built for herself, using the power of her smile to make others feel hopeful in the worst of circumstance—it was enough. He was happy that a brighter side of life could shine her way now. Just around the corner there'd be a man waiting for her—the right man.

The main road, barely wide enough for two cars, curled through the last of the slate-stone cottages and outbuildings heading toward the sea. Sheep peppered the rolling hills to the west as a hedgerow of rosehip led him to the final cluster of whitewashed cottages. The drizzle wouldn't let up.

GILLIAN BREATHED IN THE LANGUID AIR that would surely make her drop at any moment. Dizzy—that's precisely what she felt. She stopped by the rosehip to steady herself, her heart racing as she glanced down at the envelope clenched in her fingers. And as the numbing sensation in her limbs surrendered to her need for Christian, she rounded the corner. There he was, as striking as the day she first met him—his sport coat, collar turned up, and trousers now hanging suitably damp against his body, a military kit bag flung over his shoulders, and those droopy eyes held heavy in the mist. He was beautiful. And he was here.

"GILLY!" Christian said, his brow creasing at the sight of her. Her brown sweater hung sopping, dripping into her boots. She looked like a stray cat that had been caught out in a storm. He glanced past her noticing the umbrella lying on the road then hobbled toward her as quickly as he could manage, throwing his backpack on the wet ground. "What is it? What's happened?" he pleaded into her shaken expression.

Gilly tried to speak, but her words fell silent through the trembling and cold. All she could manage was to take out the envelope from her pocket. As he gingerly took it from her fingers, Christian saw the return address. *India*. A sudden weight plummeted inside him.

ONCE IN THE COTTAGE, Christian stripped Gilly of most of her wet clothes then threw a blanket around her and eased her into the lounge chair. After adding a couple logs of peat to the fire, he filled a pot with water to boil for tea. As he stood next to the stove, he glanced over at Gilly warming by the fire under the low-beamed ceiling, the envelope sitting on the hearth. He'd never seen her like this, the invincible Gillian McAllister. If he'd only had her magical way of pulling someone out of the darkness…

"Will you read it to me? The one marked with my name?" she whispered as he knelt now in front of her. He set her tea on the table next to her.

Christian took the envelope then moved to a small needlepointed footstool in front of the hearth. He'd imagined straight away the long evenings she must have spent here alone writing or crocheting. Signs were scattered everywhere: fountain pens, parchment, yarn, knitting and crochet needles, and his pocket watch slipped between the pages of a blue notebook, the notebook he'd seen in the garden the day he'd first visited, the notebook filled with poems.

Christian lifted the flap to the envelope then pulled out

the letter marked *Gillian*.

23rd of November 1943

Dear Gillian,

I am not certain when you will have this letter. It could be in two weeks or in two years. If I am lucky, you will never have to read these words. I have asked my mother to post it one day in the future when I have passed. My fifteenth birthday was a fortnight ago, and it has been eleven and a half years since we waved to each other from sea to dock. I remember that day very, very well. I held my mother's hand as a tear fell to my very English, shiny black shoes with the buckles. You chose my dress, do you remember? It had such a pretty lace collar, and you said that it was befitting a princess.

If I had all the rupees in all of India, I would snip that day from my memory, for it is the day that I left my nanny, my best friend, and I shall never meet her again.

I am a terrible person, Gillian. I have kept my illness from you, but I always planned to tell you one day of my greatest and final adventure. If you are reading this now then today is that day.

I do not need to speak of my illness. I am quite sure that my mother has told you what you need to know. Instead, I want to tell you about the angels.

My mother and father were having a small party a few years ago. It was just before the war came to be. We are controlled by Britain, you know, so it was not such a good idea to have a big party when the world was shaking like your fizzy drinks waiting to explode. But it is an important celebration for Hindus, and one that my mother and father, especially in my circumstance, wanted to hold. It is called *Raksha Bandhan*, which is a ceremony where a sister ties a sacred thread called a *rakhi* to her brother's wrist. This shows the sister's love and prayers for her brother's wellbeing and the brother's lifelong vow to protect her. Samir gave me an envelope with rupees in it and a small note that said, "Money is just money but you, Shashi, are my angel. I wish I could protect you from your sickness."

I remember we fed each other sweets in the center of the dining hall with a small crowd around us. My favorite has always been Jalebi because it is chewy like English Milady Toffee. (I know you knew that Samir and I kept a tin hidden under our bed, but you never said a word.)

Later that evening in our great dining hall when everyone was dancing and the colors of the saris swirled together like a sea of jewels, Samir and I crawled under a table and peered from behind a cloth of gold—and waited. The smell of incense danced with the flicking of wrists while an old man with a very hairy face sat in the corner smoking from a hookah. I was afraid of him, for I could see only little slits for eyes.

When all was quiet and our guests had left, we knew that our mother and father would take the carriage pulled by our oxen (we named them Sir-Trot-A-Lot and Guy) and ride about our estate under the light of the moon. We had time before they would come to check on us.

Samir and I lay down in the center of the dance floor, our arms spread apart with our hands held tightly to one another. The room was dark, but the moon cut through the tall window like your stream to the beaver dam in that great lake you were telling me about. Samir told me to look up, and for the first time in all the years that I have eaten in that hall, the four angels painted on the ceiling came alive and were flying above me. They have long black hair, just like mine, and wear saris the colors of the sea. Their wings have feathers the colors of the stone on the walls. They whirled around me smiling, each carrying a pendant… a medal. Samir told me to close my eyes for a moment while they placed the medals around my neck. He explained that one was for bravery, the other for storytelling, one for honor, and the last for a thousand smiles. When I opened my eyes, my medals felt like the large pebbles from my pond hanging on a piece of twine—just like an angel would give. Samir said that no maharani deserved such laurels as I did. He then took one of my thousand smiles and squeezed my hand.

I asked the angels why they had chosen me to be sick. I always tried to be a good girl, after all. I learned all my spellings and I have always done as I am told— mostly. Samir told me that one day I would know. I also asked if I would grow wings just like them and how that could happen if I am burned. My brother told me that because our souls go on after life, my wings will fly to my soul, so I do not need to worry.

What I did not tell my brother, what I have not told anyone until now, is that I am frightened. I am not supposed to be as a Hindu, but I am. I am terrified of fire. I don't think I am supposed to know what will happen, but I know that they will make a special bed of sandalwood for my body and cover my head. I think I will try to brush the fire from my skin. I once burned my finger, and it hurt so. The next day, they will take my bones and ashes to the sacred water of the Ganges. I am not sure, but I think my father, the maharaja, will carry my ashes until the water comes to his waist. Then he will say something while setting me free. I will imagine that I am floating to my nanny in the Irish Sea. My mother will prepare three balls of food, my favorite food, and set them at the edge of the water. If birds come to eat my food, every bit of rice holding it together, then my parents will know my soul is at peace. But Gillian... what if the birds do not come? Perhaps I can roam for eternity in your little cottage on the Isle of Man. Would you mind a houseguest terribly?

Now you know my last adventure, but I have a feeling that you would say to me that it is not my greatest—that my greatest adventures have been on this Earth. Please don't be sad for me, Gillian. As you know, I have a thousand smiles, and smiles can be seen in words. All you need to do is read my letters and take a smile from them whenever you need. Your smile was always brightest when you wrote about Mr. Right, and I borrowed those ones especially. He built you that mushroom for a reason. He loves you, just as I do.

Good-bye my nanny, good-bye my friend,
Shashi

Christian folded the letter then slid it back into the envelope. Gilly stared vacantly into the fire as he added one wood log then used the poker to stir up the peat. The crackling from the fire whispered through the room while dark seeped into the sky outside. Christian took the liberty of stepping into the bedroom for her robe, which he found hanging behind the door. She stood up, letting the blanket drop to the floor, and as he held up her robe she slipped her arms into it.

"Will you stay?"

He glanced at his backpack by the door ready for the airport. "Yes."

Then Gilly took his hand and led him to her small loveseat where they nuzzled without a word between them. Christian held her in his arms until she finally drifted into a soft pool of slumber. She'd never looked so beautiful.

DAWN BROKE as Gillian gazed out the latticed window from her bed. The sea was rowdy this morning. She could feel the misty air all the way to her bones by sight alone. Her door was left slightly ajar. And for a moment she couldn't recall how she'd made it to her bedroom until the events of last night settled. As she stared at the ceiling thinking of Shashi, a single tear dripped down the side of her face. "Christian," she soughed. She wondered if he'd stayed the whole night or if he'd snuck out. Wouldn't blame him—all that gloom. But she'd needed him, and he was there. She slid into her slippers next to the bed then threw her dressing gown over her shoulders, a cap-sleeved cotton nightgown trailing underneath.

"Good morning," she said stepping into the lounge where Christian was folding a blanket, propping it on the pillow she'd given him last night. Her eyes traveled downward noticing his large kit bag for the first time. "Are you going somewhere?"

"Home, I thought."

Gillian felt her brow kneading together. "I see."

"Well, I thought it was time." For a woman of words, Gillian didn't know what to say. She wasn't ready for him to show up out of the blue, fourteen years and one war later, but she sure wasn't ready for him to leave, either.

"Please. Will you eat something? I have an egg and a little milk. I'm sure I can create a semblance of an omelette."

Christian hatched a grin while throwing on his sport coat then topped his fair hair with a flat cap. His five o'clock shadow from the other day had turned into a scruffy jaw. She wanted to touch it, run her fingers along it.

He shook his head. "Thank you for last night. It was nice to be here."

"*I* should be the one to say thank you."

"You're welcome then," he said teetering toward her. "Listen, I'm sorry about Shashi. I know how much she meant to you. At least I think I do. It's amazing what this war has taken away, but even more amazing what it's brought. Every time you see a wildflower like the maharani described in that first letter, you'll know that Shashi's still trumpeting her music. She played it through the war, and she'll play it through you... you'll see." Christian wore a soft expression, his eyes gentle. "Thank you for letting me read the letters." He drew a deep breath. "And besides, who do you think Shashi got the musical notes from, anyway?" Gillian cracked a smile as he leaned into her, "You're extraordinary, remember that." He picked up his kit bag, approached the front door, opened it—all of it in slow motion or so it felt.

As Gillian watched him moving down her path, his walking stick in hand, the doorway framed the picture of a man she once loved—still loved—disappearing into the foggy mist and out of her life. It occurred to her in that moment as her stomach leapt to her throat that she wasn't willing to let him walk away; she couldn't. Shashi was right. Destiny was a matter of choice, not chance. Gillian deserved more and so did Christian.

With a sudden jolt, she ran unbridled down the path, her dressing gown swaying behind her until she reached him by the hedgerow. She took hold of his arm in one great pluck.

"Why do you do that?" she beckoned, steadying herself on the gravel.

"Do what?"

"Tell me I'm extraordinary then walk away. It's twice now you've done it, do you know that?"

"Is that such a bad thing—to be extraordinary?"

"Oh, you're infuriating! Haven't changed a bit, have you?"

"Me?" Christian said sniggering. "Don't push me, Gilly. I mean it."

"Why? If you've got something to say... say it!"

"I've never been able to figure you out. One day you're in love with me, the next you leave,"

"Are we on about that now?" she wailed.

"Right we are! I don't think for a second it had anything to do with your father wanting you to come home. Sure, maybe I wouldn't have been his first choice for his little girl, a Canadian who held little promise. But I think he was a good man."

"Of course he was!"

"So why did you use him as a crutch? Why couldn't you have been honest with me? Why did you leave, Gilly?" Gillian stood silent, staring into his wondering eyes, terrified to tell him the truth. "You're as stubborn as you ever were.

Even a war couldn't change that, could it?" he said crossly.

"Don't you preach about a war you know nothing about! You didn't live under its marring terror. You wouldn't know."

"Wouldn't I? How do you think I lost these?" he said pummeling on his club legs. "Are you blind? Why haven't you asked me about them? About this?" he said waving his walking stick in the air.

"Do you think I give a varmint's testicles about your legs? I didn't ask because I don't care!"

Horrified, Christian stepped back.

"Don't you see? They're just legs! I could have lost *you*." Gillian swallowed trying to catch her breath, drizzle now trickling down her face. "I know you were there, in Cuckfield, before the accident!" Christian looked bewildered. "You *did* know the war. That was unfair of me. I just meant you hadn't experienced it through the eyes of a civilian. You were stationed at Ockenden Manor, at the old Jewish boys' school in Cuckfield, weren't you?"

"How did you know that?"

"I know from an article I read only this week. You met my sister Beaty." Gillian could see Christian reeling in memories. Dates and images and accents and orders shot through the drizzly air around them, the garden filling with tension. "I was there, too, only I had left to rest my weary bones." Gillian could feel a faulty beat to her heart and feared the organ would collapse altogether. "Beaty didn't know it was you at the time. She had no idea about you. I'd never told anyone outside of my cousin Roderick and Shashi. Had I known you'd go and get yourself cut in half, I would never have left Tobermory."

"Are you mad, woman? My injury had nothing to do with you. If you had stayed in Tobermory, I would have joined the air force anyway. It's true you were incentive—maybe, just maybe I'd find you—but you're not the reason I joined. It was as if my years of crop dusting led me to it. It was something I had to do. I could feel it."

"Just like *I* could feel the Isle of Man was around the corner for me. Leaving you was something I had to do, but it wasn't because I didn't love you."

"Was it really that simple?" Christian said.

"Can't it be as simple as that? I was young. I wasn't ready for this," she motioned toward the garden, a perfect place to raise a family. "And there was something out there that I needed to do first. I hadn't a clue what it was. I just knew it was there." Tears began to swell in her eyes. "But if I had known…"

"Known what? You would have saved me?" he said, his brow now pinched together. "Just like the maharani's flower? I know Jimson weed. Seen it a thousand times. Its poison can kill if you ingest too much. Did you know that?" he said crinkling his eyes. "But with just the right amount, it's the perfect medicine. A drop more makes you delirious." He sighed, "Oh that flower is beautiful—tempting. Best to admire it from a distance, though."

His words were pointed, but they hadn't a thing to do with Shashi. She knew that. "Is that the best you can do?" she huffed. "You could have been killed!"

"Would that have made a difference?" he asked smugly.

"How dare you ask such a question?"

"Then say it!" he shouted, the dewy air muffling his roar.

"Say what? What do you want to hear? That I crumbled into nothing after leaving you? That it took forever to build myself up from the rubble? That I haven't loved another man or felt another man's breath on my skin since you? That ever since I saw that walking stick against your lorry I have blamed myself for this horrible nightmare? I was so busy taking care of everyone else that I wasn't there for *you*."

"Is that what you were doing when you left Canada— taking care of me? Protecting me?"

"What are you talking about?"

"You didn't want me to get hurt, did you?" he shouted.

"But I did hurt you. I left you, didn't I?"

"But why? Why did you really leave?"

"I don't know what you're talking about. I've already explained," she snipped.

"No. You haven't!" he said as though he'd been doused in icy water. Silence snatched the air as he calmed himself, a truth working its way into his expression. "Gilly... it was Griffin, wasn't it?" Gillian stepped back, nearly stumbling, feeling her chest crush inward. *He knew.* "Griffin touched you, didn't he?" The air felt heavy around her—the kind of air that grounds you and won't let you go. "I have to know. Please tell me." Again he stared through her. "Did he hurt you?"

Gillian felt her lips shudder before she could answer, knowing she was cornered. It was the only part of her she could feel. "No." She could see a rush of pain grip his eyes, understanding at once the meaning behind her answer. She had confirmed what he'd feared. "How did you know?" she asked.

She could see him swallow, struggling to speak. "Griffin told me," he stepped toward her, lowering his head, "when I showed him this article." Christian took a paper from his pocket. It had been torn and crumpled. He handed it to her. "When Griffin saw it was you, he whispered his wife's name. And then I saw it in his eyes."

"Saw what?" she asked.

"Fear. Shame." That's when he told me what he thought may have happened—the real reason you left. But he didn't know for sure. He'd been confused for such a long time. He was seeing things that weren't there, and you were so like his wife. That part was true… you *were* alike. He was terrified that he'd hurt you. I stood there watching him in his rocker as he crumpled into a ball sobbing—begging for your forgiveness. It was the first time I'd ever thought of him as frail, this big old man… frail. In that moment, I knew I had to come." Gillian didn't know what to think or how to feel. Her words left her. "So you don't think you were there for me? God Gilly, wake up! Forget about my legs. You sacrificed *us* for me." His eyes followed some birds in flight, a momentary reprieve before finally being drawn back to her. "You didn't want me to find out what had happened because you knew how much Griffin meant to me. Isn't that right?"

"I tried to tell you… that morning by Big Tub."

Christian crinkled his forehead. "What are you talking about? I'd remember something like that."

"When I brought up Griffin's name, the day after it happened, you must have already been feeling sentimental. You were sitting on the rocks just beside the lighthouse, staring out on the bay when I arrived. I brought you my book, *Gulliver's Travels*. I'd already finished it and wanted to give you something that brought me pleasure, something you could remember me by. Don't you recall?"

Christian arched his brow, clearly remembering. "My God, Gilly, it was the day you left me. Are you telling me it happened the day before?"

She nodded. "I planned to tell you then." Gillian sighed.

"I'd hardly slept the night before. I was so upset, and Roderick wasn't returning until the weekend. I'd nearly taken my auntie's car in the middle of the night. I thought I could reach the university before he made his way back to Tobermory. Trouble was, I didn't know how to drive."

"So you stayed."

"Only to find you. I was too afraid to go to your place in the event I might see Griffin. So I asked one of the fishermen if he'd seen you when I had wandered down to the docks. He said you'd been at the lighthouse. That was how I found you."

"So why didn't you tell me right away?"

"As I was trying to say... when I brought up Griffin's name, you started in on how he'd helped you that very morning with your dock—that even his age would never turn him away from you. You compared him to your father before he'd left for Sudbury, to a time when your father meant everything to you. Griffin took you under his wing, you told me so. And it was obvious how close the two of you had grown over the years." Gillian turned, inhaling the cool, misty air in the garden. "Had I told you, it would have been like losing your father all over again," she said soberly. "He'd have disappointed you, just like your father did. You'd never have forgiven him."

Silence. Oh, how she longed for peace. Gillian breathed slowly before continuing, "I couldn't do that to you. There really wasn't a choice at all. It was the first time I'd truly struggled to forgive someone, and truth is, it took me a long time. Years. Somewhere in my heart, I knew Griffin wasn't evil, just a lonely old man. But I was afraid it might happen again, and I was afraid of what you'd think of me." Gillian sighed. "I promise you, he didn't hurt me. But he took something from me that day, leaving a pale, lonely moon shining down on me each night. I certainly wasn't afraid of men, but it made me question my ability to judge wisely. I was eighteen years old. I thought I knew everything. Yet I couldn't even see when an old man found me attractive. At eighteen, who would think a kind old troll would do something like that? Reels of images swirled around my mind. The times we'd been with Griffin, what used to be an innocent look of fondness, my mind would churn into something ugly. Of course I see it all quite differently now. But at the time, I wanted to run as far away from there as possible. I didn't want to leave you." Gillian rubbed her arms, feeling a shiver of cold through her body. The dismal, dank air felt like retribution for hurting him. "I knew I could never tell you the truth, and that's why I wasn't there when you lost your legs, when you needed me most."

Christian snatched her arms, an unwavering countenance. "Don't you see, you *were* with me that day. *You* were taking care of me. Lucky charms can come in unexpected forms. I had you with me all along—my pocket watch. Every time you touched it, every time you wrote a poem, every time you slipped it between two pages. Gilly," he lifted her chin until their eyes met. "It wasn't the day I lost my legs. It was the day my life was spared, and I've never once thought of myself as disabled."

Spray from the sea brought in a chill as the hills were quietly pushing back the morning. Nothing stirred in the few neighboring cottages apart from the woodsy scent of smoke curling from the chimneys.

"I'm sorry," Christian said. "I'd have *given* my legs away to protect you, but I didn't know." Gilly drew closer, reaching for him, virtue and tears welling in his eyes. "There was a reason I fell in love with you that summer. I saw in you everything that was special about my mom, only *you* took it all to another level. When you laughed, you made me feel free. When you committed yourself, you never gave up. When you were stubborn, you made me feel challenged. Most of all, when you looked at me, you made me feel wanted." Tiny gasps fluttered in her throat as she held onto his words. "I know it was only a summer, but I'm here for a reason, the real reason," he said. "I love you, Gilly. I've loved you since the day I met you. And if I could, I'd bottle three days ago at Cregneash and have it for the rest of my life."

The hour when daylight dies
And lighted window through the dark,
A shining pathway throws
To welcome home a loved one,
Whose daily work is o'er.

When evening shadows fall
The fireside chair,
The loving word and smile
Wait for him the hour when daylight dies.

In the peace of a fireside glow
All troubles fade away,
He finds new strength and purpose
To face another day.

When the hours of work are past
His footsteps tread the shining path,
To meet again the love and smiles
That wait for him when daylight dies.

Chapter 21

1946

CHRISTIAN GLANCED UP at the sky noticing how it seamlessly stitched its way into the sea. He knew his words were soaking in while Gilly stood there quietly as though she was letting them find their place in her heart. She took his hand wittingly and led him up the walkway and into the warmth of the cottage where the cinders still burned low. Christian took off his cap and sport coat and set them on the back of a chair while Gilly added a log of peat to the fire then stood up, staring into the remains as though she was considering what might happen next.

After arousing the flame with some tongs, she set them down, not a word spoken as she turned to face him. The moment made Christian feel just a little bit like that boy again, the one who'd found his treasure on the beach with a quiet promise that no matter what, nothing could come between him and this amazing discovery. And as Gilly slipped her robe off her shoulders, he could hardly believe this was happening. Her hair kept its wave even in the dampness of the island, her eyes holding a familiar confidence though she was trembling like it was her first time. But it wasn't. It was how she looked that night at Bear's Rump when they'd made love for the first time. Only now something was different; her expression carried with it fourteen years of living, of independence, making her all the more intoxicating.

She reached behind her back and let loose the ribbon that had been tied on her nightgown then slipped it off her shoulders, letting it fall to the hearth. She stood naked with the glow of the fire behind her, her skin shimmery as the colors of the sunrise finally peered through the windows facing the sea. Christian swallowed hard not quite believing how divine she looked and thinking for a moment how his expression must have seemed juvenile. He was even sure she'd hear a pant escape him.

"I love you, Christian," she said soberly. "I've always loved you." How he longed to hear these words again. His chest swelled as he tried to curb the tears welling up in his eyes. He hadn't asked for much in this world, and now he was given what he wanted most. The few feet between them was too great; he found himself reaching out to her then moving her way. Christian brought his hand to her cheek then traced her lips with his fingertip. The light softened the lines of age at the sides of her eyes and around her mouth that carried with them a thousand smiles sent from India.

"You're exquisite, do you know that?" he whispered.

"I thought I was extraordinary," she said as the sides of her mouth grew faintly wider. He returned her smile, delighting in her playfulness, then skimmed his fingers along the outline of her shoulders. He leaned down, grazing her skin with his mouth. The scent of dew and the saltiness from the air outside lingered on his lips.

If ever he'd wished his legs back, it was now so he could

work his way down her body easily, supply. As though she'd sensed his wishes, Gilly brought her hand to her breast then began caressing it.

"Do you have any idea what you're doing to me right now?" Christian said.

"Well, if my intention isn't obvious, I think we might just have a communication problem here."

"Shall I order a therapist?" he said trying to suppress a grin while running his hands down her hips.

"I don't think they have such a thing for these kinds of shenanigans."

"Is that what this is now?"

Gilly didn't answer. Instead she pulled back as he tried to kiss her. He could feel the playfulness stipple into something serious. It was that look, the one he'd been waiting for. The look that terrified him, that told him she was ready... ready to see *him*, ready to touch him. He wanted this. He needed her to accept him the way he was now. He brought her hands to his chest then began unbuttoning his shirt. As she took over, he watched her chest wave in measured, anticipating breaths. When a whimper sounded from her lips, he knew that he could never want a woman more than this treasure in front of him. He reached behind his neck and pulled his undershirt over his head, tossing it on the floor.

She gazed at him. Then she lovingly murmured, "You're the exquisite one."

With the uneasiness he felt as she undid his belt, letting his trousers drop to the floor, he wondered what this moment would look like, the moment she saw his prosthetic legs for the first time. Tin and wood, how could anyone not be shaken? But Gilly wasn't just anyone. Her eyes studied them like a curious child might do, yet her face remained expressionless. She knelt down and began touching them, tapping them, almost listening for an echo as though memorizing their weight and color, feeling the joints and leather straps. He wondered what she was thinking.

"These are ghastly things, you know," she said, widening a smile and looking up at him from his shoes. He couldn't have agreed more and appreciated her honesty. What he didn't want to hear was how splendid or sensible or practical they were. She always knew the right thing to say, but even better—she meant it. "I'd rather see what's underneath. I'd rather see you," she said as she began to undo the straps. He clasped her shoulder gently, protectively.

"Are you sure, Gilly?"

"My darling, I've never been more sure of anything in my life."

Gillian led him to the settee and once he sat down, she unstrapped the leather that secured the prostheses to his upper thighs. When he was ready, she carefully removed them then set them on the floor. She could feel his vulnerability, trusting her not to cringe or pass judgment. What was left of his legs simply didn't make her feel ill at ease.

Neither shock nor sorrow crept into her. It was a new version of the man she loved—just a new version, and she would get to uncovering the mystery about how he came to be when the time suited. But right now, all she wanted was to feel his body next to hers, swaddled in his arms. She caressed his thighs. They had healed well with a few small folds at the end, and it wasn't the first time she'd seen such an injury—never in this way, mind you. She'd have her license revoked giving an examination like this!

Gillian lowered her lips to his thighs and peppered his

skin with kisses. He was beautiful in every way. It was how he looked at her, the way he trusted her that made her feel even more special, even more desirable. The rest of the world disappeared as the sun was rising just for them. She looked into Christian's eyes from where she knelt in front of him, her fingers toying with the waistband of his boxers. And as she removed them, Christian moved to the floor, taking her in his arms, then lying down on the area rug.

Gillian could feel the heat and flames snaking behind her and enjoyed how the light played on Christian's skin. She reached back almost wanting to touch them as he moved on top of her.

"Oh, I *do* prefer you like this!" she muttered.

"Do you now?" he said salaciously.

"I have you all to myself."

"So you won't get on the next ocean-liner and disappear from my life again?"

"Only if you say please!"

The look in his eyes made her fall in love all over again. And in the crackling of the fire and the smell of their passion, they both came together as one—fourteen years, a Depression and a World War dissolving into the misty air around them.

As Gillian's breath subsided, she could feel her heart begin to slow to a steady beat. She lay there braided in his arms; time and place felt dazed. Even now, the playfulness that simmered just under the surface had a way of showing up unexpectedly.

"Well, it's about time you came and got me, Mr. Christian Hunter," Gillian said smiling mischievously. He smiled back—a wide savory grin—then pattered kisses all over her face. "Now, tell me about these legs of yours."

Amidst the teeming crowds,
To cross my path along the years.
I wonder could I find just one,
To pause and heed my fears.

Fear of the years now I am old,
My friends all gone and I'm alone.
No kindly voice to wish me well,
Scarce passing glance from supposed friend.

This loneliness is what I fear,
Which must be borne, till comes a day,
When loneliness is swept aside,
And only rest and peace remain.

Chapter 22

2003

BURNT ORANGES. I can taste it on my lips now as though it were soaking in before even reaching my tongue. It's the one thing that neither age nor illness has robbed me of—taste. How divine Daddy's recipe was, though with all that wine and whiskey flaming atop, only us older niblers were granted a mouthful each. Only Seville oranges would do. Daddy was strict about that. But oh, how hard they were to come by in those days! I remember Mommy standing in the queue just to get one, a single orange for the whole family. Daddy would hunt them down like a grouse in pheasant season. That buttery sweet, edgy taste and caramelized sugar left me dreaming of fairies and leprechauns. Shame my son never took to such a traditional desert. I always wanted him to learn the finer things of Ireland, but I suppose over time, my homeland will become the distant memory of an old lady whose name is written in the family tree.

"Grandma," a voice twitters, stirring me from a rather juicy muse. I don't like the word *muse*, never have. Makes me feel mousy, as though I should be scurrying about in the earth.

"Yes, dear, I'm still here." I pat my granddaughter's hand lightly. Takes every ounce of energy just to lift these skeletal bones wrapped in purple twine, but she needn't know.

"It scares me when you just stare like that."

"I know, but I promise I won't leave without saying goodbye," I mutter, trying to sound spirited and audible. Lying on my side it's hard to do both, but the pain is something I can't hide if I lie on my back.

"I'll hold you to that," she smiles, my pretty Gilly.

"Will you take your glasses off, dear, so I can see your eyes?" Gilly slides them from her ears and sets them on the bedside table. "There you are! You remind me of me at your age. Did I ever tell you that?"

"A hundred times at least, but I never tire of hearing it."

"I was quite something, you know. Proud—but not too proud to do the Lord's work. I think He's always considered me a bit of a militant," I say, noticing how a beam of light shooting through the hospital window seems to curve straight at me. "All in good time," I whisper just loud enough for Him to hear. "Tell me, have you been here long darling?"

"Didn't the nurse tell you I had just arrived? I just popped down for this," she says eyeing her paper cup."

"Yes, that's right." But I don't remember. I want to tell her that but I can't bring myself to. I can't bring myself to tell her that she's made it just in time—time for my story to end. "Now tell me, how is Sebastian?"

"Great. Just yesterday, he reminded me of what you said to him the first time you met." Gilly sets her cup on the table.

"Well, don't keep me in suspense. What was it?"

"Hand me down the moon, you said. So I used that in my book!" Gilly says winking.

"Well, he is very tall."

"I keep a step ladder in my pocket wherever I go, just in case," she says, this time with a naughty wink.

I adore my granddaughter's spirit. "Promise me, Gilly, that you'll never lose your zest for life? It's the one precious thing we have. Without it, we may as well not live at all." Sudden concern plays with her expression but I know what I'm saying and she needs to hear these words. "Whatever you do, don't ever let foolishness or pride keep you from the man you love. I know it's Sebastian. Do you know how I know?" Her eyes are pinned to me now. "He has sat here in the very spot you are now, holding your place whenever duties whisk you away. He has visited me several times on his own. Bet you didn't know that?" I say with as firm a nod as I can manage. "I'm quite sure he knows full well that in the end it would make you happy. Sometimes we have long chats about you, other times he reads to me, but he has never asked for me to tell you of his visits. I'm telling you because you should know the gem you have unearthed. Only a man truly in love would do such a thing. I see it in his eyes when he talks about you, I know... because I've only seen it once before."

"In Christian's, right?" I know my eyes are telling her what she already knows. "I wish I knew more about him. I feel like I'm guessing sometimes in my writing."

"You have *almost* all you need to know. Book your flight today after my last breath and I promise once you have been to the Isle of Man, all you will need to do is pluck the words from the air and find their rightful place."

The streak of sunlight fades away as the end of my story

approaches and dusk begins to fall. Though how can it be dusk when dawn seemed only moments ago. Has time really been washed away from my life? I feel cold and frightened. I've never felt quite like this before. I should be accepting by now, but I'm not. Whose arms shall I fall into other than the Lord's? Which of the two men who have loved me? But I already know the answer to that. I feel my heart begin to race. *My darling Christian! Oh my darling! It's you. You're waiting for me. I can feel it.* Only then will the threads of my story be tied.

"Grandma? Are you okay?" Gilly says while wetting my lips with a cloth, a panic in her voice.

"Yes. I'm sorry, what were you saying?"

"Just that I wish you could stay long enough to know my book."

"Oh but I do. I've *lived* it."

"To see it published one day, I mean. I don't have an ending yet. Please tell me... what happens to Christian?"

Knowing in my heart my granddaughter has found my voice... a story I've always wanted to tell, to shout to the world but never knew how, a book I wanted to write but didn't, she deserves to know the ending. It's time to scrub clean that jar of pickled truths, but I will leave one morsel for her pilgrimage, the one bit she must find out for herself. Gilly pulls the vinyl chair right up to the edge of the bed and listens intently. For the first time, I believe I can hear the patter of her heart over my own.

THE SKY WAS MOODY that day, the kind of sky that makes you feel alive. We'd just made love under the ledge of a crag not far from my little cottage. Christian had had a devil of a time climbing down but we couldn't get enough of each other, and no rock face was about to stop him. We had a thrilling habit of marking our territory, and I regarded myself as quite a vixen when I felt playful and luring. The surf was only feet away and the tide was crashing in quickly. I don't know what I was thinking. The Irish Sea is nothing to harry.

I sat curled in his arms while the rumbling clouds drummed their final warning. Strangely Christian made the sound almost disappear through a whisper when he made a promise to love me for all time and never leave me. Wherever he might be, he said, I shall always feel him next to me.

I began shivering after our encounter simmered. The spray from the surf sided with the clouds so we took our clothing in one great snatch then dressed as we climbed. The rocks were now slippery and Christian wasn't managing well. His tin legs were in the cottage. He rarely wore them at home. We both preferred it. I knew he was more comfortable without them. That's why he was so lean, so strong from carrying his weight on his hands most of the time. But there was one rock that even *his* strength couldn't hurdle. It was just too high. I shouted to him over a clap of thunder to go around but he wouldn't hear of it. The surf was getting angry. We had no right to be there. I reached for him knowing full well I wouldn't be able to lift him, and I lost my own footing.

I remember the instant terror I felt as my feet slid down the rock, the cragged edges cutting through my skin while I plunged backwards into the surf. It happened so quickly until I hit the water, then my body sunk in slow motion. I was sure of it. I remember a frenzy of bubbles above me and the gray of the sky staring down at me with that look my father used to give when he was disappointed. Suddenly the beads of water calmed, the frenzy stopped, the sky still. It was strangely peaceful just for that moment, as though I was being warned that something greater was about to happen. The moment escaped and I was thrashed against the rock, my hand instantly wedged. The salty summer water clogged my throat and I began to panic until I felt my hand released then pulled upward. Christian quickly wrapped his arms around my torso and pulled me to near safety, but we weren't safe, not until the surf's snatch was out of reach. We climbed to the top of the bluff then fell into each other's arms.

That gray sky was a worm! A falsehood that couldn't be trusted. And I was right.

It was a Sunday morning, one week after our scare. I sat on the Hemsworth's stone wall watching Christian test his new crop duster, a scrappy old plane he'd fixed up for a pittance. He was playing tricks in the sky, high and low, waving to me as he swooped down, skimming the tops of their barley. I could feel his freedom. It was right for him to be up there. I suppose in some minute way he felt like he was in his Typhoon again, showing off maneuvers he'd made during that mission over Belgium—the same mission that took his legs when he'd parachuted from his fighter plane only to be the target of a "potato masher" he called it, once landed. He watched as his plane spiraled to the earth in the cold of winter, and after the stick grenade, he remembered nothing but the white of the forest. No... I could do without that show!

I told myself he needed to test it. No good having a crop duster that couldn't do the job. Then it occurred to me that the sky looked exactly like it did when I had plunged into the sea a week earlier. It's brooding clouds traced with that same warning. Panic raced through me as I heard the plane sputter through some low-lying clouds. My worst fear then seized me when there was no sound at all, hoping, just hoping, it was a mad gamble, intentional. I stood on the wall trying to see better when his plane came into sight. I thought I should die on the spot as I watched it fall from the sky like a shot pheasant, straight into the ground. No explosion, no smoke, just pieces of aircraft scattered everywhere.

I couldn't feel my limbs as I ran toward the crash. All sound was muffled and blurred except for my breathing. As the golden barley trampled underfoot in my desperate sprint, the crash seemed to move farther away. I don't remember what happened when I finally reached him, apart from holding him in my arms on the ground and screaming without a sound escaping my lips. My darling Christian draped over me—his neck broken.

Sisters are forever,
No matter the tides they bring.
Quarrels merely heighten,
Their blessed understanding.

Though rickety they grow,
As the years pass by in haste.
A giggle saved 'specially,
For a sister warmly embraced.

She sees you at your worst
And very best of days,
Despite any trials
She's there in timeless ways.

Chapter 23

Date = forever and a day or two, 1946

MY LITTLE COTTONTAIL,

Do you notice how I'm giving you the benefit of the doubt, inferring that you are soft? Or have you gone prickly, my dear, as a result of your frolicking in the hay with that Canadian of yours? I still have yet to hear from you, and my intuition has never failed me before! So either you write to me this very instant or I shall be pummeling your door down by the rise of the sun on the morrow! I want to meet this Mr. Christian Hunter so I can stare... him... down.

On a more curious note, I received a card from a Mr. and Mrs. Percy Spooner thanking me for a packet of humbugs. Whoever is Percy Spooner? And why on this blessed Earth would anyone name their child Pickles? Apparently, she's welding some sort of monstrosity for our garden and wanted to know its square footage. Christian's name slipped between the lines so I thought I should inquire? Do me the favor, dear, when you've untangled yourself from the throes of gloppy passion and ask that swain of yours for details.

Other oddities have been whirling around me these past weeks, queer I tell you! A letter from that hillbilly called Griffin arrived not two hours ago. It could only have been Roderick who slipped up and let loose my address. He's come after me, this Griffin, I'm sure of it. Probably carries a tomahawk in his pocket. He wanted to know of your Canadian's whereabouts. How shall I respond when my own sister refuses to answer my telephone calls and written pleas for acknowledgement? It's been weeks! My only strand of communication seems to be through Mrs. Hemsworth, and I daren't say I want to put up with all her dribble. She muttered something about a plane crash earlier then hung up on me. Can you believe it? That breedy louse!

Now I must say it's very strange, but this Griffin's sent a package for you. It rattles as though there are bones inside. I managed to accidentally tear a corner of the wrapper and had a little sneaky peek—a lovely carved box inside but I've mended the paper the best I could so you wouldn't think I had prying eyes. You know me better than that. I shall forward the box today by special delivery.

But if I hear from you before I make way to the post, I shall bring it with me to Port St. Mary—pummeling or not, I miss you, dear sister, and Horatio's chest is much better now. Besides, I can't wait to meet this man again who's looped your heart into a right mess.

Ah, I see my threats must have worked for the telephone is finally ringing.

Love and hugs,
Beatrice
Post Script—I'm on my way, darling. Hold tight.

And when the sun sinks in the west,
The silent shore by waves caressed.
Awaits the coming of the night,
When moonlight turns to silver bright.

Chapter 24

"YOU KEPT YOUR PROMISE that day and said good-bye," Gilly mutters, kneeling in the icy cold of winter next to her grandma's headstone. "You were right about Sebastian, too. I knew it the moment he turned the corner in the hospital on that fateful day with a book tucked under his arm—a book I learned later he'd been reading to you. You were right about a lot of things. And my trip to England? You were right about that, too. Auntie Beaty didn't disappoint. Even at ninety-eight, she owned the sidewalk with that mobility scooter of hers. She seemed to enjoy bowling down anything in her path," Gilly says, unable to feign her admiration. "But when I told her I was planning on going to Cuckfield, everything changed. She was hiding something. Why else would she try to steer me away? I knew it had to be a place of significance after it had crept into at least a dozen of your most recent tales. That, combined with her reaction, was when I knew I had to go there and that's when I knew I couldn't tell her I was also going to the Isle of Man."

As icy clouds puff from her mouth, Gilly gathers her

thoughts. "Sebastian didn't come with me. I suppose somehow you know that. He knew it was something I had to do on my own. Yet I couldn't help but remember you'd be tripping over me every step of the way. Every now and then I'd find myself giggling just at the thought. How are your wings anyway, Grandma? Black and blue, no doubt, after that journey."

Indeed, like the slow clanging of a church bell on a quiet Sunday, the crackling of the trees summons her attention. *Now you listen to me!* They seem to be saying. *Tell me about the Isle of Man.*

"It all started at Ockenden Manor in Cuckfield. I went despite Auntie Beaty's wishes. A hotel and spa now! Did you know that? But I kept asking myself why your own sister wouldn't want me to find out about Canadian troops being housed there during the war. Why would that have been such a secret? I was able to get some information on a plaque in the lobby, but what I really wanted was a roster of the soldiers stationed there at the time." Gilly sighs, fighting her urge to tell every detail, already feeling her bones turning crumbly in this cold.

"But when I took off my shoes on a quiet lane in Port St. Mary in the dead of winter and felt the damp, frigid cobblestone under my toes, just as you had suggested, I realized that even if I had found a roster in Cuckfield, only this place would give me the answer." Gilly feels her mouth widen to a grin. "I had asked myself a hundred times why it was so important that *I* discover the answer. Why me? But I knew the reason was waiting for me in a little cottage by the sea. And even though you could have just told me yourself, the swashbuckler in you didn't dare keep the thrill of discovery from me. 'What a bore!' I can hear you say about telling me the conventional way. I'm right, aren't I, Grandma?" she says patting the headstone.

"I found your cottage by following the picture I'd painted in my mind, the cottage I'd created in my novel." She smirks knowing it wasn't magic but rather tying together all the pieces she'd heard over the years, all those nights by the campfire when she was a young girl. She hadn't realized at the time how she soaked in every word, every description of her grandma's life. That was why words had become so important to her, just as they were to her grandma. It didn't hurt either that half the waterfront knew exactly which cottage it was and even recognized her grandma in her. "It felt strange, as though I was coming home," she says, her brow furrowed. "Two old ladies live there now. Best friends their whole lives. But what was odd was that even though they were originally from the north, they knew who I was as well. Said they'd been waiting for me, waiting for the person on the envelope."

As though expecting her grandma to clarify, Gilly reaches into her coat pocket and takes out the envelope. "It's your handwriting, Grandma, with my name on the front. I sat on the hearth, two floorboards over from where the ladies found your letter years earlier, hidden underneath until the floor was nearly rotting through. They never opened it, said it didn't belong to them," she sighs. "To entertain themselves on cold winter nights, they'd imagine what was in the letter—usually a love letter, sometimes filled with betrayal, other times a mystery involving a smuggler. But always, they said, 'in the end the rightful owner will come looking for it.'"

"I'm not sure when you hid it, but I learned that you had kept the cottage for most of your life before selling it when

I was a child. You can't know how much I wanted to read the letter then and there. Instead, the ladies left me to my thoughts and I just sat there wavering. *Should I open it now or shouldn't I?* Selfishly, I thought it could add to my book, but then I considered that the words inside this envelope were written for my eyes only. So I tucked it away unopened. I waited until it was time to bring it here. Just breathing the salty air on the Isle of Man and walking through the barren barley fields of winter, all I had to do was close my eyes anyway. I could see you perfectly standing on that stone wall waving to Christian as he swooped down in his crop duster, both of you as happy as the day you'd met. That was for my book. This letter," Gilly says waving it lightly then tearing the seal, "is for me."

23rd of May, 1991

My dearest granddaughter,

When you find this letter, you will likely be a grown woman and I will likely be a memory. A happy one, I hope. When I held your tiny hand for the first time, I knew that I would never let go. And so here we are. I have told you my story as I always planned to. I don't know where or how, but I know the good Lord would not have taken me before I had the chance to tell you. The remainder of my secret that I have kept for most of my life can finally be set free. I have waited for very good reason, but before I tell you what that is, I want to begin with the day I came to exist only.

Living was something Christian's memory had to teach me all over again. That beautiful man belonged on the Bruce Peninsula, not on the Isle of Man. Can you feel my breathy sigh rise from this paper Gilly, feeling right about my choice? So I took him home and buried him by his butterfly cove under a nest of sycamore trees. It was the place, he'd say, where all his troubles would float away on a fluff of silky milkweed floss.

It was there after a quiet funeral that I met your grandfather, his name as sorry as the first time I met him though it made me smile. He didn't know at the time, but I was pregnant. When I told him, he promised to love Christian's child as his own and to give an unwed mother-to-be a stable life. At the time, it felt like the right choice. I needed a soft place to fall, for my recent losses were cruel. He explained to me that he and Christian had become friends and that he was there the day Christian's plane was shot down over the forests of Belgium. He, in fact, had parachuted from the same aircraft.

Gilly, can you feel me squeezing your hand? If you can't, close your eyes for a moment before I go on. Can you feel it now?

Your grandpa, darling, was Christian's gunner.

Somehow I know there is a long silence wherever you are reading this. It seems to be weaving into the afterlife. But I must go on.

Your grandpa had never really forgiven himself for Christian's injury. He had nightmares for years, and although I know he grew to love me, I am quite sure that he married me to ease his mind… a sort of reprieve, if you will. That is why I have always kept a very special photograph next to my bed. But for you, my sweet, I have removed it from my Bible and tucked it in this envelope. When you look at it, I think you'll understand.

It may have aged with time but it's a photo of the two men whom I have cherished most in this world for two very different reasons. Christian is in the foreground sitting on the wing of his Hawker Typhoon with your grandpa standing by the rear of the plane, both wearing their flight suits. It is the only photograph the two had ever taken together. But if you look closely, you'll notice that the Tiffy only had a single seat. It was your grandpa who had arranged for Christian to abandon his plane and fly with him that day in a two-seater fighter, destined for ruin.

As Gilly examines the photo, she can't help but recognize it from her own writing. Though it differs in setting, it's more or less the photo that has already woven its way into her novel. Perhaps it's an anomaly of sorts, but maybe, just maybe, she considers, it was something divine. When a chill runs through her, she pulls her scarf higher, suddenly feeling the grip of winter.

Do you see it now, Gilly? Just as I realized the truth through my poems, "the gift of their love was never mine, just lent to me for a short spell of time."

That day at the field, I planned to tell Christian my news, that we would have a child together. I know he was happy when I whispered it in my cries all that evening. Do you want to know how I know? Because all these years I've watched his smile in your father who bears his name and in your smile, my dearly treasured granddaughter who bears my name.

Now comes the hard part: forgiving your grandma

for burying the truth for so long. The reasons may not outweigh the injustice, but it is important that you know how much I desperately wanted to tell your father all these years. Granted, it was more important not to hurt the ones I loved than to ease my own conscience.

Why now? you might be asking yourself. Angus' love for your dad was bewitching. I'd say it was almost a crusade that he provide this child the life he deserved, the life that your grandpa believed he had nearly robbed him of. As he grew into his role, the deception grew larger than life. I've asked myself countless times if your dad needed to know the truth. After all, Angus has been the only father he's ever known, the only father who has had a chance to love him, to nurture him. And as the years still pass, I know I can't hurt your grandpa by telling your dad the truth. I actually think Grandpa has forgotten what the truth is. Moreover, when your dear grandpa passes away one day, I know in my heart that even then I will not be able to tell your dad. I pray to the good Lord that this knowledge will not burden you but instead make you smile knowing that you were the lucky one to have had an extra grandpa.

So I hope you can understand why it has to be you who tells my story. You have inherited my love for words. I know because you never stop talking. Can you feel my smile now? You are a little girl full of wonder, and I know that as you read this in the future you are now a woman of wonder. Equally as important, my story cannot happen in your grandpa's lifetime, and it has to be gentle enough to coo my darling son when the time comes for him to read your words. Only you have such finesse.

My love to you for all time,

Grandma

"So that's what it was," Gilly whispers softly, finally understanding why Auntie Beaty didn't want her to go to Cuckfield. "She didn't want me to find out who my real grandfather was. She was trying to protect me, wasn't she?" she says now cutting through the air. "But I'm glad to know the truth. And I'm glad I waited till I came here." Gilly breathes deeply, feeling the cold snatch her lungs. Yet as she lets the news fall softly around her, a loon's song fills the distant air with an eerie, wistful cry. Saddened for a moment, wondering if it had lost its way in migration and was left to fend for itself, a surge of emotion fills Gilly, making her shudder in the cold. When she turns her head at the flapping of wings from shore, a rush of freedom takes Gilly to another place when she witnesses the bird's mate land by its side.

"Hardly a burden," she finally concedes with soppy eyes. "This day is even more magical than expected. I got two packages in the mail this morning. That's why I've come all this way today. One from you and one from my publisher. But I haven't opened yours yet. Like the envelope, I thought I'd wait to do it here," Gilly says reaching into a bag for the small package.

As she strips the box of its brown paper and twine, she finds a dish with a silver lid inside wrapped in blue velveteen cloth. Gilly's brow kneads together, a sudden tingling dancing down her arms. Could it be? Is it really possible? And when she lifts the lid, her heart skips a beat—a tarnished pocket watch! She lifts it out, letting the chain hang over her palm, not quite believing her eyes or daring to open it. When she does, she understands for the first time the marvels of love, for inside she finds a brittle four-leaf clover.

Tears well in her eyes as she takes her newly published novel, the very first copy, then drapes the chain along the book's spine... where it belongs.

"This is for you," she says setting the book down between the graves.

Gilly's eyes travel the snowy curve of the cove while feeling proud of her grandpa. He knew that he was the one lucky enough to grow old with her grandma, yet he still asked for her to be laid to rest here one day... where she belongs. As Gilly turns to leave, her eyes fall on the only neighboring stone on the shores of Georgian Bay. She kisses her fingers lightly then places them on his name.

CHRISTIAN DEAN HUNTER

1912-1946

WHERE ALL YOUR TROUBLES FLOAT AWAY

AND ONLY REST AND PEACE REMAIN!

As GILLY WALKS through the wooded path, trees like naked statues, a gust of wind swirls around her and whoops through the branches and over to her grandmother's grave where it throws open the pages of her story.

To Grandma
For your poems, your Irish jigs and
making me laugh till tears spilled from my eyes.
And this story?
I could feel your hand on mine with every word.

Acknowledgements

I WOULD LIKE TO THANK my grandma, Gertrude Beck, for the amazing gift she placed in my trust just weeks before she died. "Maybe you can do something with these one day," she said. Nine words that sent me on a creative journey ten years later for which I will forever be grateful. This book would not exist without her. I hope that I have captured your spirit in Gillian's character, but most of all I hope that I have made you proud.

My sister, Julie Blain. Thank you for your constant support and friendship and for drilling into me to dream big and make it happen. In her words, "Never give up!"

Stephanie Harper, a treasured friend since high school, had just five words for me when I showed her what my grandma had left me, "THIS is your novel, Susan!" I am indebted to Stephanie for all those e-mails, phone calls and chapter critiques. Thank you for being my literary guru, and for always supporting my dreams.

A special thanks goes to my dear friend, Barbara Rörqvist whose son gave me the inspiration for Christian, and whose character bears his name. I know he walks with you every day.

Many thanks to my friend and colleague, Shashi Sethi for sharing her culture and photos from India with me. Who would have known the beautiful story those photographs would paint in my mind? Thank you!

Thank you to my editor Elizabeth Turnbull for believing that this story needed to be shared and for seeing it through an objective eye. It has been a long journey of drafts and edits, but you've been instrumental in helping me fine-tune the manuscript. Thank you.

Thanks to my two children, Alexander and Isabelle for craving my bedtime stories while growing up. You fed my imagination then and inspire me today as you grow into incredible young adults. I am so proud of you both. Thank you for always believing in me.

Most of all, thank you to my husband Staffan whose unwavering support and love have helped me turn my dreams into attainable goals. You're my sounding board, my best friend, and quite frankly, a gift from the Swedish rain gods. You are amazing.

Lastly, I am indebted to a number of books and websites for the insight and stories of Britain's Internment camps on the Isle of Man, life in Britain during WWII, and Hindu traditions, coupled with information by friends and colleagues. A full listing of these sources can be found on my website: www.susanornbratt.com/books.

About the Author

SUSAN ÖRNBRATT was born in London, Canada and grew up on the dance floor until her brother's high school rowing crew needed a coxswain. Quickly, she traded in her ballet shoes for a megaphone and went on to compete in the Junior and Senior World Championships and the XIII Commonwealth Games in Edinburgh, Scotland.

A graduate from the University of Western Ontario in French and the University of Manitoba in elementary education, as well as attending L'Université Blaise Pascal Clermont-Ferrand II in France while she worked as a *fille au pair*, Susan has gone on to teach and live in six countries.

Although a maple leaf will forever be stitched on her heart, she has called Sweden her home for the past sixteen years with a recent three-year stint in North Carolina, USA for her husband's work. It was there where Susan wrote *The Particular Appeal of Gillian Pugsley*.

Susan lives in Gothenburg with her husband and two children and an apple tree beloved by the local moose population. If she isn't shooing away the beasts, you can find her in her garden with some pruning shears, a good book, and always a cup of tea. If Susan were dried out, she could be brewed.

A reader's guide and interview
with the author are available online:
lightmessages.com/susanornbratt

If you liked this book...

Check out these other women's fiction titles from Light Messages Publishing:

How to Climb the Eiffel Tower *by Elizabeth Hein*
This moving, delightful, sometimes snarky novel about life, friendship & cancer proves life's best moments are like climbing the Eiffel Tower–tough, painful & totally worth it.

A Sinner in Paradise *by Deborah Hining*
Winner of the *IndieFab Book of the Year Bronze Medal* in Romance and the *Benjamin Franklin Award Silver Medal.* Readers will quickly fall for Geneva in this exquisitely written, uproarious affair with love in all its forms, set in the stunning landscape of the West Virginia mountains.

A Theory of Expanded Love *by Caitlin Hicks*
A dazzling debut novel. This coming-of-age story features Annie, a feisty yet gullible adolescent, trapped in her enormous, devout Catholic family in 1963. Questioning all she has believed, and torn between her own gut instinct and years of Catholic guilt, Annie takes courageous risks to wrest salvation from a tragic sequence of events set in motion by her parents' betrayal. **Coming June 2015.**